A FATHER'S WORST NIGHTMARE . . .

Fred's insides clenched as if someone had punched him in the stomach. Enos couldn't believe this. Douglas wasn't *capable* of murder. Fred studied Enos's face, hoping to find a trace of hope there, but found none.

He dragged in a breath and tried to steady himself. This couldn't be happening. Not to his boy. Not to Douglas. Tears stung Fred's eyes, threatening to spill over and make everything worse. He blinked rapidly, trying to force them back, trying to regain control.

He had to get Douglas out of here and . . . and what? What could he do?

He could take Enos's advice and find Douglas an attorney. It was a necessary step, but one that wouldn't make Fred feel much better. He wanted to *do* something, like . . .

Find the murderer.

Don't miss Fred Vickery's
first foray into murder in . . .

NO PLACE FOR SECRETS

Fred is the only person in Cutler who doesn't believe
that Joan Cavanaugh committed suicide.
And what he uncovers when he begins to snoop around
proves that wisdom does indeed come with age.

MORE MYSTERIES FROM THE
BERKLEY PUBLISHING GROUP . . .

DOG LOVERS' MYSTERIES STARRING HOLLY WINTER: With her Alaskan malamute Rowdy, Holly dogs the trails of dangerous criminals. "A gifted and original writer." —Carolyn G. Hart

by Susan Conant

A NEW LEASH ON DEATH   A BITE OF DEATH
DEAD AND DOGGONE   PAWS BEFORE DYING

DOG LOVERS' MYSTERIES STARRING JACKIE WALSH: She's starting a new life with her son and an ex–police dog named Jake . . . teaching film classes and solving crimes!

by Melissa Cleary

A TAIL OF TWO MURDERS   SKULL AND DOG BONES
DOG COLLAR CRIME   DEAD AND BURIED
HOUNDED TO DEATH   THE MALTESE PUPPY
FIRST PEDIGREE MURDER   MURDER MOST BEASTLY

CHARLOTTE GRAHAM MYSTERIES: She's an actress with a flair for dramatics— and an eye for detection. "You'll get hooked on Charlotte Graham!" —*Rave Reviews*

by Stefanie Matteson

MURDER AT THE SPA   MURDER AT THE FALLS
MURDER AT TEATIME   MURDER ON HIGH
MURDER ON THE CLIFF   MURDER AMONG THE ANGELS
MURDER ON THE SILK ROAD

PEACHES DANN MYSTERIES: Peaches has never had a very good memory. But she's learned to cope with it over the years . . . Fortunately, though, when it comes to murder, this absentminded amateur sleuth doesn't forgive and forget!

by Elizabeth Daniels Squire

WHO KILLED WHAT'S-HER-NAME?   REMEMBER THE ALIBI
MEMORY CAN BE MURDER

HEMLOCK FALLS MYSTERIES: The Quilliam sisters combine their culinary and business skills to run an inn in upstate New York. But when it comes to murder, their talent for detection takes over . . .

by Claudia Bishop

A TASTE FOR MURDER   A DASH OF DEATH
A PINCH OF POISON

THE REVEREND LUCAS HOLT MYSTERIES: They call him "The Rev," a name he earned as pastor of a Texas prison. Now he solves crimes with a group of reformed ex-cons . . .

by Charles Meyer

THE SAINTS OF GOD MURDERS   BLESSED ARE THE MERCILESS

FRED VICKERY MYSTERIES: Senior sleuth Fred Vickery has been around long enough to know where the bodies are buried in the small town of Cutler, Colorado . . .

by Sherry Lewis

NO PLACE FOR SECRETS   NO PLACE LIKE HOME

NO PLACE LIKE HOME

SHERRY LEWIS

BERKLEY PRIME CRIME, NEW YORK

NO PLACE LIKE HOME

A Berkley Prime Crime Book / published by arrangement with the author

PRINTING HISTORY
Berkley Prime Crime edition / February 1996

The Putnam Berkley World Wide Web site address is
http://www.berkley.com

ISBN: 0-425-15185-9

Berkley Prime Crime Books are published by
The Berkley Publishing Group,
200 Madison Avenue, New York, NY 10016.
The name BERKLEY PRIME CRIME and the BERKLEY PRIME CRIME design are trademarks belonging to Berkley Publishing Corporation.

PRINTED IN THE UNITED STATES OF AMERICA

10 9 8 7 6 5 4 3 2 1

For my sister and best friend,
Sandra Lewis Preysz

Acknowledgments

A special thank-you to friends and family who have helped my dreams take flight: Kathy Lloyd (teacher and friend); Jennie Hansen (critiquing partner and friend); Deloy Barnes (designated mature individual) and Heather Horrocks (designated slow reader) of the Wednesday night critique group; my friend Robert (Slim) Brinkman (whose imagination knows no bounds); Dan Weinrich, Cindy Beuhler, and Deneen Nunn (for being honest with me and keeping one foot firmly rooted to the ground); to Gene Lewis, Vanda Lewis, Sandra Preysz, and Heidi Preysz (for helping me keep everyone in character); all the court security officers (who share their combined decades of experience in law enforcement with me); and, finally, to Valerie Brown and Vanessa Brown (for tolerating deadlines and an eccentric mother and for becoming *my* mother whenever I need them to).

A very special thank-you to my agent, Patricia Teal, and to my editor at Berkley, Gail Fortune, for taking a chance on me and helping my dreams soar above the clouds.

one

Fred Vickery adjusted his step to keep up with his youngest son, Douglas, who led the way down the boardwalk of Main Street. Douglas set a quicker pace than Fred's usual one, but not an impossible one to match.

"It never changes here, does it?" Douglas asked.

Fred squinted into the early spring sunlight and surveyed Cutler's tiny business district and sparse morning traffic. "There have been more changes than you think."

Nestled in a narrow valley, cut into the forest, the town huddled on the shores of Spirit Lake, high in the Colorado Rockies. Even in its most densely populated section, it felt more like a nick in the timber than a town.

Lodgepole pines towered over most of the buildings, aspen trees shivered in the high mountain breezes, and the chatter of forest creatures broke the silence almost as often as the sounds of human occupation. Yet there were subtle differences Fred could sense, even if Douglas couldn't see them.

"I haven't been home in over a year," Douglas said, "and everything's exactly the same." He grinned, looking more like he was eighteen than thirty-six. He'd grown tall as a teenager, but the height suited him better at this age than it had then. His deep brown eyes held their usual twinkle, and tiny smile lines creased the skin around them.

"Not exactly," Fred insisted. "Change is in the wind."

"Well, let's just say I'm not likely to get lost around here. You've got a long way to go before you catch up with Seattle."

"Who said we wanted to?"

Douglas laughed. "Got to leave us some place to come home to, huh?"

"As long as I have any say in the way things are done."

Douglas laughed again and threw an arm around Fred's shoulder. "After we see Alison, let's drop by Maggie's, okay?"

"Did you call her this morning?"

"Who, Alison? Or Maggie?"

"Either. Both." Fred tried to keep exasperation from sounding in his voice. Douglas didn't believe in making plans, but his way of dropping in on people unannounced didn't always go over well. Margaret had always argued against her brother's easygoing manner, and Fred thought Alison deserved more consideration from her father.

But Douglas didn't seem concerned. "No, I didn't."

"Don't you think you should have let Suzanne know you're back? You're divorced now, son. She might not appreciate—"

"She knows how I am," Douglas broke in. "It'll be fine. Besides, she's been all right with you, hasn't she?"

Fred refrained from pointing out the flaw in Douglas's thinking. Suzanne knew only too well how Douglas was. After fourteen years of marriage, she'd stopped complaining about Douglas's habit of leapfrogging from job to job. She'd abandoned her efforts to change him and moved from Seattle to Portland, taking Alison with her. Then, less than a month ago, Suzanne had moved back to Cutler. And late last night, Douglas had shown up unannounced.

"She's seemed pleased to see me every time I've been over there, but you can't expect her to feel the same way about you."

Douglas patted Fred's shoulder. "You shouldn't worry so much. She's come back to Cutler, hasn't she? And she knows I'll come here to visit you. If she didn't want to see me, she wouldn't have come back. Besides—" He broke off suddenly and grinned. "Is that Enos?"

Fred followed his gaze. Less than a block away, Enos Asay, Cutler's sheriff, stood in the street, talking to Grady Hatch, one of his deputies. Without another word, Douglas sprinted toward the two men. Fred followed, without the sprint.

Still facing the other direction, Enos tilted his battered old cowboy hat back on his head and gestured toward the east end of town. Grady nodded and walked away just as Douglas reached Enos's side.

Enos glanced at Douglas, did a double take, then whooped loudly and threw his arms around Douglas. "Doug? Good billy hell, what are you doing here?"

Douglas returned the embrace, and the two men laughed and pounded shoulders and patted backs, both talking at the same time.

Stretching to see over Douglas's shoulder, Enos shouted to Fred, "Why didn't you tell me he was coming home?"

"I didn't know myself. He just showed up last night."

Enos looked back at Douglas. "How long are you going to stay? I'll tell Jessica to figure out a good night to have you over for dinner."

"That'd be great. How is she?"

"Same as always. But tell me about you. What brings you back home?"

"I just needed a visit."

"Have you seen Alison yet?"

"Not yet. We're on our way there now."

"Does she know you're coming?"

Douglas shook his head.

"Well, I'll be dipped. I guess Suzanne doesn't know either?"

This time when Douglas shook his head, he looked a little sheepish. "No."

Enos glanced at Fred. "Well, I'm sure it'll be all right. She's not the type to keep you from seeing your own daughter."

Douglas shot Fred a look of triumph. He obviously thought Enos agreed with his methods.

Fred didn't say a word. Arguing with Douglas usually proved fruitless. The boy had a way of flying by the seat of his pants that had always driven Fred to the point of distraction, and Fred had never been able to convince him of the wisdom of keeping both feet on the ground.

"Well, if you're going, you'd better get on over there before someone else tells her you're here," Enos said. "I'll give you a call about dinner."

"Sounds great," Douglas said, taking a step or two away. "Tell Jessica hello for me."

Enos settled his hat into place and patted Fred's back. "Will do. Now go on, and let me get my coffee. Grady's saving me a table at the Bluebird."

Douglas laughed. "See? I told you nothing had changed around here."

"Only because he gets his coffee free there. If he weren't the sheriff, it might be another story," Fred argued.

Enos shook his head. "No, I'll go to the Bluebird as long as Jessica keeps buying that fancy flavored stuff. Who ever heard of drinking chocolate-mint coffee?" He made a face and shuddered. Enos often served as a guinea pig for his wife's experiments with products she saw advertised on television. And Fred sympathized.

Douglas took another couple of steps across the street, turned back and called, "It's good to see you, Enos." Then he turned toward his father and asked, "Are you coming, Dad?"

Fred shoved his hands in his pockets as they turned down Ash Street, and he smiled when he realized Douglas had done the same thing. He knew Douglas was eager to see Alison again, and understood that. The two of them had always been close, and Alison would be thrilled to see her father.

Fred, however, wished Douglas could be more realistic when it came to Suzanne. Douglas never was anxious to hear fatherly advice, but Fred had to say something. "How long has it been since you saw Suzanne last?" he asked.

"I saw her for a minute on Thanksgiving."

"So, nearly four months?"

Douglas nodded. "If you count that as a visit. It's been a long time."

"I don't think you should expect too much when you see her."

"What do you mean?"

"Divorce can do strange things to people. She might not be too happy when you come knocking on her door."

Douglas's face clouded. "I have a right to see my daughter, don't I?"

"Yes, you do."

"Well, then . . ." he said, as if that settled something. But he looked away from Fred and made a point of studying the tops of the pines at the side of the road; the air was strained between them.

They walked in silence until they reached the block that housed Cutler's elementary and junior high schools. Trying to ease the tension, Fred asked, "Helen Digby passed away right after Christmas, did I ever tell you that?"

Douglas made a noncommittal sound.

"Wasn't she your second-grade teacher? Or am I thinking of Jeffrey?"

"No, it was me. But it might have been Jeff, too."

"Well, she passed away. Had an aneurysm, if I remember right. It was real sudden."

Douglas nodded, but said nothing more.

"They'll have to hire a new teacher now, I guess."

Fred had spent a lifetime working for the school district, and he'd loved almost every minute of it. Even though he'd retired eight years ago as building and grounds supervisor, he still knew just about everyone, and he still had his opinions about what the district needed.

But Douglas didn't share Fred's interest. He still said nothing.

"Don't know who they'll get. It'd be best to get someone younger, don't you think?"

This time Douglas made a noise that Fred took as agreement. But when they turned onto Arapaho Street, Fred gave up his efforts at conversation.

Within minutes they reached the house where Suzanne had lived with her Aunt Celeste until she married Douglas.

The house was small and pink with white trim and a narrow porch, and sat well back from the street.

Watching Douglas quickly walk up the stretch of uneven cement that split the winter-brown lawn in two, Fred battled a twinge of envy. Fred had always been an active man— "vital," Phoebe'd called him—but in the nearly three years since his seventieth birthday, he'd started to feel his age. He'd been just Douglas's age when Douglas was born— young and strong and sure of himself. Now it was hard to imagine himself so young.

Douglas rang the doorbell and waited only a second or two before pressing it again. A heartbeat later, the door opened and a large woman with a halo of hair tinted an unrealistic color of red filled the entrance. Fred had heard that Suzanne's aunt, Celeste Devereaux, had come back to Cutler, but he hadn't actually seen her since Douglas and Suzanne's wedding.

In all this time Celeste hadn't changed a jot. She had to be creeping up on sixty by now and, as always, she was too brightly made-up, too heavily perfumed, and too colorfully dressed to suit Fred's taste. And she still jingled; he could hear her from here.

Celeste's lips, glossy and pink, curved into a smile. She pushed the screen door open and threw her arms around Douglas. "You dear, *dear* boy. What a *wonderful* surprise."

Douglas staggered a little under the attack, but returned the hug as soon as he recovered.

Celeste pulled away when she saw Fred, straightened her clothing, patted her hair, and smiled. "Hello, Fred."

"How are you, Celeste?" He stayed well back, just in case a need to repeat the embrace overwhelmed her.

"Pushing deadlines," she said and waved them both inside. "Twenty-five books in print now, and I've got three *more* coming out this year. I've always got too much to do, but you'll never hear *me* complain." She led them into a boxy living room stuffed with too many chairs, tables, and bookcases.

On every available surface she'd stacked awards or novels—hardcovers and paperbacks tottering in uneven columns—evidence of her career as an author of erotic romance novels. Phoebe had always enjoyed a good love story, so she'd tried reading one of Celeste's books years ago. After only a few pages she'd proclaimed it too steamy to finish and had tossed it into the trash to keep it out of Margaret's young hands. But Celeste obviously enjoyed some measure of success if she had twenty-five of the things in print.

She waved toward the chairs, delicate, antique-looking pieces that didn't look like they'd support a man for long. Fred perched on the edge of one, and Douglas settled onto the other.

"How is everybody?" Douglas asked softly.

"Fine. Wonderful." Celeste moistened her lips and looked over her shoulder as if checking for listening ears. "I'm sorry about the divorce—*so* sorry."

"Me too."

Celeste checked behind her again. "Such a shame. You're one of the *good* ones, Doug. It's too bad Suzanne can't see that." Tears glistened in her eyes, and she ducked her head.

Douglas looked down at his hands. "Is Alison around?"

Celeste dabbed at her eyes and nodded. "Of *course*. I'll run and tell them you're here." She sighed heavily, then tried to smile. "I'm sorry I can't stay and chat, but I've got to get back to my galley proofs. But I *will* talk with you in a couple of days. All right?"

"Yeah. Sure. Good to see you again, Celeste."

"You too, Doug." She patted his knee, then looked over at Fred. "And it's *wonderful* to see you again."

"Wonderful," Fred agreed without enthusiasm.

With one last despairing glance at Douglas, Celeste disappeared into a room at the end of a narrow corridor. A few seconds later, Suzanne emerged.

Fred rose to embrace her. Small and dark with vivacious brown eyes and a lively face, Suzanne had always been one of Fred's favorite children-in-law. He already missed her snappy conversation, ready wit, and the almost comical way she'd kept Douglas in line.

Suzanne endured Fred's hug, but her attention never

wavered from Douglas, who remained stubbornly settled in his chair. "What are you doing here?" she demanded of Douglas when Fred released her.

"I came to see Alison."

"How long have you been in town?"

"Since last night."

"You should have called first." Her voice sounded frosty.

"Oh, come on, Suzanne—" Douglas didn't move a muscle, but his eyes snapped with hostility.

"I mean it. You can't just drop in anytime you feel like it. I have the right to my privacy, and Alison has the right to a little common courtesy."

Fred hadn't seen them together in at least two years, and the disintegration of their relationship sickened him. Where they'd once used words as the bridge between them, now every syllable worked like a loaded weapon.

Douglas flushed. "I'll call next time."

"Fine. Next time." Suzanne hesitated, then shrugged with a slight degree of elaborateness. "I guess I can ask Alison if she wants to see you."

A muscle jerked in Douglas's neck as Suzanne disappeared. He kept his eyes trained after her, almost as if he expected some kind of trick. But when Alison stepped into the living room a few minutes later, Suzanne hadn't returned with her.

With her light brown hair cut shoulder length and the sprinkling of freckles across her nose and cheeks, Alison looked enough like Phoebe to make Fred's breath catch. The resemblance had always been there, but he noticed it more lately—either because Phoebe was gone or because the seven-year-old's likeness to her grandmother had suddenly become more striking.

Alison smiled uneasily, almost as if Douglas and Fred were strangers. She leaned against the wall and looked at Fred with the same honey-brown eyes Phoebe had passed on to their daughter Margaret.

Douglas bolted out of his chair and bounded across the room. He gathered her into his arms, lifting her off the ground and spinning her around. "It's my little brown-eyed cinnamon roll!"

"Daddy—" Alison protested, but a flicker of delight danced through her eyes. She peered at Fred over Douglas's shoulder. "Hi, Grandpa."

"Make that big lug put you down this instant," Fred groused, but his objection carried no conviction.

Fred expected her usual giggle, but he earned only a timid smile. And where Alison would once have tried to wriggle out of Douglas's grasp, now she made no move to get away. She'd grown even more withdrawn since Fred's last visit, and it hurt him more than he could ever have imagined.

Slowly, as if sensing the change in her, Douglas put her down. "You okay, sweetheart?"

"Fine, Daddy."

He took her hand and pulled her toward the couch. "Come and tell me all about life here in the big city. What's school like? Who's your teacher?"

"It's fine. Do you want to see my workbook for reading?"

Caution had replaced warmth in her relationship with her father. Fred closed his eyes, hating the price divorce demanded of everyone, and opened them just in time to see Douglas send him a look of pure confusion over the top of Alison's head.

"Sure, sweetheart, in a minute or two." Douglas lowered his voice. "Are you happy here? Do you like it?"

This time Alison stiffened. "I like it very much." Her tone was every bit as inflexible as her shoulders. Suzanne must have warned her not to say anything to Douglas that he could use against them in case he had ulterior motives for returning to town. "I'll go get my workbook for you." She escaped down the hallway, and when she came back, Suzanne followed her.

Suzanne watched while Douglas studied the thin book Alison handed him and made a comment or two, then she said, "Alison and I have to leave now, Douglas. I'm sorry you couldn't visit longer. If you call first next time, this won't happen."

Douglas's face darkened, but he gave Alison a quick hug.

"Okay, then. I'll call you tomorrow. Would you like that?"

Alison nodded, but when Douglas hugged her again, she remained limp in his arms.

Silently cursing the heartache they'd all endured, Fred hugged her next. "See you tomorrow, okay, cupcake?"

She nodded again.

Straightening, he patted Suzanne's shoulder and stepped behind his son back into the weak March sunlight.

Douglas didn't speak until they'd put several houses behind them; but when he finally did, the words snapped like taut wire. "Dammit. Can you believe that?"

Fred's compassion stretched between them all, but centered on Alison. Being torn between two loving parents couldn't be easy. "It's terrible."

"She's turned her against me—her own father!"

"Don't jump to conclusions. Alison's confused and upset about the divorce—everybody is."

Douglas swore again.

"Give her time, son."

"Time. What the hell's time going to do for me if her mother's turning her against me?" Douglas stormed off, setting such a grueling pace that Fred had to demand a respite before the end of the block. With a glare of annoyance, Douglas complied, and they walked the rest of the way home in uneasy silence.

Fred turned his face to the sun and tried to recapture his pleasure in the early spring weather, but somehow the day didn't seem quite as bright as it had before their visit with Suzanne and Alison. And watching Douglas march beside him, Fred's internal alarms sounded. The divorce had been ugly enough before, but Fred had the uneasy conviction that the hostilities had just escalated.

two

Steam wafted up from Fred's coffee cup and teased his nostrils. Still hungry after a skimpy serving of chicken and broccoli, Fred leaned back in his chair and watched Douglas stir sugar into his own cup.

After their disastrous visit with Alison this afternoon, Douglas had disappeared into his old room for a couple of hours. He'd finally emerged with an offer to buy tonight's dinner at the Four Seasons, the area's newest restaurant, and Fred had agreed, though he'd have preferred the Bluebird Cafe.

The Four Seasons had only been open a few months, since just after Christmas, but it had already grown enormously popular with the younger generation.

Albán Toth had taken his profits from the Copper Penny Lounge and turned the old Mason Marina into one of those places where he could charge outrageous prices for meager portions of food with unpronounceable names. The restaurant had a nice atmosphere, but Fred would take one of Lizzie Hatch's country fried steaks with mashed potatoes and bacon gravy anytime.

Pushing aside the hunger pangs that came with thoughts of Lizzie's food, Fred lifted the delicate cup and hoped he wouldn't crush the thing between his fingers. "So, are you ready to talk to me yet?"

Douglas smiled. "Can't I take you out for a birthday dinner without you thinking something's going on?"

"My birthday's not until next month."

"I know. And you're what—seventy-two?"

"I'll be seventy-three. Now talk."

"About what?"

"You've been home twenty-four hours, and the only thing I can say for sure is you aren't here for a casual visit. What are you trying to do?"

"I came home to see my daughter. Are you going to tell me there's something wrong with that?"

"No. That's fine. But I don't think that's your only reason for being here. How long do you plan to stay?"

"What?" Douglas asked with a laugh. "Are you going to kick me out?"

"No." Fred dragged in a deep breath and tried again. "You're always welcome at home. But I've known you all your life, and I know the way you think. Something's going on that you're not telling me."

With a shrug, Douglas leaned back in his chair and a pained look of resignation crossed his face. "All right. What would you think if I told you I was coming home—for good?"

"To Cutler?"

"Yeah. I miss it here."

Now Fred *knew* something wasn't right. "What about your job?"

"I'll find another one. Look, Dad, I'm fed up with all the competition, the dog-eat-dog mentality out there. I'm not cut out to spend my life clawing my way up some corporate ladder."

That much was true, but even when Douglas put his job instability down to career decisions, the real story lay somewhere else.

Fred felt his face settling into lines of disbelief. "Do you think that's smart?"

"I don't know. But it's the only chance I have of being near Alison—and Suzanne."

And Suzanne? Just a few hours ago Douglas had been blaming her for Alison's strained response to him. "If I were you, I'd take some time to think this over. You can't just walk away from a decent job."

"It's a decent job, but it's not what I want to do with the rest of my life."

Fred had heard that from Douglas a time or two. Everyone who knew Douglas had heard it. It's what finally drove Suzanne to leave him. And now Douglas was ready to uproot himself and do the same thing all over again, as if somehow he'd impress her this time.

"You'd better figure out what you *do* want before you make another move. You're not in any position to just walk away from another job and start over again."

Douglas fiddled with the handle of his cup and refused to look up. "It's a little late for that."

"You already quit?"

Douglas nodded.

For Pete's sake, what was he thinking of? "And you didn't say anything about it before now?"

Looking defensive, Douglas met Fred's eyes. "I knew what you'd say."

Damn right, Fred thought. They'd argued many times about this before, though obviously nothing that Fred had said had made a speck of difference to the boy. Clutching the edge of the table, he drew a steadying breath and waited several seconds before he spoke again. "Just how do you plan to get by?"

"Well, I . . . I don't have any savings. I mean, with the divorce and child support . . ." Douglas's voice trailed away.

"So you're planning to stay at home?" Fred lifted his cup, pleased that he'd maintained enough control to keep his fingers from trembling. "Well, I won't turn you away," he continued, "no matter what I think of your decision. But you're going to have to do something to support yourself while you're here. No free rides."

Douglas tried to smile. "Yeah, well, that goes without saying. I've already put out a few feelers."

"In Cutler? What do you expect to find here?"

"Like you said, Cutler's growing. It's going to come out of the dark ages yet. And I—" Douglas stopped abruptly, and his face darkened at something he saw over Fred's shoulder.

Twisting slightly, Fred checked behind him. At a small

table in a dimly lit corner of the restaurant, a man leaned
toward a female companion. Tall and dark, and only slightly
stockier than he'd been as a boy, Garrett Locke appeared
impressive. But then he'd always been good-looking, and a
ladies' man.

Fred looked back at Douglas. "Did I tell you Garrett's
running Locke's Furniture now? He came back home after
Richard had his stroke last year."

"You mean he's living in Cutler again?" Douglas's face
contorted.

"Built himself a place out on the highway, on the way to
Estes Park." Fred had almost forgotten how much Douglas
disliked Garrett. Still, after nearly twenty years, he'd have
thought the rivalry would have faded.

"How long has *this* been going on?"

"What?"

"Don't you see who's with him?"

Fred looked again. Small, dark, shoulder-length brown
hair. It couldn't be anyone else.

"Suzanne and Garrett? I haven't heard a thing—"

"Well, I'm going to put a stop to it right now." Douglas
shot to his feet.

"I think you'd better sit down, son."

"Like hell I will. Look at them. Look at the way he's
touching her—"

"Sit back down."

"—like they'd never left off. Maybe they never did."

"Don't be ridiculous. You and Suzanne were living a
thousand miles away."

Douglas sent him an angry look and started across the
room. As he passed each table, diners stopped eating and
paused to watch. Most of the faces belonged to long-time
Cutler residents. Most of them probably remembered the
way Douglas and Garrett had acted over Suzanne twenty
years ago.

Fred pushed away from the table and stretched his aching
knees. He didn't want to interfere, but he couldn't sit back
while Douglas embarrassed himself.

Before he made it halfway across the room, the sound of

angry voices shot toward him. Ignoring the curious glances of the other customers, Fred reached Douglas's side just as Garrett jumped up.

"You're a loser, Doug. Always have been and always will be."

"Me? At least I'm not trying to take over another man's family. I'm telling you, Garrett, stay away from my wife and stay away from my daughter."

Fred groaned. Now that ought to go over well with Suzanne.

Just as he'd expected, Suzanne's face colored and her eyes snapped. "Oh, stop it, Doug. I'm not your wife anymore."

With a wave of his hand, Douglas dismissed her protest. "You know what I mean. Just stay away from this guy, he's bad news."

"Don't you dare come in here and start telling me what to do." Suzanne snatched her purse from the seat beside her. "Get me out of here, Garrett."

"Of course." Garrett smirked, looking smug and confident, the exact opposite of Douglas at this moment.

As Suzanne brushed past him, Douglas grabbed her arm and pulled her around to face him. "Don't go with him."

"Let go of me." As it always did when she got angry, Suzanne's voice tightened and rose a couple of notes—and a look of pure venom filled her eyes.

Fred had never been one to interfere in the lives of his children. They could only learn by trying and failing and trying again. But every once in a while one of them did something so stupid that he couldn't help but step in.

Laying his hand on Douglas's arm, Fred tried to draw the boy away. "Come on, son, we're going home."

"Stay out of this, Dad."

Suzanne shrugged out of Douglas's grasp and headed for the door. With a final glare Garrett followed, tossing a couple of bills on the table on his way out.

Smothering a sigh of relief, Fred muttered, "Let's give them a minute before we leave."

"I don't intend to give Garrett Locke ten seconds alone

with Suzanne." Pushing past Fred, Douglas hit the door at a trot and disappeared into the night.

That boy didn't have an ounce of patience, Fred thought, and his temper flared at the drop of a hat. Phoebe used to say the trouble between Fred and Douglas was that they were too much alike; but to this day Fred couldn't see where she'd gotten that notion.

Fred grabbed his coat from the rack near the door and shivered as the cold air bit through his shirt and pants. In the still night air, the sound of raised voices guided him to Garrett's black Audi. As Fred approached, Garrett shoved Douglas away with both hands.

Douglas stumbled, regained his footing, and lunged at Garrett, catching him on the jaw with his fist.

Slightly dazed, Garrett responded slowly, and before he recovered completely, Douglas landed another blow; but neither did more than stun Garrett.

The two men squared off like a couple of bantam roosters and eyed each other warily. Taking advantage of the momentary lull, Fred pushed himself in between them, hoping neither one would decide to take a punch before they realized what he'd done.

"Now listen, you two, this has gone far enough. Garrett, get in your car and take Suzanne home. Douglas, you come with me."

Douglas tried to shake Fred off. "I'm not letting him get her alone."

But this time Fred didn't let go. "You're acting like a couple of schoolboys. Why Suzanne would want a thing to do with either of you is beyond me, but you're not taking this any further tonight. Go on, you two, get out of here."

Looking as if he'd won this round, Garrett took Suzanne's arm and led her to the car. But even that simple act set Douglas off again. "This isn't over, Garrett. Not by a long shot."

Using enough force to spin the boy around, Fred firmly guided him toward the Buick at the other end of the parking lot.

Douglas struggled against Fred's hold on him, twisting

back toward the Audi. "You lay a hand on her and I'll kill you," he shouted.

"For Pete's sake, Douglas, shut up." They'd only been outside a minute or two, but already a small crowd had gathered near the door of the restaurant. Milton Gold. Nanette Whitaker and that fellow from Winter Park she'd been seeing lately. Albán Toth stood in the doorway, his arms folded across his chest and a scowl tightening his features. Bill and Janice Lacey peered over his shoulder. Wonderful. With Janice here, everyone in the county would know about this before sunup.

Fred couldn't help wishing Suzanne had been a little more discreet. Surely she knew Douglas would immediately head for the most popular place around. Wouldn't you think she'd try to avoid him? Unless she wanted to cause trouble.

Once they were inside the car, Fred settled himself behind the wheel and turned the key in the ignition. Purred like a kitten, even in this cold. His habit of starting the car three times a week just to keep it working well certainly paid off in the long run.

He drove home slowly, watching for black ice and giving Douglas time to calm down. By the time they reached Lake Front Drive, Douglas's breathing had slowed almost to normal.

Fred turned into his driveway and slowly brought the car into the garage. "You settled down now?"

"I'm fine. Don't worry about it." Douglas flung himself out of the car and slammed the door behind him.

Fred closed his own door more carefully and searched his key ring for the key to the back door. "I sure hope there was more going on back there than a little jealousy over Suzanne having dinner with Garrett. If *that's* all it was, you made a mighty big fool of yourself in front of half the town over nothing."

Douglas glared at him; but Douglas always pouted when things didn't go his way. Fred flipped the last key over and started back through the ring.

Douglas shoved out his hand. "Let me see the keys."

"I'm perfectly capable of finding the key to my own

backdoor." Fred squinted in the half-light to make sure he had the right one and then fitted it into the lock. "I think we ought to get back to this idea of yours," Fred said as he entered the house.

"Which idea?" asked Douglas as he followed his father inside.

"The one about coming home."

"Now I suppose you're going to say I shouldn't do it."

Actually, that's exactly what Fred had been planning to say, but the look on Douglas's face stopped him. "No . . ."

"Try to understand how I feel, Dad. I've lost my wife and my daughter. If I come home, at least I'll see Alison once in a while, even if Suzanne and I can't work things out."

"Which you probably won't after tonight. What on earth got into you?"

Waving away Fred's concern, Douglas made an angry noise in his throat. "She doesn't have any idea who she's playing with."

"She's a grown woman."

Douglas snorted and started to take off his coat.

"She can make her own decisions, and you're not in a position to give her advice. Heaven only knows that's not wise when you're married. But after a *divorce* . . . ?"

"You just don't get it, do you?" Reversing his actions, Douglas jammed his arms back into the sleeves.

"No, I guess I don't."

"All right. I *was* jealous tonight. I can't stand the thought of Suzanne with anyone else—especially that jerk. Did you see her face?" A spasm of anger and jealousy twisted Douglas's features. "And he sat there like the lord of the castle—just like always. She couldn't wait to get back together with him. The ink's barely dry on our divorce decree, and she's practically sitting on his lap. You can't imagine how it made me feel to see them together. I'd like to smash in his smug face, that's how much I hate him."

"You need to calm down, Douglas. Take your coat off and—"

"I can't." Stomping across the room hard enough to rattle the glass in the windows, Douglas turned at the door. "I'm getting out of here. Maybe if I take a walk I'll cool down." He wrenched the door open. "Don't wait up."

The door slammed behind him, and Fred listened to his footsteps until they faded away. He then looped his coat over a hook on the backdoor and lowered himself onto a chair.

He unlaced one boot and stared at the back of the door, as if its painted surface could tell him what to do. Douglas was grown, but he still acted like a child. Why? Was it just the boy's personality? Or was it because he was the youngest of their four children and Phoebe had pampered him and had been reluctant to part with him as he grew older? Would he have been so . . . spoiled if he'd been the oldest? If he'd been Joseph?

Joseph wouldn't act so impulsively. Neither would Jeffrey. In fact, they wouldn't have acted this way at eighteen. Fred admired Joseph and took great pride in Jeffrey's accomplishments, but he had to admit neither of them had ever been as full of life as Douglas. But that zeal, if uncontrolled, would land Douglas in a heap of trouble.

Fred kicked off his other boot and pushed himself to his feet. Half of him wanted to let Douglas lie in whatever mess he created for himself. The other half didn't want the boy to be humiliated. If Douglas wanted any chance at all to save his relationship with Suzanne and Alison, this wasn't the way to go about it.

If Phoebe had been here, she'd have known just what to do. She'd had a way with their youngest son that Fred hadn't ever been able to match. And he obviously hadn't gotten any better at it since she passed on. The chances that Douglas would listen to anything Fred said were slim to none. Used to be his word carried a lot of weight with his kids, but not anymore.

Well, maybe by morning Douglas would be willing to listen to reason. But the knot in Fred's stomach told him that if Douglas didn't rein himself in soon, there'd be hell to pay, and Douglas would expect Fred to help pay it, as always.

three

Fred stomped the mud and snow off his boots and slipped out of his heavy coat. Even on a morning as nippy as this one, he could still get outside for his daily constitutional around the lake. It started the day off right, got the blood pumping through his veins, and kept him feeling young. Younger than seventy-two, anyway.

He'd wanted Douglas to walk with him, but since he'd heard the boy sneak in sometime after two in the morning, he'd decided to let him get his sleep. They'd have other chances. Douglas would probably be around for quite a while, at least until something new lured him away.

Fred hung his coat on the hook by the door and poured himself a cup of coffee. The can in the cupboard indicated that it was a brand of decaf, and Margaret didn't put up a fuss anymore as long as she believed that's what he drank. Fred didn't see any reason to disillusion her. She was a wonderful daughter, but she had an irritating tendency to coddle him and to poke her nose into places where it didn't belong—like his kitchen cupboards. After her first couple of raids on his pantry, Fred had started locking the house when he went out for the first time in his life.

He held the cup in his stiff fingers and let the warmth seep into his bones. Checking the clock on the stove, he stifled a sigh. By the time Douglas dragged himself out of bed, the day would be half-over. Of course, sleep might do the boy some good. Maybe when he woke up he'd have come upon a dose of common sense.

Fred found his reading glasses on top of the refrigerator, tucked the *Denver Post* under one arm, and walked into the living room. Opening the curtains to let the sun in, he settled into his rocking chair by the front window and browsed through the paper until the sound of Margaret's car distracted him in the middle of reading a story about a man and his grandson who'd been killed in a drive-by shooting.

"Listen to this," he said without looking up when he heard her come in from the kitchen. "It says, 'Seventy-four-year-old Enrico Chavez—'"

"Where is he?"

At the sound of her voice, Fred lowered the paper. A head taller than Phoebe had been, Margaret was a striking woman. With her dark hair and usually serene face, she often made Fred think of Olivia DeHavilland—until she got angry.

She waited impatiently for his answer, her eyes radiating with that peculiar golden light that had always signaled irritation in her mother. She must have heard about last night.

"Douglas?" Fred asked.

"Yes, Douglas."

"In bed."

"At this hour?"

"It's not that late."

Margaret crossed the room and stood over him. "Were you with him at the Four Seasons last night?"

"Yes."

"And you *let* him act like that?"

"Well, now, I couldn't hardly stop him, could I? Besides, it all happened so fast. One minute we were talking, and the next minute he was over there shouting at Suzanne and Garrett—"

Margaret turned away and shook her head in disbelief. "Suzanne and Garrett? And now Douglas? It's like they're all sixteen years old again."

"Hormones," Fred said and shook out a section of the paper.

"What?"

"Hormones. It was hormones then, and it's the same story now."

Margaret perched on the arm of the couch. "Suzanne and Garrett. I couldn't believe it when I heard. And you can bet Janice Lacey didn't waste any time calling me this morning to fill me in."

"It wasn't as bad as she made it sound."

"No?" Margaret narrowed her dark eyes as if assessing the truth of his statement, seemed to accept it, and shifted her attention to the mug in his hand. "Is that decaf?"

"What else would it be?"

She hesitated over that one for a second longer before turning away. "Maybe I'll have a cup."

"Help yourself." She was only forty-six. At her age a little caffeine wouldn't hurt her any.

Fred pushed himself out of the chair and followed her into the kitchen. He might as well get breakfast started. With Margaret making all this racket, Douglas would be up any minute. "Are the kids in school already?"

"All but Deborah. She's got that flu that's going around."

"You should have brought her with you."

"When she's feeling better." She stopped with her hand on a mug in the cupboard and tilted her head as if listening to something.

A second later the kitchen door opened and Douglas appeared, his hair poking straight up, his face puffy from sleep. He shuffled into the room, sent Fred a blurred smile, and kissed Margaret on the cheek. "Morning, sis. Is there any coffee left?"

"Of course." Margaret stepped away from the counter.

"What's for breakfast? I'm starved." He wore only a white undershirt and a pair of too-large sweatpants hanging from his waist, and he moved in that fuzzy, unfocused way of someone not completely awake. Blinking rapidly several times, he peered into the bottom of a cup as if trying to tell whether he'd found a clean one.

Fred started to open the refrigerator, but Margaret stepped in front of him. "What's for breakfast? Dad, don't tell me you've been doing all the cooking since he's been here."

Douglas blinked again and tried to focus on the coffee-maker. "What's the matter with *you* this morning?"

Maybe Douglas didn't remember how his mother had looked when she got angry, but the expression on Margaret's face should have warned him. He poured coffee into a mug, added sugar, and stirred. "Where's the milk?"

Flinging open the refrigerator door, Margaret snatched the milk carton from the shelf and slammed it onto the counter. "I don't believe this! Do you expect Dad to wait on you like this when I'm not here?"

Finally Douglas began to realize something was wrong. He hesitated for half a second, his cup halfway to his lips, before he took a wary sip and watched Margaret over its rim. "Are you mad at me?"

Margaret shot an exasperated look at Fred. "He wants to know if I'm mad at him."

Fred dug a handful of potatoes out of a sack near the back door. "She's mad at you, son."

"Why?"

"Janice Lacey called her this morning to tell her about last night."

"Oh."

"Oh? That's all?" Margaret's voice sounded shrill.

"What do you want me to say?"

She threw her arms up in the air and looked at Fred for help. "Well, something more than 'oh.'"

Douglas took another sip and looked around for the table. "Okay. How about 'I was right.' I don't want Suzanne to have anything to do with Garrett Locke."

"Since when did you become her keeper?" Margaret opened a cupboard door and searched for something, finally taking out a box of high-fiber something-or-other she'd expect Fred to eat. "I can't even imagine how foolish you looked last night, carrying on that way."

"Is that what Janice told you?"

"Among other things." She sighed in exasperation and yanked a bowl out of the cupboard.

"I don't care." Douglas sat and rubbed his face with his hand. "If Suzanne could even think of getting involved with Garrett again, she obviously needs someone to tell her what to do."

"Look, Garrett might not be the nicest guy in the world, and maybe Suzanne is making a mistake by going out with him, but it's none of your business anymore. What's the matter with you?"

Douglas put on an indifferent face and made a show of studying the cereal box. "I don't want to talk about it anymore. It's none of your business."

"You *have* to talk about it. You can't come home and act any old way you want and leave Dad and me to deal with it when you waltz away again."

"I'm not going anywhere. I've come home."

"That's what you say now, but you'll find some reason to leave. You always do."

Fred pulled out a chair and placed himself between the two of them. "Now, Margaret—"

"*He's* not the one who's going to have to listen to everybody talking about him."

"Is that what this is all about?" Douglas shoved the cereal box away and leaned back in his chair. "You're worried what people are going to think? Since when did that matter to you?"

"That's not what I meant—"

"You've changed, Maggie."

"I have not. And it's not about what people think. It's about you screwing up again. You're thirty-six years old and you still haven't grown up."

Fred didn't like the turn this conversation was taking. "Now listen you two—"

"Why? Because I don't act like you?" Douglas pushed his fingers through his hair and his face darkened.

"No, because you're irresponsible."

"And if anybody would know about being responsible, it's you." If he'd said it in any other tone of voice, it might have been a compliment.

Margaret turned a deep shade of red and opened her mouth to retort, but Fred didn't wait to hear what she had to say.

"Enough! Both of you." He slammed his fist on the table

and both of his children shot him a surprised look. But it shut them up. "I don't want to hear one more word."

For one long moment they both stared at him, and it wasn't until they heard the pounding on the backdoor that Margaret reluctantly dragged her eyes away. After the intensity of their argument, the silence hung heavily in the room as she walked toward the door and pulled it open.

From where Fred sat it took him a second or two to focus on Doc Huggins's face. "Doc?"

"Fred." Doc wiped his feet on the mat and nodded to Margaret. "Maggie, Doug. Mind if I come in for a minute?"

Margaret stepped aside. "Of course not."

Doc checked in at a few years younger than Fred, but he had the disposition of a cantankerous old man. For some reason, he'd decided to share his diagnosis of Fred's condition with the rest of the town and had cautioned everyone to help Fred cut back on caffeine, cholesterol, and sodium.

But Fred had no intention of spending the rest of his days eating cardboard-tasting cereal, salad without dressing, and an endless procession of chicken parts dressed in low-fat sauces, and he'd been a little angry with Doc ever since Lizzie, down at the Bluebird, started rationing his egg consumption.

Doc pulled off his hat and made a vain attempt at smoothing what was left of his hair. "I wanted to stop by and tell you the news myself. Told Enos I thought it should be me, considering your dad's health."

Panic flashed across Margaret's face. "What's wrong? Is it one of the kids?"

"No, nothing like that. Don't worry. But why don't you sit down here by your Dad." Doc settled his bag on the table and leaned an arm across it, but the look on his face convinced Fred that the news wasn't good. "I've just come from Locke's store. Considering what happened last night, I thought maybe you ought to be told right away."

Fred's pulse stuttered. "Told what?"

"Rusty Kinsella called Enos over at the sheriff's office

first thing this morning. Seems he went in early to open the store and found Garrett in his office—dead."

Margaret gasped, but Douglas didn't make a sound.

Fred didn't need to ask the next question. He knew, just the way he'd known he was looking at a murder victim when he found Joan Cavanaugh in the lake last fall. But he asked, anyway. "What happened?"

"He's been murdered. Somebody hit him in the head and crushed his skull."

four

A stunned hush filled the room, broken only by the ragged sound of someone's breathing, and Fred couldn't be certain it wasn't his own. "Any idea who did it?"

Doc shook his head. "None. Yet. Enos is still going over the scene and looking for clues."

Margaret murmured something, and a muscle in Douglas's jaw clenched and unclenched repeatedly, betraying his anxiety, but he didn't speak.

Garrett hadn't been a likable fellow, but Fred couldn't imagine anyone wanting to kill him. Maybe there had been some sort of trouble at home—except that the Locke family had been whittled down to almost nothing, what with Richard's death last year. Maude had been gone at least ten years and now, with Garrett gone, that left just what's-her-name, Garrett's sister. And an ex-wife somewhere or other—it seemed like she and Garrett's daughter had been gone a good five years. Would one of them have wanted Garrett dead?

Or was it something else? "Any problems at the store that you know of? Or maybe a robbery?" Fred asked.

Silence greeted his question. Silence and three pairs of narrowed eyes.

Margaret leaned toward him, her face tight. "Don't even think about sticking your nose into this, Dad."

Doc cleared his throat pointedly. "As a matter of fact, Enos did ask me to make it perfectly clear that you're not to go getting any big ideas this time."

Ideas. They made him sound like an old fool. The thought of Enos sending such a message with Doc—the idea of

Doc's coming by at all—made him angry now that he stopped to think about it. "Why are you here, Doc? Why have you made a special trip just to tell us about the murder?"

"I thought you ought to know."

"Why?"

"It's just that after last night . . . I mean, with Doug and Garrett fighting again . . ."

"We had an argument—" Douglas's face flushed an angry red.

"The way I heard it, you were fighting in the parking lot."

Fred cut in before Douglas could say anything foolish. "Well, for Pete's sake! They got a little testy, that's all. Nothing more to it than that. It was all over in a minute, and after Garrett and Suzanne went on their way, Douglas and I came home."

"We were worried about all the excitement, that with Douglas's visit, and last night's trouble—and now this," Doc said. "Enos and I both thought I should be the one to break the news. Just in case."

Fred hated the way people fussed over him as if they expected his heart to give out any minute. He'd had that one little scare, but he'd been fine ever since. "Well, you've told us, and I'm still alive."

Doc's face puckered into a scowl.

Margaret patted Fred's hand. "Don't get upset with Doc. People care about you, that's all."

"Nothing but a crotchety old fool." Doc snapped his case shut and shook his head. "Show a little concern, and what does it get you? Snapped at by a crotchety old fool. You have my sympathy, Maggie, having to deal with this all the time."

Fred snorted.

Doc pointed a finger at him. "You just remember what Enos said about keeping your nose out of his investigation."

Feigning a look of innocent surprise, Fred met Doc's holier-than-thou expression. "Then you've ruled out the idea that he might have killed himself by whacking himself on the head?"

In spite of herself, Margaret smiled. "Don't start in on Doc. It's not his fault you were the only one who believed Joan Cavanaugh didn't commit suicide."

Not Doc's fault, she said, when any fool could have seen it if he'd just looked hard enough. At least, any fool but Doc.

"Does Suzanne know? About Garrett?" Douglas asked quietly.

Doc's face softened. "I don't know. Enos sent Ivan and Grady to notify the family, but I don't know whether anyone's planning to tell Suzanne."

"Then I've got to tell her."

Margaret pushed herself away from the table. "That's not a good idea."

"I *have* to tell her."

"Can't you understand she doesn't want you hanging around? Let someone else tell her, Doug."

"I can't."

"Margaret's right, son. Leave her alone."

Douglas shook his head. "I can't. I have to keep trying. For Alison."

Margaret screwed up her face in a look of disbelief. "For Alison? Please." She turned away, saying more with the set of her shoulders and the tilt of her head than with her words.

"I have to let her know right away—before she hears it from someone else." Douglas's voice carried enough conviction to make Margaret look at Fred for support.

He agreed with Margaret, but Douglas did have a point. Somebody ought to tell Suzanne, but it ought to be somebody else. Fred didn't want Douglas getting involved. Let sleeping dogs lie, that's what he thought. He opened his mouth to say so, but Douglas cut him off.

"I won't be gone more than an hour."

Doc shook his head. "I have to agree with Maggie and your dad. Let me call Enos and have him get on the horn to Grady and Ivan. They can swing past Suzanne's after they've talked with Olivia."

"Oh. Olivia." Margaret dropped back in her chair. "How's she going to take it?"

Olivia—that was the sister's name. Same age as Margaret, if Fred remembered right. Well, he didn't envy Grady and Ivan the task of telling her about Garrett's death. She wouldn't take it well.

"I have to tell Suzanne before Olivia gets to her." Douglas insisted, and, thinking about it that way, Fred had to agree.

If Olivia knew Garrett had been seeing Suzanne, she'd probably call her as soon as the deputies left. It would be far better for Suzanne to hear the news from Douglas than from Olivia. Fred had heard Olivia say she didn't believe in sugar-coating things. What she meant was, she didn't have an ounce of tact. "Maybe Douglas is right—"

"Absolutely not." Margaret leaned toward him, her eyes bright.

"—we've got to think about Alison. We can't let—"

"Exactly." Douglas shot to his feet. "That's exactly why I need to tell her."

"But I don't think you should go over there." Fred reached for the telephone and held it toward Douglas. "You can say everything you need to over the phone. Later, when things cool down a little, you can see her again."

With a show of reluctance, Douglas took the receiver from Fred. But it took him several seconds before he focused on the list of telephone numbers Fred kept by the phone and found Suzanne's new number. Under other circumstances, Fred would have given the boy some privacy for this conversation, but in his current state of mind, there was no telling what kind of fool thing he might say.

It must have taken Suzanne several rings to get to the telephone, and Douglas looked just about ready to hang up when his face brightened. "Suzanne? Doug."

His face fell and flushed with color, and he replaced the receiver slowly. "She hung up on me."

Fred had almost expected as much. Suzanne wouldn't be in any hurry to speak with Douglas again after last night.

"I knew I should have gone over there. She couldn't hang up on me then."

"No, but she could slam the door in your face." Fred

reached for the telephone again. "I'll talk with her. Give me her number."

Douglas rattled it off and Fred punched the numbers in, half-convinced Suzanne wouldn't answer this time. Her tentative hello after the second ring surprised him. "Suzanne, it's Fred. Now don't hang up, this is important."

"What is it?"

"Doc Huggins just stopped by with some news we thought you ought to hear right away."

"You mean about Garrett." Her voice sounded low and flat—unemotional.

"You've heard?"

"Yes."

"Well, I'm glad. We didn't want you hearing about it somewhere in town."

"That's kind of you." He couldn't remember ever hearing her voice so controlled before, so devoid of feeling.

"It wasn't my idea, really. Douglas was worried about you." He might as well put in a good word. It couldn't hurt.

"Worried? Why?" A trace of emotion Fred couldn't define tinged her voice.

"Like I said, he didn't want you to hear about it at the store or—"

"Tell him I'm touched." Sarcasm. Bitter sarcasm, that's what it was.

"He really is concerned."

"That was obvious last night."

Without warning Douglas reached for the receiver and yanked it from Fred's hand. "Suzanne? We've got to talk." He paused to listen, but obviously didn't like what he heard. "You can't refuse to see me, I'm your husband." Another long pause. "Maybe not, but I'm still Alison's father. We can tell her together."

Fred could hear Suzanne's voice sounding shrill and tinny at this distance. Then silence.

Douglas slowly lowered the receiver to his lap. "She hung up again."

"Well, at least she knows." Doc hoisted his bag off the table. "Should I give you a quick check, Fred?"

"Not now." He waved Doc away. He felt fine, but the look on Douglas's face concerned him. "What's wrong?"

Douglas turned slowly, panic evident in his eyes. "She thinks *I* did it."

"Did what?" Margaret took the phone from Douglas's limp fingers and replaced it on the hook.

"She thinks I killed Garrett."

"That's ridiculous." Margaret whipped around to face Fred, her eyes pleading with him to agree. Which, of course, he did.

"Ridiculous," he echoed, and patted Douglas on the shoulder. "Ex-wife talk, that's all it is."

But Douglas's shock had frozen into his expression. "She really thinks I did it. How could she think that? She knows me."

Doc fumbled with the catch on his bag and extracted his stethoscope, and Fred waved him off again. He was fine, for Pete's sake. Douglas was the one who might need attention. Fred gripped Douglas's shoulder hard enough to make the boy raise his eyes.

"She's angry, son. Hurt and angry. And you have to stay away from her for a little while. Give her some time to calm down before you try to see her again."

The pain on Douglas's face tore at Fred's heart. He tried to imagine how he'd have felt if Phoebe had ever thought him capable of something terrible. He knew it would have broken him.

In spite of the divorce and the bitter feelings between them, Douglas obviously still loved Suzanne. If anyone else had said those things, Douglas would have laughed them off. But Suzanne's lack of faith in him, her belief that he could have murdered a man, and her accusations that he'd actually done it, had staggered him.

Margaret, bless her, wrapped her arms around Douglas. "Ignore her. We know you didn't do it. Everybody knows you didn't do it."

"Suzanne thinks I did."

Fred couldn't sit still and watch this. "Now just a minute. Suzanne doesn't really think you killed Garrett. She's upset.

She's still angry and embarrassed about last night, and she's going to say the first thing that comes to her mind that will hurt you back. That's all."

For a second or two Douglas's eyes flickered with hope, but just as quickly it died away. "I'm sorry."

"For what?"

"For everything."

"Nothing to be sorry for," Fred insisted.

Margaret gave Douglas a gentle shake. "Don't pay any attention to her, Doug. She knows what's going to hurt you the most. It happens when you've been together for a while. And since the divorce, you can't expect her to have any faith in you, or even particularly like you."

But Douglas didn't look convinced. Fred suspected nothing they could say would make a lick of difference right now. In fact, he doubted whether anyone but Suzanne could make a difference. And he knew that if Suzanne was angry enough to say such things to Douglas, she wouldn't be ready to take them back anytime soon.

Doc was still fussing around with his bag, and Fred saw no sense in letting him hang around any longer. "Why don't you go on home? I'm fine."

Doc hesitated.

"Do I look like I'm ready to keel over? I'm fine. Besides, aren't your grandkids coming today? Get on home and spend a little time with them."

"They'll be here for two weeks. Charlotte and Ted are leaving them while they go to Mexico," Doc protested, but he looked at Margaret as if seeking her permission to leave. When she gave it with a slight nod, he repacked his bag and reached for his coat. "Things will blow over soon, Doug," he said. "Your dad's right. Just give her a few days to calm down and she'll come to her senses." He gave the boy a pat on the shoulder and, with a curt nod at Fred, left them alone at last.

But after Doc left, none of them spoke. Fred poured himself another cup of coffee, wishing its soothing warmth could help straighten out the jumble in his mind.

For Suzanne to even suggest Douglas had killed Garrett

was ridiculous. Nobody else would even *think* of something
so absurd. But if they didn't prove that to Douglas, he'd
mope around the house all day. So if Fred could just get
Douglas out and about—over to the Bluebird, for instance,
and around other people—surely his spirits would rise.

With fresh enthusiasm, Fred slapped his palm on the
counter. "Douglas, go get dressed, I'm taking us all out for
breakfast."

Margaret shot him a look of disbelief. "Out to breakfast?"

"Out to breakfast." Fred switched off the coffeepot and
rinsed his cup. "What Douglas needs is a healthy dose of
good old common sense. Get up, Douglas, and get dressed."

Responding obediently, Douglas pushed himself away
from the table and shuffled down the hall. When he returned
a few minutes later, his hair was only half-combed and he
wore a pair of faded jeans and a ratty-looking sweater. No
matter. He didn't need to look like a million dollars. He just
needed to get out and talk to people who could help him feel
better. He'd see soon enough which way the wind blew.

five

Fred pushed open the front door of the Bluebird Cafe. He took a deep breath of the heady aromas of bacon, sausage, fried eggs, and hash browns, the earthy scent of freshly brewed coffee—a real breakfast—the kind of meal Margaret would choke over and nobody wanted him to eat anymore.

The Bluebird had been part of Cutler for almost as long as Fred could remember. It had always been the Bluebird, but when Lizzie Hatch bought it a few years back she'd changed it considerably. She'd ripped the yellowed ivy-twined wallpaper from the walls and replaced it with posters of Elvis Presley young and old. She'd replaced most of the songs on the jukebox with the King's greatest hits, and once an Elvis song found its way onto Lizzie's jukebox, it never left.

Now *this* was a restaurant. Lizzie did most of her own cooking, and one of her meals could stick to Fred's ribs all day. Looking forward to a decent breakfast, and knowing Margaret was too upset over Douglas's troubles to argue much over his order, Fred led the way through the crowded tables to a booth at the back under the *Girls! Girls! Girls!* poster.

He'd just settled himself onto the bench beside Margaret when Lizzie approached and greeted them with a nod of her head.

"Morning, Lizzie," Fred said.

Margaret looked up from a study of her silverware and smiled. "Good morning, Lizzie."

Lizzie nodded again, then let her eyes light on Douglas. "Doug."

Looking miserable, Douglas tried to paste on a smile. At least you had to give him marks for effort. "How've you been, Lizzie?"

But she'd obviously reached the limit of her conversation for the morning because she only nodded, as if to indicate she'd been fine, and raised the coffeepot with a silent question at them all. Without waiting for Margaret to do something silly like order a pot of decaf, Fred turned over his cup and settled it onto the saucer, smiling his answer.

Now this ought to help Douglas feel better, Fred thought. Just look how warmly Lizzie had greeted him. From across the room Sophie Van Dyke gave them a little wave. George Newman turned in his seat at the counter and nodded, and several other friendly faces acknowledged them.

As Elvis started singing "Moody Blue," Fred happily settled back against the seat. He'd known this would do the trick. In a few minutes, Douglas would have forgotten all of Suzanne's foolishness and he'd be his old self again.

Fred ordered biscuits and sausage gravy, earning little more than a scowl from Margaret, who ordered whole wheat toast and cereal. Lizzie waited, pencil poised in hand, for Douglas's order, but he didn't seem to be aware of her.

Fred prodded him gently with his foot. "Tell Lizzie what you want, son."

Douglas didn't even bother to look up. "Nothing."

"You were starving a few minutes ago. What's the matter, do you need a menu?"

"I can't eat."

Lizzie stuck the pencil into her hair behind her ear and slipped her order pad into her apron pocket. "Must be all this murder talk upsetting him."

"What murder talk?" Fred knew better than to think the town wouldn't be buzzing with the news, but he didn't want to think that anyone else might share Suzanne's opinion as to who was the guilty party.

But Lizzie merely picked up the extra cup and saucer and turned away. She'd said her piece. She'd let them know there had been talk, interrupted for the moment by their arrival. Maybe bringing Douglas out hadn't been such a good idea after all.

No, if Douglas hid away at home, tongues would just wag more. This way he didn't look as if he had something to hide. They'd done exactly the right thing. But Fred wished he could figure a way to get the boy perked up a little. His hangdog expression alone would cause speculation.

Fred made an attempt or two at conversation, and Margaret made an effort to pick it up, but Douglas didn't show any interest in the kids, their school, Sarah's almost-lead role in the musical, or the problems with Fred's brakes. By the time Lizzie arrived with their breakfast, Fred welcomed the diversion. At least now they could turn their attention to food and have an excuse for the unnatural atmosphere at their table.

In spite of Douglas's refusal to order, Lizzie had brought him one of her ham and cheese omelets with hash browns, toast, and raspberry jam—Douglas's favorite meal. Whatever anyone else might think, Lizzie believed in Douglas. She always had, even when he was young and getting into trouble. Leave the boy alone, she'd said time and again. And this morning, in her own way, she'd said it again.

Smiling in gratitude for her support, Fred picked up his fork just as the front door opened. Amidst much stomping of feet and noise about the cold, Enos and his two deputies made their appearance.

Beside him, Fred sensed Margaret straightening her posture a little. They might have been married to other people for over twenty years, but there'd always been something between Margaret and Enos, and Fred imagined there always would be. He didn't for one minute believe they'd ever done anything about it, but the attraction was there, and if anything ever happened to both Webb Templeton and Jessica Asay, Fred intended to see that Enos and Margaret got together.

Shrugging out of his heavy coat, Enos surveyed the room. Fred watched him notice Margaret and then send the deputies to a table on the opposite side of the room.

Enos crossed quickly to Fred's booth and slid into the seat beside Douglas with a smile and a nod for everyone and a soft look in Margaret's direction. "Morning everybody. Did Doc get by to see you?"

"Yes, he dropped by." Fred knew he sounded sharp. He might think of Enos as a fourth son, but that didn't mean he had to like everything the man did. "Why did you send him?"

Enos glanced at Douglas out of the corner of his eye. "I had three calls last night about the argument at Albán's place. Well-meaning citizens wanting the local officials to be aware of the hostilities. You know how it is, Fred, it happens all the time."

"You don't think Douglas had something to do with the murder?"

"Of course not. But I do need to ask the two of you a couple of questions."

Douglas looked up, finally. "What about?"

"I've got Ivan and Grady asking around. Maybe somebody saw something. Did either of you hear Garrett say anything about meeting someone at the store?"

"Nothing." Douglas shook his head.

"We didn't exactly chat about his plans," Fred said. Silly question, he thought. If you're busy accusing a man of stealing your ex-wife, you don't waste time on small talk.

"So he didn't say anything to either of you?" Enos said, looking at Douglas, then Fred.

Douglas shook his head again, and when he lifted his cup Fred noticed his hands were trembling. This must be harder on the boy than he'd imagined.

"It didn't come up."

Enos sighed and leaned back in the seat. "At least I found some evidence in Garrett's office that ought to help tie things together."

"Then you'll solve this case quickly?" Margaret asked, her voice low.

"I expect to."

Good, Fred thought. The sooner everything got straightened up, the sooner Douglas could get on with his life. And putting his difficulties with Suzanne behind him ought to be his number-one priority. Any woman who'd accuse the man she'd been married to for over a dozen years, a man as gentle as Douglas, of killing someone . . . well, it didn't bear thinking about.

The front door opened again and, almost as if Fred's thoughts had conjured her up, Suzanne made her appearance. Even at this distance she looked pale. With her lips compressed in a straight line and her dark eyes hooded, she looked troubled. For a second Fred wondered whether she'd come looking for Douglas, but when her aunt Celeste followed her through the door, he changed his mind.

What were they doing here? Every eye in the place had looked up to identify the new arrivals, and now they turned to Douglas for his reaction.

His eyes lit up. "Suzanne."

"Stay right here," Fred instructed.

"No, I've got to talk to her."

Had Douglas lived in Seattle so long he'd forgotten what a small town like Cutler could be like? "Not *here* you don't."

Douglas slowly focused and looked around the cafe. "But she won't see me, she won't even talk to me. I have to convince her I didn't—" He broke off suddenly and stared wide-eyed at Margaret.

"Sorry." She gave him a tight-lipped smile. "My foot slipped."

"Didn't what?" Enos looked from Douglas to Margaret and back again.

"Nothing," Douglas said quietly.

"Convince her you didn't what?"

Sometimes Enos could stick his nose into family business in the most irritating way. Fred tried to think of a diversion, but at that moment, Celeste made a great show of noticing them. Patting Suzanne's hand, she murmured something to her niece and then sent meaningful looks in Douglas's direction. She raised her arm to call Lizzie over to their table and pointed with a clattering of jewelry toward a booth on the opposite end of the cafe.

The place fell silent: no silverware scraping against plates, no ice tinkling against glass—even Elvis had stopped singing.

Fred cringed. If he'd had any idea something like this could happen, he never would have asked Douglas to leave the house. Well, there was no sense making him stay any longer. With Suzanne and Celeste here, things could only get worse.

Scraping up and eating the last of his biscuits and gravy, Fred looked at Margaret. She hadn't eaten much, and Douglas hadn't done more than push his omelet around on the plate. Fred wiped his mouth with his napkin. "Ready?" he said.

Margaret nodded almost eagerly, but Douglas didn't look anxious to leave. "Not yet."

Enos shifted around to face Fred. "You heading out?"

But Douglas answered. "Not until I've talked with Suzanne." He started to rise as if he wanted to leave the booth.

And, like a fool, Enos stood to let him pass. "If you see Lizzie, send her back this way with the coffee."

Fred stifled a groan. Not here—this was not the place or the time for a confrontation with Suzanne. If Douglas dreamed another attempt at conversation with her would go smoothly, he must have his head further up in the clouds than Fred imagined.

From the way Margaret watched her brother cross the room, Fred knew she felt the same sense of rising panic that he did. But short of tackling the boy and dragging him out by his collar, they couldn't do a blasted thing. At least now Margaret could see how easily the situation last night had gotten out of hand. Once Douglas made up his mind, he was like a steamroller. Every one of Fred's children had inherited that annoying, stubborn streak from their mother—it just showed up differently in each of them.

Enos settled back in his seat and rubbed his face with his palm. "I could sure use a nice cup of coffee. I've been up all night . . ."

Douglas was almost there. Suzanne looked up and she

saw him. Fred tried not to wince at the look of anger on her face. He waited for the explosion.

"Seems next to impossible to have three murders in such a short time in a place like Cutler," said Enos, his voice dropping low as he leaned across the table toward Margaret.

Celeste put her hand on Suzanne's arm. She must have asked Douglas to sit down. Maybe there was hope.

". . . don't think it was premeditated, really," Enos continued. "Now if there'd been poison or a gun involved, it'd be different. But there weren't any signs of a robbery or forced entry, so Garrett must have let whoever did it into the store . . ."

Douglas tried to touch Suzanne's shoulder, but she jerked away and said something. Fred could tell by the way her face twisted, and the way Douglas looked as if he'd been slapped, that it hadn't been kind.

"No, I haven't found a murder weapon yet, but I've got an idea or two. All Doc can say is that it's a blunt instrument. And whatever the killer used, he didn't leave it in Garrett's office . . ."

Enos's last words drew Fred's attention away from Douglas and Suzanne. "Did you say you haven't found the murder weapon?"

Instead of just answering the question, Enos scowled and got that funny look on his face. "You're not getting involved."

"I didn't ask to get involved. You're sitting at my table. You're discussing the murder with my daughter. And you said you hadn't found the murder weapon. I'm just trying to make polite conversation."

Enos looked skeptical.

"What earthly reason would I have for wanting to get involved in your murder investigation?" Fred asked.

Margaret made a rude, choking noise and Enos looked suspicious. "I can't imagine," he said. "That's what worries me."

Before Fred could defend himself, loud voices erupted on the other side of the room. Douglas. Again. Fred slid out of the booth, but Enos shot up and made it across to Suzanne's table before Fred even got upright.

"Stay away from me, Doug," Suzanne hissed. "Don't come anywhere near me again. And stay away from Alison. The last thing she needs right now is you." She threw down her napkin and snatched up her purse.

"Suzanne, please—"

"I mean it. If I see you anywhere around my house or my daughter, I'll file a formal complaint."

She'd made it almost to the door when Douglas broke the shocked silence by shouting, "You can't keep me away from Alison. No matter what you do, you can't keep me away from my own daughter."

Suzanne stopped and turned, her eyes spitting fire. "Why do you insist on hurting Alison like this?"

"I haven't done anything that would hurt Alison—"

"What about Garrett? You've always hated him, everybody knows that. And last night only made it worse."

"I didn't do anything—"

"Save it, Doug. Nobody else had any reason to kill him." She stormed out of the door, leaving a stunned audience in her wake.

Watching her, Fred felt his world crumble at his feet.

six

Fred wiped his feet on the mat and opened the door to the sheriff's office. Enos sat behind his battered desk, his sandy head bent over his paperwork. Country music played softly from the clock radio at his side.

He didn't even look up. "Don't bother asking, Fred. You're not getting involved."

"I didn't come here for that."

In spite of himself, Enos looked interested. "Really? What did you want, then?"

"I wanted to be sure you don't believe what Suzanne said this morning."

Enos lifted his eyebrows. "You worried?"

"Not really."

"Good." He bent back over the desktop.

"It's just that Douglas is letting Suzanne's crazy accusations bother him, and I was hoping you could tell me something that would put his mind at rest."

This time Enos leaned back in his chair and studied Fred for a moment, tapping his pencil on a file. "Tell him I'm real careful about arresting folks based just on the words of an angry spouse. Hell, if I did that, half the town would be in jail."

"*You* tell him that. He won't listen to me."

Enos grunted his understanding and closed the file folder. Sliding it toward one corner of his desk, he reached for another from a small stack at his side. "What I wish is that the two of you could tell me something. I don't have much to go on."

"I thought you said you'd found some evidence."

"One little button. No murder weapon. No eyewitnesses. Nothing but a button on the floor near the body. Even if I knew who it belonged to, there's no way to prove how it got there."

"How about blood? If somebody crushed his skull—"

Enos shook his head. "Crushed it, but didn't break the skin. A little bleeding from his nose and ears, but that's all. No convenient bloody footprints leading to the alley, no chance of blood on the murderer's clothing—nothing."

"Fingerprints?"

Enos hesitated for a second and looked suspicious. "No. There are fingerprints all over the place, but nothing we can use. Every person in a hundred-mile radius has probably been inside that store."

"And no murder weapon?"

This time Enos didn't answer. He pushed the file folder away and fixed Fred with a no-nonsense look. "I know what you're trying to do, and I'm not saying another word."

"I don't want to get involved in your murder investigation. I only want my son to stop fretting."

"Uh-huh," Enos said in that tone of voice that meant he didn't buy it.

"Believe it or not."

"I tend toward not." He pulled the file folder toward him again and made a show of opening it.

"Did I ask to get involved?"

"Not yet, but it's only a matter of time."

"Now listen, Enos—"

"Don't bother. I remember what you did last time, and I'm not letting you get away with it again. This is an official investigation. Stay out of it. Do I make myself clear?"

Fred bit back the protest from the tip of his tongue and nodded. "Absolutely."

"Fine." Enos turned his attention to the folder again.

Fred let him work in silence for a minute. "Guess I'll run along then."

"You do that."

"I don't suppose you'll just tell me whether you have any suspects in mind."

"And have you race off trying to interrogate them? Not on your life."

Very funny. Fred decided to ignore the comment. "Mind if I borrow your phone for a minute?"

Enos shook his head without looking up. "Go ahead."

Fred punched in the first six digits of Margaret's home number, rocked back on his heels, and acted like he expected someone to answer. After the amount of time he figured several rings would take, he checked his watch and muttered, "That's funny."

Enos didn't look up.

He disconnected and repeated the procedure. He waited again. "That's odd," he said a little louder. "I wonder where she's gone."

Enos turned his head a fraction of an inch. "Who?"

"Margaret. I promised to call her after I talked to you." He disconnected again.

This time Enos looked out from under his eyebrows. "She's not home?"

Fred shook his head and tried to look worried. "Well, no matter, I guess. I just hoped I'd have something to tell her that would make her feel a little better. I wish she wouldn't worry about it so much. You'll do your job and arrest the killer soon enough."

Enos checked his watch. "Isn't it about time for her kids to come home for lunch?"

"And Webb, too." Fred gave the desktop a pat with the palm of his hand. "Yep. And Webb. Guess he was right, after all."

Enos's eyes darkened. His lack of regard for Webb could be measured directly against his affection for Margaret. "About what?"

"He just said she'd be smart not to count on you to tell her anything. He thought you'd want to keep everything you knew under your hat . . ." Fred hesitated and then shook his head. "Never mind the rest." He didn't let Webb's comparative innocence this time bother him. Webb never hesitated to voice his opinion of Enos when the other man's name came up, and Fred wouldn't repeat most of what he said.

Enos flushed and Fred could almost hear his mind working. He'd never want Margaret to think she couldn't rely on him, especially not if Webb suggested it.

Margaret had made a big mistake when she threw Enos over for Webster Templeton, and Enos had answered by rushing off and marrying Jessica Rich within six months. Fred liked to think that if Enos had waited a while, Margaret would have seen her mistake and things would have worked out between the two of them. As it was, he'd had to watch them mooning over each other from a distance for nearly thirty years. But once in a while their mutual admiration came in handy.

Enos tossed his pencil on the desk. "You tell Margaret that Douglas isn't under any more suspicion than anyone else, and he won't be unless I come across some pretty compelling evidence."

Fred tried to keep his face composed, but relief overwhelmed him. "I'll let her know. She'll be glad to hear it."

Enos nodded in satisfaction, reopened the file, and picked up his pencil. "Tell her to call me if she has any other questions."

"Sure." Fred paused with his hand on the doorknob. "And Enos?"

"Yeah?"

"Thanks."

Their eyes held for a moment before Enos nodded. "No thanks necessary. Like I said, I don't arrest people on the word of angry ex-spouses."

Fred turned, but had to sidestep around Ivan Neeley, Enos's youngest deputy. Ivan's excitement radiated from his face and animated his stocky body as he pushed gently past Fred and stepped into the office.

Ivan's uniform looked as if it had seen better days, and his face was layered with a fine growth of whiskers he didn't usually wear. "We hit pay dirt," he announced with satisfaction. "Albán Toth saw somebody running from Locke's last night, and he thinks he can make a positive ID. Grady's bringing him over so you can question him."

Fred hesitated at the door. A positive ID? Surely knowing what Albán had to say would clear Douglas's mind. Maybe he ought to stick around . . .

But before he could take two steps back inside, Enos came around from behind his desk and escorted him through the door. "Not now, Fred. This is official business."

As the door shut between them, Fred tried to convince himself it didn't matter. He wanted to stay and hear what Albán had to say, but he'd obviously pushed his luck with Enos far enough for one day.

Albán wasn't the type to accuse someone without good cause, so if he said he saw someone leaving Locke's, the case was as good as wrapped up. And Fred would just have to pretend to be content and wait for the news.

He took a deep breath and headed across the street. Enos's office sat at the west end of Main Street, near the dead end at Spirit Lake. Since Fred lived only about half a mile down Lake Front Drive, this particular walk home was one of his favorites. He loved watching the lake through the trees and listening to the sounds of nature, but he hated the pallor Garrett Locke's murder threw over the landscape. Nothing felt the same.

The weak March sun danced off the water's placid surface and the air carried a hint of warmth. Within a few feet, Fred slipped out of his coat and draped it over his shoulder.

Every year more people discovered the Spirit Lake region. With Rocky Mountain National Park only a few miles away, and several ski resorts already in the area, growth was inevitable. The people of Cutler had managed to elude most of the tourists until now, but Fred knew their quiet days were numbered. He hated to see expansion coming, but they were already experiencing the side effects. An element of violence had crept in from Cutler's edges. Between the Cavanaugh murders and this one, the total came to three in less than six months. A chilling thought, that.

Fred tried to push away the dark thoughts and concentrate on something more pleasant. If Cutler grew, he reckoned, Douglas might find a job that would keep him interested for a while. But Fred wouldn't hold his breath waiting for any career to tie Douglas down permanently. He just hoped Douglas would find *something* that could hold his attention for more than two years.

Loralee Kirkham waved to Fred from her living room window, and he stopped for a quick chat with Arnold Van Dyke all dressed up and driving his new Ford Taurus. This was what Fred loved about living here. Funny, when he loved the town so much, how all his boys had bailed out of Cutler almost as soon as they could.

He rounded the last curve before home and stopped again, this time to scratch with a pocket knife the bark on a willow to see if the sap had started to run. Phoebe's garden would need the soil turned any day now. If she were still alive, she would have circled a date on the calendar for him to aim for. Maybe he'd circle one for himself, for old time's sake.

He started up the driveway, but hesitated at the sight of an unfamiliar car parked behind Douglas's in the driveway. Who would come calling that he didn't know?

Glancing quickly into the car's interior for some clue, but finding nothing, Fred hurried up the drive and across the deep front lawn toward the house. He stepped onto the porch, and he could hear a woman's voice through an open window. When he opened the front door, Celeste's perfume hit him and his confusion evaporated.

"Fred!" Celeste Devereaux bounded up from the couch the second he opened the door. "I'd almost given up on you."

Douglas had claimed the other corner of the couch. He usually draped himself in some comfortable position wherever he landed, but today he sat upright, hands in his lap, shoulders slightly hunched.

Celeste and her jewelry clinked their way across the room, gestured a glossy pink kiss near Fred's ear, and took his arm. "I was just telling Douglas how *sorry* I am about what happened with Suzanne earlier. You know, I just don't understand that girl." Celeste walked with him as he headed toward his chair and she hovered while he settled in. "I don't know what she's *thinking*, accusing Alison's dear father like that. 'Don't be ridiculous,' I told her. 'Do you know how serious an accusation like that can be? You could *ruin* that dear boy's life—'" she broke off and shook her head. "I'm sure she doesn't have *any idea* what she's done."

Fred set his rocker in motion. "Don't let it worry you too much, Celeste. She hasn't actually done anything."

"Oh, but she has. She's practically accused poor Douglas of murder."

Practically? She *had* accused him. But knowing her bitter words couldn't harm Douglas gave Fred solace and made him charitable. "Enos has it under control, and he's not going to be swayed by an argument between Suzanne and Douglas."

Celeste lowered herself onto the couch again, looking uncertain. "You don't think so?"

"Not for a second. Everything's fine."

Without shifting his position, Douglas asked, "Are you sure?"

"Absolutely. No sense making a mountain out of a molehill. Let's just try to put it behind us."

Celeste sighed and smiled a little. "I can't help feeling *bad*. I guess if it was *anyone* but Douglas—" she broke off and patted Douglas's knee. A second later, she brightened and leaned forward, eager to gossip. "I can't say I'm sorry about what happened to Garrett. When I came back and found out Suzanne had *taken up* with him again—" She waved a hand in front of her as if dismissing an unsavory thought.

With that sentence she'd strayed onto uneasy territory, and Fred didn't want to let Douglas join her. "Ivan came in as I was leaving Enos's office and said something about finding an eyewitness."

Celeste had leaned back in her seat, but the news brought her upright again. "An *eyewitness*? You're kidding?"

"I guess he saw somebody running out of Locke's about the time of the murder."

"Who?" Douglas asked, but he didn't look as relieved as Fred expected.

"I didn't stick around to hear. Good news, though. This business can't go on much longer now."

"Do you know who the witness is?" Douglas's voice sounded harsh. Maybe he just didn't comprehend what this meant.

Fred reached for a section of the paper where he'd left it on the floor that morning. "Albán Toth. And if Albán says he saw someone leaving Locke's—"

Douglas shot to his feet. "Albán?"

"Albán?" Celeste echoed. "What was Albán doing there?"

"Ivan said he was driving over to the Copper Penny."

Douglas paled.

Fred lowered the paper slowly and stared at him. "What's wrong?"

Douglas shoved his fingers through his hair and walked toward the window. "I think I'm in big trouble, Dad."

Fred didn't like the sound of this. He didn't like the way Celeste hung on every word. And he didn't like the bloodless look on Douglas's face.

"What is it?" His voice sounded as if it had traveled from a distance to reach him.

"I think Albán saw *me*."

Fred could hear his heart beating in his ear, drowning out Douglas's voice and Celeste's gasp.

Douglas turned from the window to face him, eyes wide with anxiety. "I was at Locke's the night of the murder." He hunkered down in front of the chair and gripped Fred's hands. "I didn't kill him, Dad, but I was there. And I saw a car as I was leaving. It must have been Albán's."

Celeste made a soft moaning sound and a second later Fred could tell she'd started to cry. He wanted her to leave so he could think clearly. He wanted Douglas to let go of his hands, and he wanted to wake up and discover he'd only imagined Douglas in the middle of this mess.

But the increased pressure of Douglas's hands forced him to admit he wasn't dreaming. And the knot of anguish in his heart convinced him the nightmare had only begun.

seven

Fred pulled open the living room curtains to let in the morning sun and then lowered himself into his rocking chair. Douglas had spent the rest of yesterday and all last night in his room, refusing to eat dinner or to speak to anyone. They hadn't heard from Enos yet, so maybe Albán's testimony hadn't been bad news. But Douglas seemed to believe it was only a matter of time before Enos arrived, and Fred was beginning to agree.

He felt old this morning, older than he had in a long time. Not even his usual two cups of real coffee had perked him up much.

Only the occasional flush of the toilet and the sound of mournful music from Douglas's room assured Fred that he hadn't disappeared completely. When sudden footsteps sounded from within the sanctuary, Fred held his breath to listen. He didn't want to force Douglas out of his room, but he couldn't let him mope around this way, either. And he couldn't just sit here in his old rocking chair listening to the evidence of such unhappiness.

If Douglas was in as much trouble as Fred feared, his only hope was to do something. Hiding away and worrying wouldn't accomplish a thing. The next time Douglas emerged for any reason, Fred intended to be at his door.

Footsteps sounded again, but this time they came from outside. Quick, heavy footsteps. Enos. Fred pushed himself up and started for the door. From the other side, muted voices reached him. Realizing Enos hadn't come alone made Fred's apprehension grow.

He pulled open the door and came face to chest with

Grady Hatch. Behind Grady, Enos stood at uneasy attention.

"Enos. Grady. Come on in, it's cold out this morning." Fred turned away, expecting them to follow him inside.

"Hold on a minute, Fred." Enos's voice sounded funny. "I've got to tell you first that we've come with a search warrant."

"You won't find anything here."

Enos didn't seem to hear him. "We're looking for clothing that might match pieces of evidence we found in Garrett's office. We're also looking for a murder weapon. We have reason to believe we may find them here."

"I said, you won't find anything here. But come in and look around all you want."

Without answering, Grady held a folded piece of paper in front of Fred's face.

Fred waved it away. "I'm telling you there isn't any murder weapon here. But if you have it in mind to play it this way, go right ahead." He stood away from the door and waited for them to come in.

"I don't want to do this, Fred, but I have an eyewitness who places Doug at the scene at the time of the murder." Dark circles rimmed Enos's eyes, and his shoulders sagged as if they were carrying the weight of the world. "And we have probable cause to think that some of the evidence we found might match the clothes Doug wore that night. Enough to force me to check it out."

Fred had been expecting this, but the reality of it threatened to buckle his knees, and he had to grip the doorknob for support.

Enos got a worried look on his face. "I knew we should have brought Doc with us."

"You keep that old goat away from me. I'm all right. Come on in and look around. I've got nothing to hide, and I'm getting too damn old to stand here in the cold all day."

Grady looked back at Enos, who pulled his ratty old black cowboy hat from his head and nodded. Without meeting Fred's eyes again, the two men passed into the house.

Once inside, Enos twisted his hat in his hands. "We're going to need to look through Doug's bedroom."

Only the pain on Enos's face kept Fred's anger at bay. He wanted to refuse, but if they had a search warrant, it wouldn't do any good. And protesting would only darken Douglas's situation. Despite his misgivings, Fred led them down the hallway and knocked on Douglas's door. What this would do to the boy after Suzanne's nonsense, he didn't even want to guess.

It took Douglas only a few seconds to answer. His face hadn't regained its color, and his fingers trembled where they rested against the wall.

Stepping forward, Enos touched Douglas on the shoulder. "I'm sorry, Doug, but we're here with a search warrant."

Douglas stepped aside and folded his arms across his chest. Without another word, Enos and Grady set to work systematically searching the dresser, the closet, and under the bed.

Fred watched in horrible fascination for several minutes before turning back to the living room. He needed to sit. They wouldn't find anything—there wasn't anything to find—but his insides twisted with foreboding.

He rocked and looked out the window, but he didn't see a thing. The steady creak of his rocking chair, the agitated beat of his heart, and the ticking of the clock echoed until he wanted to shout—to do something—to break the tension. But he couldn't make a sound.

Before long Grady called to Enos, and Fred knew without being told that he'd found something. Enos's heavy footsteps crossed the room and for several minutes the deep rumble of Enos's questions alternated with Douglas's soft-voiced answers, but Fred's heartbeat drummed out the words. He waited, almost unable to breathe, until Enos came back down the hall.

Regret made Enos look old, more like Fred's age than his own. "It's here."

"What is?"

"The jacket Doug wore that night. It's missing a button, and the ones that are left match the one we found on the floor by the body." He rubbed his face with his open palm and let his shoulders droop. "Good billy hell, Fred, I'd give anything not to have to do this."

"You know he didn't do it."

"I hope not. But I can't ignore the evidence."

"That's all you've got, right? A button?"

"No, it's not all. But I *don't* have a murder weapon, and I'm praying I won't find it anywhere near Doug. Or that when I do find it, his fingerprints won't be on it." He rubbed his face with his hands. "Look, Fred, I don't have enough evidence to force me to arrest him, so I'm going to leave him here with you. But you'd better not let him go anywhere until this is cleared up."

A million separate emotions churned around inside him. His hands and legs tingled. He could feel the hair on the back of his neck. But he couldn't say a word about it or everyone would think he was having a heart attack.

He couldn't bear thinking that Enos was this close to arresting Douglas for murder. It was the most ridiculous thing he'd ever heard.

"Promise me you'll keep him here," Enos insisted.

Fred nodded.

Grady reappeared with Douglas's jacket in hand, and Fred somehow made all the appropriate responses as he let Enos and Grady out the door. He heard Douglas shuffle down the hall and come to a stop somewhere behind him, but he watched Enos and Grady cross the lawn and follow the driveway to the street before he forced himself to look at his son.

Douglas's shoulders slumped forward in defeat and his face looked ghostly pale. He averted his eyes to avoid Fred's gaze, alerting Fred he wanted to keep something hidden.

But Fred would be damned if he'd let him. "Well?"

"I didn't do it, Dad. I swear."

"You'd better tell me exactly what happened."

Douglas dropped onto the couch and buried his face in his hands. "I was there, I told you that."

"Why?"

"You know how upset I was when I left here. I wanted to

make Garrett agree to leave Suzanne alone. He wasn't the right kind of man for her—"

"What in the hell's the matter with you?" Fred pounded his chair with his closed fist. "Why do you care who Suzanne sees? She's not your wife any longer. Don't you see what a mess you've got yourself into because of her?" Fred might not like divorce, but he didn't believe in begging a person to let you stay once they decided they didn't want you around.

"None of this happened because of her."

"It happened because you won't let her go." Fred dragged in a deep breath, brought himself under control, and tried again. "Let her go, son."

"I can't. I love her."

Fred tried not to groan aloud. He hated seeing his children unhappy. Margaret's life with Webb had always been tough. And now, watching Douglas agonize over Suzanne, Fred wondered whether it was his fault—his and Phoebe's. Maybe because they'd had such a good marriage their children had grown up without realizing what hard work it could be. Fred's other two boys, Joseph and Jeffrey, seemed content, and he hoped they'd stay that way, but he didn't like to take anything for granted.

"What happened when you got there? Did you go in?"

Douglas nodded. "I argued with him, but he refused to listen to reason. We got into a fight—that must be when he tore the button off my jacket. But that's all that happened, and he was still alive when I left, I swear to God."

"What about Suzanne?"

Douglas's head snapped up. "What about her?"

"Did you see her?"

"No."

"She didn't—"

"She doesn't know anything about this, and I don't want her to."

"Then why is she so adamant about accusing you?"

Douglas turned away. "I don't know."

Something didn't feel right. Douglas wasn't telling him everything. "Maybe I ought to drop over and talk to her—"

Douglas whipped back so fast he nearly lost his balance. "Don't."

"But—"

"Just leave her out of it, all right?"

Fred didn't know if he could agree to that, so he didn't answer. He couldn't figure why Douglas insisted on leaving Suzanne alone when she was so busy pointing a blaming finger at him. If Douglas was keeping secrets from Fred, chances were he hadn't told Enos the whole truth, either. But would Enos see through Douglas's story, or would he accept it at face value?

"Tell me what Albán saw," he demanded.

Douglas shrugged. "I don't know. Me leaving Locke's and coming home, I guess."

"Except you didn't come home until after two. So tell me again what he saw."

Surprise flickered across Douglas's features. "I walked around for a while after I left Locke's, but I don't remember where I went—I was upset." He looked as if he thought that answer would satisfy, and Fred's temper rose.

"What do you mean you don't remember? How many places are there to go in Cutler?"

"I don't remember," Douglas insisted. "I walked around."

Douglas didn't really expect him to believe that, did he? In this early spring cold, Douglas would have been aware of every step he took. "Well, you'd better start working on remembering."

"I can't." Douglas had that same obstinate look on his face Fred remembered from the boy's childhood. Douglas spun on his heel, and left the room.

Fred watched him go, realizing only after Douglas had slammed his bedroom door how tightly his own fists were clenched. And for the first time in twenty years, Fred had to fight the urge to use them on some inanimate object to wipe out his anger.

He snatched his jacket from the coatrack and headed out the door. He could either spend the rest of the day arguing with his obstinate son or follow his urge to do something.

He walked rapidly up Lake Front Drive, not wanting to

admit how limited his options were. He couldn't actually *do* anything.

But he could talk. He could nose around a little. He could visit Albán and find out what he saw.

Fred hesitated. Enos would have something to say about that. Fred and his boys had known Albán for years, but Fred didn't frequent the Copper Penny, and he'd only been to the Four Seasons once. If he sought Albán out, Enos might get angry with him. And Fred didn't want to tip the delicate balance out of Douglas's favor.

So what could he do?

He reached the intersection with Main Street in record time and turned toward town. A block ahead of him he could see Janice Lacey washing the front window of Lacey's General Store. He certainly didn't need Janice poking her nose where it didn't belong.

Wanting to avoid her, Fred stepped off the boardwalk, checked for oncoming traffic, and caught a glimpse of Rusty Kinsella standing in the front window of Locke's Fine Furnishings. Like a bolt from the blue Fred realized what he could do.

In a town the size of Cutler, a man couldn't just ignore another man's death. Wouldn't he be expected to offer condolences to those closest to Garrett? He knew he'd eventually have to visit Olivia, but as long as he was already here, he might as well stop by the store and pay his respects. And if he happened to get a chance, he'd try to get a look at Garrett's office. He just might see something that would shed a little light on the subject.

eight

Fred waited for Grandpa Jones to go by in his battered old truck and then crossed the street, checking for signs of Enos, Grady, or Ivan before he slipped inside Locke's.

Rusty turned from his sentry post at the window and offered a tiny smile. "Morning, Fred. What can I do for you?"

Short and stocky with a ruddy complexion and red hair, Rusty Kinsella was probably somewhere in his early forties, but he looked much older. He'd lost one job after another for the past several years, but a year ago he'd landed this one, and it looked as if he'd finally found his niche.

"Thought I'd stop by and pay my respects," Fred said as he walked further into the interior of the showroom and looked around. No other customers, he noted. Good. "How's Eileen? And the kids?" he asked.

Rusty's smile warmed. "Eileen's fine, but Kelsea and Andrea were exposed to chicken pox at a birthday party the other day, so we're just waiting for things to fall apart." The six Kinsella children ranged from early teens all the way down to diapers, staggered about two years apart. Except for the oldest boy, they'd all turned out as red as Rusty.

"Sounds like Eileen'll have her hands full."

Rusty snorted a laugh. "Eileen's always got her hands full." He looked away, and when he turned back some emotion lurked behind his eyes. "Have you heard our news? We're expecting again."

Fred's heart sank when he recognized the anxiety in Rusty's expression. The last thing in the world Rusty and Eileen needed right now was the burden of another child.

Rusty obviously knew it, but Fred suspected Eileen did not. "How soon?"

"End of the summer." Rusty shoved his hands into his pockets and tried to straighten his shoulders. "Eileen's hoping for another boy."

"I'll cross my fingers for her. Hope everything goes all right."

Rusty's smile flickered. "Yeah." This time he managed to straighten his posture. "So what can I do for you?"

"I saw you in the window and thought I'd see how you're holding up."

"I'm all right."

"I heard you're the one who found Garrett's body. It must have been quite a shock."

"Oh. Yes. I can still see him lying there."

"In his office?"

Rusty nodded. "Next to the desk."

"Why was he here? I mean, didn't it happen in the middle of the night?"

"Enos said they figured it was about midnight."

Fred tried to sound casual as he repeated his line of questioning. "Why was he here at that time of night?"

"Who knows? There wasn't anything big going on. We had a defective shipment from a supplier in New York, but he'd already taken care of it, and the replacement tables weren't scheduled to come until next week."

Fred took a couple of aimless-looking steps toward the back of the store. "I guess Enos and the boys went over everything pretty thoroughly?"

Rusty gave a sharp laugh. "With a fine-tooth comb. They were in here this morning, and now they're out back digging through the dumpster and searching the alley."

"What are they looking for?" Fred took another two steps further into the store. Knowing that Enos and his deputies were looking someplace other than Douglas's bedroom brought Fred a little comfort.

"The murder weapon, I guess," said Rusty. "They figure it was a leg from one of those coffee tables we got in last week. Garrett had me take all the legs off and stack them in his office so we could package them up—" He shuddered and gave an embarrassed laugh. "Sorry, it still gets to me a little."

"So the legs are missing?"

"One of them is. The rest are still here. Doc said something about having to measure and compare them to the mark on Garrett's head."

The murderer must have grabbed the first thing he saw and used it to smash Garrett's skull. Which meant that the murder probably hadn't been premeditated. But whoever did it had been thinking clearly enough afterward to carry the weapon away.

Fred skirted a flower-print living room set and he caught a glimpse of the door to Garrett's office. It stood open, but yellow crime-scene tape stretched across it and marked it off-limits. Still, it couldn't hurt to just look . . .

After a second Fred became aware of Rusty watching him in silence, and he saw curiosity dawning in Rusty's eyes. Fred turned his back on the office and scanned the show-room. "Who's going to run the place now?"

"I'd guess it'll be Olivia. There isn't anybody else left except his ex-wife and daughter. Garrett wouldn't have left anything to Yvonne—he hated her. And Jenny's so young— she can't be more than thirteen . . ."

"Hasn't Olivia said what they plan to do?"

Rusty laughed and looked away. "Olivia? I'm the last person she'd discuss her plans with."

"I didn't know there were bad feelings between the two of you."

"Olivia and I aren't exactly friends, but there aren't *bad* feelings between us. I don't think she approved of Garrett giving me this job, but he was willing to take a chance on me and that's all that mattered."

"She's a lot like Garrett was," Fred said.

"At least Garrett had his money to make him happy—she doesn't even have that."

Fred didn't respond, but he couldn't help thinking that if Olivia inherited anything from Garrett, she'd have money on her side soon. Maybe a great deal of it. He suppressed a smile. He really ought to pay that condolence call on Olivia sometime soon.

A shadow crossed in front of the window and a second later Grady Hatch pushed open the door and ducked inside. When he saw Fred, he stopped quickly and a puzzled expression crossed his face. "When did you sneak in, Fred?" he asked.

Fred abandoned all hope of getting a look at Garrett's office and instead tried to pull off a nonchalant look. "I just wanted to pay my respects."

Grady raised an eyebrow and fixed him with a look of disbelief. "Enos said he thought you might be coming around."

"Why would he think that?"

"Oh, I don't know. Call it intuition."

Smart young whelp. "There's nothing wrong with a man offering his condolences after someone dies."

"Maybe not, but between you and me, it's probably not a real good idea. See, Enos thinks you're going to start poking around like you did with the Cavanaugh murders, and he's a little worried about it."

Poking around? Fine thing to say when he'd done all of Enos's work for him, and solved the murder to boot. Fred shook his head. "Let him know he doesn't need to worry."

But Grady didn't look convinced. He reached behind him and pulled open the door. "I'll tell him you said so. Now I'm sure Rusty appreciates your stopping by, but you'd probably be smart to catch up on the rest of your news some other time."

"Are you asking me to leave?"

"Yep." Grady kept his stance casual, but his shoulders tensed as if he expected Fred to argue.

Not for the life of him would Fred let Grady think he had the upper hand. He shrugged casually and headed for the door. "Give my best to Eileen, Rusty."

Grady smiled and gestured a mock salute. "Good decision."

Ignoring him, Fred stepped outside and started for home. It looked like he might have to find some reason to stop by the Four Seasons again, after all. It might take a bit of imagination to come up with a believable story, but he'd enjoy the challenge.

The visit to Locke's hadn't been wasted. He knew a lot more about the murder now, and every detail he'd learned reinforced his belief in Douglas's innocence.

Douglas *might* occasionally lose control of his temper, but he would *never* attack a man from behind. Fred could never prove it, but it gave his spirits a much-needed lift. Whatever Douglas was hiding from him, it wasn't a guilty conscience.

He stopped at the intersection with Lake Front Drive and looked back over his shoulder, not a bit surprised to see Grady standing in the sunlight, watching him.

Fred pull out the garlic salt he kept in the salt substitute container from its hiding place at the back of the cupboard and sprinkled some over the chicken. He intended to apply a generous coat, but rapid footsteps warned him to ditch the evidence before he could finish.

A second later, Margaret burst through the backdoor. "What in the hell do you think you're doing?" She slammed the door and faced Fred across the kitchen. Her eyes glittered and her breath came in quick, shallow gasps the way it always did when she got angry. Grady hadn't wasted any time getting to Enos, and Enos, apparently, hadn't wasted a second contacting Margaret.

Fred held up the package of chicken breasts for her inspection. "Fixing dinner."

"I'm not talking about that, and you know it. Enos just called to let me know you're already snooping around in this murder."

"I'm not *snooping around*."

"You went to Locke's today to ask Rusty Kinsella all sorts of questions."

"I only asked one or two." He spooned flour into a bowl and added a little pepper.

"Dammit, Dad—"

His patience cracked. He dropped the spoon into the bowl

and faced her squarely. "Did Enos also tell you that he and Grady stopped by here this morning with a search warrant? Did he tell you how they searched your brother's bedroom and took his jacket away as evidence?"

"That doesn't give you the right to start sniffing around again."

"And what are you going to do if they arrest Douglas? What will you say then?"

She hesitated a split second. "Enos won't do that."

"I certainly hope you're right."

"You're changing the subject. Of course I don't want Douglas arrested, but don't you remember what happened last time you got involved in a murder? You almost got killed."

"This is different."

"How? You started off this same way—just trying to find out a couple of answers."

He picked up the spoon and tried to focus on the floor and chicken breasts. "Nothing's going to happen."

Margaret crossed the room and sat in one of the chairs at the table. She used her big brown eyes to their best advantage, letting them pool with tears as she stared up at him. "Two people got killed last time, and you were almost the third. When I think how close you came—"

"This is different," he insisted, and tried to avoid looking at her.

She stood up abruptly and jerked the bowl away from him. "You keep saying that, but it's not different. You just think it's all some big game, don't you?"

"This is no game. Your brother's in serious trouble. I can't let him deal with this alone any more than I could if it were you." He snatched the bowl back and finished coating the piece of chicken.

She rolled her eyes and shook her head. "I wish somebody could make you see reason."

Fred tossed the chicken breast into a baking dish. "Why don't you tell me what you'd do if Benjamin was accused of murdering somebody."

She ignored him. "Let Enos handle this, Dad."

"Is that what you'd do? Sit in your rocking chair and let Enos handle it?"

"Let him do his job."

"Answer my question, Margaret. What would you do if Benjamin was in the same boat? Or Sarah? Or Deborah? Would you bail them out, or watch them sink? Rely on someone else to get there in time, or swim after them yourself? And if you tell me you'd sit back and wait for help, I'll know you're lying." He picked up another piece of chicken and stared at it, not quite certain what he needed to do next.

"What do you want from me? You want me to condone this? I can't. You almost got yourself killed last winter, and I'm not going to sit here and keep my mouth shut while you start the same thing all over again."

Margaret looked so much like her mother at that moment that Fred knew he wouldn't be able to stay angry for long. He'd been angry with Phoebe plenty of times during their forty-seven years, but his anger had never lasted, and it didn't sustain itself with Margaret either. He sent Margaret a teasing smile. "Shut your mouth? You wouldn't be your mother's daughter if you did that, now would you?"

"You're impossible," she snarled, but the anger in her eyes faded a little. "How did Mom ever put up with you?"

"I made her laugh."

"Oh, I'm sure you did."

"That's what she said," Fred insisted.

"Well, she wouldn't be laughing now." Apparently nothing was going to make Margaret smile. "Where's Douglas? Does he know what you've done?"

Fred shrugged. "In his bedroom, I imagine." He ignored the second question completely.

Without another word she jumped up and disappeared into the living room, obviously searching for backup. But Fred doubted Douglas would be as concerned about this as Margaret. Douglas had other things on his mind.

Knowing she'd be gone for at least a minute or two, Fred retrieved the garlic salt and sprinkled it generously over his dinner. Margaret knew that he resented Doc Huggins' suggested changes in his diet, but she didn't know how often he disregarded the advice. And her behavior tonight over a couple of innocent questions certainly didn't encourage him to fill her in.

Re-stashing the garlic salt in its usual place, Fred closed the cupboard door without a sound. He listened for Douglas and Margaret in the other room but couldn't hear anything. Either Douglas was asleep, or he'd refused to answer his door, or they were whispering. He'd bet on the latter.

He understood why Margaret was so upset. It hadn't been smart for him to chase Tony Striker out to the quarry last year, but it had been the only thing he could do. And he'd survived. He wasn't as old and feeble and useless as Margaret seemed to believe.

He'd never admit this to her, or to Enos for that matter, but he'd enjoyed getting involved and feeling useful again. Sitting in his rocking chair and watching the world go by could no longer keep him content.

After Phoebe's death, he'd almost fallen into the trap of complacency. He was no spring chicken, he admitted, and he moved too slowly, and his heart caused everyone a great deal of concern. And he'd almost let himself turn into an old man. If not for the Cavanaugh murders, he would have. But now that he'd caught himself, he had no intention of letting himself slide again.

Crossing to the door that separated the kitchen from the living room, Fred tried to eavesdrop on their conversation, but no sound carried through the heavy wood.

He pushed the door open an inch or two. Still he could hear nothing. They must be in Douglas's bedroom.

Margaret would tell Douglas, again, about the part Fred played in the Cavanaugh murders. She'd cry. She'd grumble about how close Fred came to dying. And she'd play up their responsibility to keep their aging father under control.

Douglas would listen sympathetically. He'd nod his head a lot and look like he agreed. He'd make all the appropriate noises, and then he'd say something that would make Margaret laugh. He'd calm her down and argue, convincingly, that Fred didn't require constant supervision—yet.

Fred let the door close softly, and he went back to preparing dinner. No need to worry, he could leave this in Douglas's hands. And maybe tomorrow he and Douglas could try the lunch menu at Albán's Four Seasons. It would be Fred's treat.

While he waited for Douglas and Margaret to emerge, Fred finished coating the chicken, opened a can of green beans, and found some Rice-a-Roni in the cupboard. Measuring two cups of water into a saucepan, he let himself anticipate asking Albán a few questions. He measured the margarine and added an extra dollop for flavor. The doorbell broke the silence and Fred jerked, nearly burning himself on the pan's side.

He lowered the burner and then walked toward the living room. But Margaret made it to the door first and opened it just as Fred came into the room. Douglas had followed his sister, but obviously more slowly, because he watched from the hallway.

Enos stood on the porch, hat in hand, face set in stern lines, his posture rigid. Something was wrong.

"Enos, what are you doing here?" Margaret's voice betrayed her delight. She stepped away from the door. "Come on in."

"I need to see Doug." Enos's tone didn't match the warmth in Margaret's.

"Come on in," she repeated, but she sounded wary now.

Enos stepped inside, hesitating only slightly when he saw Fred, stiffening noticeably when he saw Douglas. Something was definitely wrong. "I came here tonight by myself because of how I feel about you all. I didn't want the boys in on this. I—" his voice cracked a little and he paused. "I'd give anything not to have to do this."

nine

Fred's throat constricted and his pulse raced. Douglas looked away and Margaret's face turned pale.

"We found some new evidence today in the trees behind Locke's. Much as I might want to, I can't ignore it. Doug, I'm going to have to ask you to come down to the office with me."

"No!" Margaret cried.

"What evidence?" Fred heard the echo of Margaret's distress in his own voice.

Enos locked eyes with him for a split second. "We found the table leg that was used to murder Garrett."

Douglas looked from Fred to Margaret and swayed against the wall.

"So why do you need Douglas? Are his fingerprints on it?" Fred demanded, but he knew they couldn't possibly be.

"Yes."

Fred's pulse thudded in his ears. "Impossible. You've made a mistake."

Enos flushed an angry red. "I've got witnesses who heard Doug threaten Garrett. I've got one who saw him running away from the scene of the murder. I've got proof positive—and his own admission—that he was on the scene. And I've got a weapon with enough of Douglas's fingerprints to make a positive identification. I haven't made a mistake."

"So you're arresting me?" Douglas interrupted.

Enos shook his head. "Not yet, but I need to take you in for questioning."

Douglas shuffled slowly down the hall and Enos took him by the elbow.

Margaret pushed herself between them and the door. "This is ridiculous, Enos. You know Douglas couldn't murder somebody. If you have questions to ask him, ask them here."

But Enos couldn't even look at her. "Please step out of my way, Maggie."

Bile rose in Fred's throat. "You know he didn't do it," he repeated uselessly.

Enos didn't spare him a glance, either, but concentrated his attention on Douglas. "You want a jacket or anything?"

Douglas shook his head, and when Margaret reluctantly moved away from the door, he followed Enos outside.

At least Enos hadn't used handcuffs. Fred didn't think he could have watched his boy hauled off in handcuffs. He grabbed his jacket from the coat tree by the door and trailed them. "Wait a minute. I'm coming with you."

"No." The word cracked in the stillness of the night. Then, softly, Enos said, "I'll send someone to pick you up in the morning. There's nothing you can do tonight."

"In the morning? What are you talking about?"

"Look, Fred, I have enough evidence to detain Douglas for twenty-four hours. Long enough to get a warrant for his arrest. Unless he can give me something more than he told me last time, he's not going anywhere tonight."

"And you expect me to sit here in my rocking chair while you haul my boy off to jail?"

Enos didn't answer.

"Come on, Enos. Who's going to care if I ride with you?"

Enos wheeled around. "Everybody in the county knows how I feel about you. You're like a second father to me. I grew up with your kids. Hell, I almost married your daughter. People will watch me like a hawk, and if I don't do every little thing by the book, somebody somewhere will make an issue of it. You can bet on it. I'll send Grady for you in the morning."

"I don't need you to send Grady for me. My own two legs are perfectly capable of carrying me half a mile to your office. Tonight."

Enos's face closed down the way it always did when he

made his mind up about something. "Until I charge him, I don't even have to let you see him."

Fred hesitated. He'd known Enos long enough to recognize that tone. Further argument would get him nowhere, but he couldn't stand the thought of sitting at home uselessly when Douglas needed him.

With a sinking heart he watched Douglas walk across the lawn and down the driveway to Enos's truck. He waited until he heard the engine turn over before he pushed the door shut.

He expected Margaret to fall apart, to huddle on the couch and cry, to look to him for the answers. Instead, she waited for him at the door to the kitchen. "We can take my car."

His surprise must have shown on his face.

"Well, don't tell me you plan to sit here? Come on."

"What about Webb?"

"What about him? Come on, Dad. Are you coming or not?"

Fred hustled into the kitchen to turn off the oven and find his keys. Knowing how frigid the night air could be this time of year, he slipped on his winter coat and the fur-lined hat Jeffrey and Corinne had given him for Christmas, and then followed Margaret to her car.

Her tires squealed lightly when she backed onto the highway. "Do you think Enos will let us bail him out?" she asked.

"I don't know what to think anymore."

Margaret tore her eyes from the road for an instant. "They can't keep him in jail."

They could, and they probably would. There was no telling what might happen next. Fred stared out the window, seeing nothing, but imagining what Phoebe would have done if she'd been here. For the first time since her passing, Fred was glad she'd gone. This would have torn her apart.

Fred waited with Margaret in Enos's outer office for so long that he lost track of the time. In desperation, he pulled out a pen and a notebook and tried making a list of the questions he wanted to ask, but his attempt at concentration failed him.

Enos stomped through the office every few minutes, but he refused to speak with them, and his face warned Fred not to push it. Fred just didn't want to wait forever.

After nearly twenty minutes without a sound, the door to the cell area opened again. Fred looked up hopefully. But instead of Enos, Grady ducked through the doorway.

"How much longer?" Fred demanded.

"I couldn't tell you."

"Then let me talk to Enos."

"He's tied up right now." Grady's voice carried a hint of a challenge.

Fred struggled to keep his own voice calm. "How much longer does he expect me to wait out here?"

"The point is, Fred, I don't think he expects you to wait at all. I think you ought to go on home now and let one of us give you a call—"

"We'll wait," Margaret said.

Grady's face flushed a little. "Look, Maggie, I know how upset you and your dad are—"

"We'll wait," Fred echoed. "We're not leaving here without Douglas."

"Enos already told you he's going to hold Doug for twenty-four hours. You won't be able to take him home tonight."

"We'll wait."

Grady let out his breath in an exasperated sigh. But that didn't hold a candle to how Fred felt.

"Sheriff Asay told me to send you home. You can't do anything until tomorrow morning."

"That's a bunch of hogwash." Fred leapt up and started for the door to the cell area.

But Grady sidestepped quickly and blocked his way. "I can't let you go back there."

"Oh, you can't? I'll tell you what you can't do. You can't keep me from seeing my son or talking with Enos. We've been patient long enough. Now get the hell out of my way." But he had a hard time getting around Grady.

Before he could reach the handle, the door creaked open and Enos appeared. He didn't look happy. "What's the trouble?"

Grady looked relieved to see him. "They say they won't leave until they see Doug."

Enos came into the room and pulled the door shut behind him. "I'll bend the rules enough to let you see him tomorrow morning, Fred. Not sooner than that." His gaze traveled to Margaret and softened slightly. "My best advice for you right now is to find him an attorney."

"An attorney? Do you really think that's necessary?" Margaret asked as she crossed the room and took Fred's arm, squeezing tightly as if she thought she'd find reassurance there.

"I'll be honest with you, everything's against him. Witnesses. Evidence. And I've got to see Judge White in the morning about a warrant."

Fred's insides clenched as if someone had punched him in the stomach. Enos couldn't believe this. Douglas wasn't *capable* of murder. Fred studied Enos's face, hoping to find a trace of hope there, but found none.

He dragged in a breath and tried to steady himself. This couldn't be happening. Not to his boy. Not to Douglas. Tears stung Fred's eyes, threatening to spill over and make everything worse. He blinked rapidly, trying to force them back, trying to regain control.

He had to get Douglas out of here and . . . and what? What could he do?

He could take Enos's advice and find Douglas an attorney. It was a necessary step, but one that wouldn't make Fred feel much better. He wanted to *do* something, like . . .

Find the murderer.

He looked at Enos quickly, almost afraid the other man could read his thoughts. Enos would blow a fuse if Fred tried to figure out who really committed the crime. But with Enos only too ready to accept Douglas as the guilty party, Fred couldn't worry much about keeping Enos happy.

He stole a glance at Margaret. She would raise holy hell. After the Cavanaugh murders she'd given him his way for a few weeks, but it hadn't taken long for her to go back to her old way of thinking. If anything, she worried about him more.

Joseph . . . Well, Fred would have to avoid Joseph's telephone calls. But that couldn't be helped. He couldn't just remain idle while Douglas sat in jail.

And Jeffrey . . . But somehow Fred didn't worry so much about Jeffrey. Jeffrey would understand. Jeffrey would probably do the same thing.

Fred turned away, and Enos immediately came to attention. "Where are you going?"

"I thought you wanted us to leave."

"I do, but it isn't like you to give up so easily."

"I'll come back tomorrow."

"Fred—"

Stuffing his notebook into his pocket, Fred slipped into his jacket.

"What are you planning?"

"What makes you think I'm planning anything?"

"I know you too well. Maggie, you'd better talk to him—"

Margaret looked from one to the other several times, but she didn't say anything.

Fred found his gloves and worked his stiff fingers into them, suddenly glad of their warmth.

Enos perched on the corner of his desk. "Talk to me, Fred."

"Nothing to talk about, is there? I'll be back in the morning." Fred picked up his hat, settled it on his head, and pulled the flaps down over his ears.

"Don't you walk out of here without telling me what you're thinking." Enos sounded angry. He'd get over it.

Fred started for the front door.

Enos jumped up. "You'd better not get any big ideas about interfering with this murder investigation. I'm warning you—" He broke off, then added quickly, "Maggie, you'd better not let him do anything stupid."

Enos still got overly excited at times. It seemed to Fred

like Enos's system hadn't calmed down yet, even after more than three months without cigarettes.

Fred waited at the door until Margaret stepped outside, then pulled it shut with a little more force than might have been absolutely necessary.

Margaret had that suspicious gleam in her eye, but she waited until they'd walked on a bit before she spoke. "What are you up to, Dad?"

"What makes you think I'm up to anything?"

She snorted in a most unbecoming way. "Don't pull that with me, it won't work. I saw that look on your face and I know how your mind works. You only backed off because you've decided to do something else. Now, out with it."

"Don't worry, sweetheart. Everything's going to be fine."

But Margaret had never been the complacent type, and she didn't like, figuratively speaking, being patted on the head and sent away. "Oh, no you don't. Spill it."

Fred stopped walking and turned to face her. "The first rule is that you never let the other side know what you're going to do."

"What other side?"

He jerked his head toward Enos's office.

"Enos isn't the other side," she said.

"He is as long as he believes Douglas is guilty of murder."

She looked back at the light spilling onto the boardwalk from Enos's window, and when she spoke again her voice had lost its hard edge. "What are you going to do?"

"Come back tomorrow, just like Enos told us to."

"That's it?" She didn't look as though she believed him.

"That's it. But we'll keep him wondering all night what we're up to."

A smile tugged at the corners of her mouth, sabotaging her efforts to look stern.

Fred smile at her and patted her shoulder. "So, go home, give the kids a kiss for me, and get some rest. Tomorrow's going to be a big day."

Hesitating only a second longer, she nodded. "Come on, I'll give you a ride."

But he shook his head. "Thanks, sweetheart, but I need the walk."

Hugging him quickly, she whispered, "I love you," and turned away.

He stood on the boardwalk, watching her drive away until her taillights disappeared, and loving her so deeply it hurt a little.

Crossing the street, he walked a while in the shadows of the old Canary house that now served as the volunteer fire station. A slight breeze stirred the tops of the trees, and the air was filled with the scent of the earth just coming to life after winter.

He walked slowly, trying to capture his usual enjoyment in the silence, until a whiff of something flowery brought him to attention. A split second later he heard a voice. "Fred?"

Overpowering perfume. The jingle of costume jewelry. Celeste Devereaux. Not now.

Her essence threatened to overtake him as she scurried to match her pace with his. "Is it true they've arrested Doug for murder?"

"No." He didn't want to talk about it.

"But I heard Enos brought him in."

"To answer a few questions, that's all."

"I hope it wasn't because of what Suzanne said."

"Suzanne had nothing to do with it." He rounded the corner, hoping to get away from her.

She followed, her plump hands waving in the air. "I don't know *why* she's so angry with him. He's a wonderful father to Alison—a really *good* man."

After everything he'd suffered today, he didn't need to listen to Celeste's commentary on his son—good or bad. He suddenly wished he had his car or that he'd accepted Margaret's offer of a ride.

Celeste maneuvered herself in front of him and tilted her head almost flirtatiously. "You know what *I* think?"

"No." And he didn't want to.

"*I* think the reason she's so upset is because she still *feels* something for him."

"For Douglas? Are you crazy? A woman who cares about a man doesn't accuse him of murder in front of half the town."

But Celeste just nodded enthusiastically. "I'm absolutely serious."

"You're wrong." He tried to step around her.

"Everybody *knows* Doug couldn't have done it. Why, Doug's never really *done* anything, has he? Why would he suddenly rear up and *kill* someone like that? I mean, Doug *talks* big, but—"

Maybe she meant well, but he couldn't listen to another word. Not from her, not from Enos, not from anyone who couldn't help clear Douglas of these ridiculous accusations. He took her by the shoulders as gently as he could and guided her out of his path.

But it didn't stop her. "Take my word for it. Suzanne *needs* him."

Fred's legs began to ache and every muscle in his body suddenly felt tired.

"It's all about love, Fred. *L'amour*. And I'm telling you, it's up to you and me to keep those children together. They *belong* together, and nothing should keep them apart."

The nerves in his neck felt pinched, as if he'd slept wrong. This woman wore him out. The way she talked, emphasizing every other word, the way she waved her arms—and rattled, for Pete's sake. The way she *smelled*.

He tried to keep his tone level. "I don't care about them staying together."

"Well, of *course* you don't. You can't think of anything else but getting him out of jail, can you?"

"He hasn't been charged with anything," he insisted.

"No, of course not." She looked thoughtful. "He really *needs* Suzanne at his side right now, doesn't he?"

"That's the last thing he needs."

"Don't be silly, of *course* he needs her. And Alison needs her parents back together."

A few months ago he might have agreed. Now the idea left him cold.

Celeste rubbed her hands together and set off the rattling

of her jewelry again. "The *first* thing we need to do is make sure Douglas gets clear of this trouble. I'll help you . . ."

He shuddered.

". . . nothing *better* to do until I have to start my next book, and I've got absolutely *weeks* until I hear back from my publisher about the proposal I just submitted . . ."

"Absolutely not."

". . . once we get Douglas out of this little bit of trouble *we* can work together on getting *them* back together . . ."

"No."

"It will be such *fun* spending time together, you and I. What should we do first?"

"Nothing." He raised his voice almost to a shout to get her attention.

"*Nothing*?"

"He hasn't been charged with anything, and I'm counting that he won't be. Now if you'll excuse me, Celeste, I'm going home." He increased his pace.

She came after him. "Fine. I don't mind. We don't need to discuss this out here—"

He didn't turn around. "I'm tired, Celeste. I don't want any company."

"You want to be *alone*?"

"Alone. Thanks for your concern."

"But—"

"Give Alison a kiss for me."

He walked faster, tensing as he listened for her footsteps to come after him, relaxing slightly when he heard her walking the other way. Whatever he decided to do for Douglas, he'd do alone. He'd have enough of a headache when Enos and Margaret figured out what he was up to. Adding Celeste to the total would equal infinite trouble.

No, the less said about his plans, the better. Especially since he had no clear idea what his plans actually were.

ten

Fred walked quickly in the dappled sunlight of early morning, checking the boardwalk in front of the sheriff's office for signs of Celeste Devereaux before he came out of the cover of the trees on the corner. Enos had called him half an hour ago, finally giving him permission to speak with Douglas. He didn't intend to waste any of his precious time dealing with that woman.

He hadn't slept well, but he hadn't expected to. Worry about his children always kept him awake, and the fact that they were all nearing middle age didn't change anything. Phoebe had always been able to sleep despite any crisis, claiming that she needed the strength sleep provided to get her through. But trouble gave Fred insomnia, kept his head from finding comfort on the pillow, and made his legs too nervous to lie still.

Sleeplessness took more of a toll at this age than it had when he was forty. It made everything hurt. This morning every muscle ached with the effort of walking, and his eyes burned in the sunlight. But Douglas needed him, and Fred wouldn't have trusted this first visit to anyone else.

When he'd satisfied himself that Enos had no other visitors, he crossed the street quickly and ducked into the office. Enos sat at his desk before a jumble of papers, but his attention was focused on a half-eaten doughnut on a paper towel.

Fred pulled off his cap and unzipped his jacket. "What's the matter? Jessica refusing to make you breakfast since you arrested Douglas?"

"Very funny." Shoving the doughnut into his mouth, Enos devoured it, leaving little flecks of glaze on his lips.

"You're still insisting on doing this?"

"I have no choice, Fred. None. I wish you could understand that."

"I might some day, but Margaret won't. What are you going to tell her?"

Enos shook his head and looked miserable. "Me? I'm not going to tell her a blasted thing. What good would it do me to try?"

Fred couldn't answer that. Margaret wasn't unreasonable, unless she felt a threat to the well-being of her family. Then nothing anyone said could make any difference to her. "Can I see him?"

Enos jerked his head in the direction of the backdoor. "He's in the back."

Without wasting any more time, Fred pushed open the door and stepped through. The back room consisted of two small cells separated by a narrow concrete walkway. Though not exactly cold, the place could have used more heat.

Douglas sat on a cot, his back against a wall. His eyes were bloodshot and dark-rimmed, his hair tousled, his skin pasty. He looked horrible.

Enos came in after Fred and snagged up the keys to unlock Douglas's cell. "Have you called an attorney yet?"

"Not yet."

Douglas swung his legs up onto the cot and looked away. "I don't want an attorney."

"You'd better get one," Enos insisted.

"I don't need an attorney. I didn't kill Garrett."

Fred lowered himself to the cot and touched Douglas's knee. "Of course you didn't. But maybe we should talk with someone, anyway, just for the peace of mind."

"I can't afford an attorney, Dad. And I'm not going to let you pay for one."

"What about a court-appointed defense attorney?" Enos asked.

Douglas waved his suggestion away and made a face. "I'm not a charity case."

"Of course you're not," Fred agreed. "The family can take care of the expense."

With a heavy sigh, Enos replaced the keys and crossed to the door. "Do me a favor, Fred. Don't refuse to take this seriously. I'll do everything I can, you know that, but most of it's out of my hands. All I do is gather the evidence. If the county attorney decides to prosecute, there's nothing I can do but testify." He pulled the door closed behind him and left them alone.

Tension radiated from Douglas, creating an almost visible barrier around him. Fred wanted to gather him into his arms and weep. He wanted to shake some sense into him and make him agree to talk to an attorney. More than anything else, he wanted to promise him everything would be all right. But he couldn't.

"All right," he said. "Suppose we start over at the beginning. What happened when you left the house that night?"

Douglas blinked several times, looking confused. "What?"

"The only way to get you out of this trouble is to prove that you didn't kill Garrett. If we can find another witness, someone who saw you somewhere else, it might give an attorney something to work with."

"No attorney."

"You need to at least—"

"No attorney, Dad. Not unless it becomes absolutely necessary."

"You're about to be arrested for murder. It's absolutely necessary right now."

Douglas turned away, looking more like a stubborn little boy than a grown man.

"You left the house a little before nine. You didn't come in until after two. What happened? I need to know everything."

Douglas shifted toward the wall.

"We're talking about five hours. You weren't at Locke's the whole time."

Fred willed the boy to meet his eyes, but Douglas didn't look up. It was a standoff. Battling the old nervous feeling in his legs, Fred pushed himself up from the cot and tried to pace in the tiny enclosure.

Silence hung between them for several minutes until Douglas finally spoke, his voice so low that Fred had to stop walking to hear him.

"I went to Locke's that night, I already told you that. You know how upset I was. I didn't start out to go there, but when I was walking along Main Street and I saw the lights on at the store, something snapped. I crossed the street and pounded on the door. Garrett was there and he let me in."

Fred sat again beside Douglas on the cot.

"We argued, like I said. He'd been drinking—he had a bottle on his desk. Everything came out—Suzanne, Alison, things from twenty years ago. We fought, and this time there wasn't anybody there to step in. This time, I got the best of him. I hit him, but only with my fist, and he was still alive when I left, Dad. I swear it."

"What about your fingerprints on the murder weapon?"

Douglas shook his head, seemingly puzzled. "I don't know. I might have touched it while I was there—I can't remember."

"Think," Fred insisted.

"I'm trying."

Fred drew in a breath and pulled back his impatience. "What time did you get there?"

"I don't know."

"How long did you stay? What time did you leave?"

"I didn't check my watch. It never occurred to me that I'd need an alibi. Garrett was pretty drunk. We talked for quite a while, but I couldn't say for how long."

"You talked? I thought you argued. How long could that take? As upset as you were, it was probably over in a minute."

"We talked. We argued. I don't know how long it took. I must have been there a while."

"Five hours?"

Douglas didn't bat an eye. "Maybe."

"Then what?"

"Then I guess Albán saw me leaving. He says it was around midnight because he was on the way back to the Copper Penny to close up."

"So we've only got to account for three hours in Locke's and two hours afterward." He intended his sarcasm to affect Douglas, but it didn't.

"Yeah. I guess so."

"He might have been mistaken. Maybe he saw someone else and just thought it was you."

But Douglas shook his head in resignation. "Albán knows me too well. You remember the year he and Jeffrey were on the high school ski team together—I was around them all the time. I thought Albán was so incredibly cool. He'd survived the Hungarian revolution and escaped from a communist country—I couldn't get enough of him. If he says he saw me, he did."

"Of course he did. I'm grasping at straws, that's all." Fred leaned his elbows on his knees and battled the weariness that threatened to overtake him.

Douglas frowned and looked miserable. "I'm sorry, Dad."

This time Fred gave in to instinct and pulled the boy to him. He told himself Douglas's story would fall into place later, when he wasn't so upset. And he tried to make himself believe that.

The muffled sound of raised voices in Enos's office reached Fred through the closed door. Patting Douglas's shoulder, he pressed the boy away from him a second before the door flew open to reveal Margaret at the entrance. Shoulders stiff, face set in a mask of disapproval, she came to the door of Douglas's cell. "Do you realize we can't get Douglas out yet?" she said to Fred.

Enos followed her inside, equally stiff, equally disapproving.

Fred forced himself to his feet. "What do we have to do to get the ball rolling?"

"You're just going to have to be patient," Enos said.

"But I thought we could get him out this morning."

"I promised to let you see him. I didn't say anything else."

"Have you arrested him—officially?"

Enos shook his head. "Once Ivan gets here, I'll send him after the warrant."

"I can't believe this," Margaret snapped.

"I can't ignore the evidence, Maggie. I have to do my job. If I could do *anything* else, I would." Enos fumbled with the key and pulled open the door to let Fred out.

Fred put an arm across Margaret's shoulder. "We'll work something out. There's no way Douglas is going to spend another minute in jail once bail is set. I promise you that." Fred looked over his shoulder at the figure of his youngest son. He ached for him, and his determination to find the person responsible grew. "I'll be back as soon as I can, son. Are you going to be all right?"

Douglas nodded, but with little conviction.

Enos pulled the cell door closed and the clang of metal on metal sent a jolt through Fred. Forcing himself to walk forward, he led Margaret into the outer office. He'd only felt this helpless and hopeless once before—when he'd walked away from Phoebe's grave after her funeral.

Now neither he nor Margaret said a word until they stepped outside and closed the door behind them.

"Nobody's going to believe this nonsense," he said softly.

A tiny spark of hope lit up her eyes. "You don't think so?"

"Not for a minute." He wrapped an arm around her shoulder. "Come on back to the house with me. We'll put on a pot of coffee—decaf—and everything will look better." He tried, unsuccessfully, to force a smile to his lips.

"This is all just so unbelievable," she said as her hope faded and tears filled her eyes.

"Look," he said, forcing steel into his voice, "Douglas did *not* kill Garrett. You and I know it, the rest of the town knows it, and, in his heart, Enos knows it. We just have to believe that the truth will come out. We *have* to believe that Enos will find the real killer and that Douglas will be home soon."

"I hope you're right." She wiped the tears away with the

tips of her fingers. "I keep thinking I should be able to *do* something."

For about half a second he considered telling her what he wanted to do, but thought better of it. "All we can do right now is try to find him an attorney, whether he wants one or not."

They walked toward the end of the boardwalk where Margaret had parked her car. Just before they stepped down, the sound of a horn interrupted them.

"Fred! Yoo-hoo, Maggie—"

Cringing at the sound of Janice Lacey's high-pitched voice, Fred weighed the odds of ignoring her successfully.

"Fred—"

Her car door slamming shut and her feet tapping in their direction helped him decide. As co-owner of Lacey's General Store with her husband Bill, Janice had access to the ears of everyone in town. Those who didn't visit the store when she had information to impart were treated to a telephone call. Ignoring Janice would only postpone the inevitable.

With her short gray curls bobbing in the early spring sunlight and her stretch pants doing exactly what they'd been invented for across her ample middle, Janice quickened her pace toward them. "I just heard. My gracious, what a horrible thing for the two of you to bear."

From the stiffening of Margaret's back, Fred knew that she welcomed Janice about as much as he did. Janice's urgent little eyes darted from Fred's face to the spot on Margaret's shoulder where his arm rested. Knowing Janice could interpret it as proof that Margaret needed comfort, he pulled his arm away.

"I was on my way to the store when I saw the two of you, and I just had to stop and let you know that if I can do anything, I'd just love to help."

Margaret smiled sweetly, though how she managed it Fred couldn't imagine. "That's very thoughtful."

"The worst part of this whole thing is the talk. You know how people in this town can be. And I want the two of you to know that if I hear one word of gossip, I intend to nip it in the bud. There are a few women in this town," her voice lowered as if she were sharing a secret with them, "Emma Brumbaugh for example, or Cleo Winkler . . . Well, you just don't want either of those two to get started talking."

She had a point there. Unfortunately, both Emma and Cleo usually got most of their information straight from Janice.

"So, is he here? Is Enos keeping him in our jail? What about bail? Is Enos going to release him?"

Margaret smiled again, but some of the sugar had melted. "I'm sure you can understand that we just can't talk about it right now."

Janice's eyes clouded, but cleared quickly. "Well, of course you can't. And I'm not trying to pry—you know me better than that."

Yes, they certainly did. Fred touched Margaret's elbow and she responded eagerly. "If you'll excuse us, Janice, we were on our way home."

"Well, of course you were. Is there anything I can send over?" She followed them a few more steps toward Margaret's car. "I should talk to one or two of the ladies from the church and have them bring dinner for you tonight. Would that be good?"

"Unnecessary," Fred said sharply, then added a tight smile. "But thanks."

"Anytime. That's exactly what friends are for. Why, it could be any of us in this situation," Janice said in a tone that suggested she believed otherwise.

Fred wanted to get out of there, to flee from the sound of Janice's voice, and to sit for a while in the silence of his own living room. He wanted to convince himself that things weren't as dire as they seemed. He wanted to believe Enos would find Garrett's real killer, and that Douglas would be home by tonight.

He tugged at Margaret's elbow again.

"This whole thing is such a tragedy," Janice said. "I heard that Olivia is absolutely prostrate with grief. She isn't taking this well at all. And the funeral. Do you know when the funeral is going to be?"

Garrett's funeral was the furthest thing from Fred's mind.

"Because I think we should provide a luncheon for afterward, don't you? I'm assuming Yvonne and Jenny will come back. Have you heard anything about that? Surely Yvonne will come back for the funeral. You can't just ignore the murder of a man you were married to for that long. Besides, she'd have to bring Jenny back for her own father's funeral, wouldn't she?"

Fred didn't think there were any laws governing it.

"Yes, I think a luncheon would be perfect. How many salads do you think we should have, Maggie?"

Margaret's eyes met Fred's and for a second he thought she was going to laugh. She looked as if she were about to speak, to respond to Janice's question, when the sound of another car door and more footsteps behind them caught their attention.

Ivan Neeley, Enos's other deputy, lumbered across the boardwalk in the direction of the sheriff's office. He wore a look of self-importance and tossed Fred an almost hostile glance before he stepped inside.

Fred tried to cling to his belief that the town would rally to Douglas's defense, but already he could see the handwriting on the wall. Some would stand by Douglas. Some would indulge in idle gossip and speculation. But some would be eager to believe the worst. And those were the ones who frightened him.

Well, he wouldn't just sit back and wait like some helpless old man. No matter what Enos said, no matter what *anyone* said, Fred had to do something. He'd never been one to let someone else bail him out of trouble, and he wouldn't start now. Somehow he had to help Douglas prove his innocence, and talking with Albán Toth about what he saw the night of the murder sounded like the most logical thing he could do.

eleven

Fred dragged the Buick into action for his trip to the Four Seasons. As he cruised up Lake Front Drive toward the junction with the highway, a soft promise of spring slipped into every breath and shimmered between the bare branches of the trees, casting thin shadows over the pavement.

The Four Seasons sat almost five miles outside Cutler, beyond Spirit Lake and Snow Valley on the narrow southern shore of Winter Lake. Fred made the trip in less than fifteen minutes. Scanning the parking lot, he breathed a sigh of relief at its relative emptiness.

Albán Toth had invested in the Copper Penny a few years ago when Sam Waters left town. He'd turned it from a so-so beer joint into a decent sort of place, if you liked bars. But he'd always said he wanted to open a restaurant where he could feature European food, mainly Hungarian dishes made the "real" way, and he'd been wise enough to wait for the right location to open the Four Seasons. On the shore of the lake, he'd do four times the business he would have done in any town. People would pay extra just to look out his windows.

Albán must have seen him pulling in, because before Fred could get to the front door he was waiting with his hand extended. "I'm impressed, Fred. You're here twice in one week. We must have done something right the other night."

At just under six feet, Albán wasn't a tall man. He had the kind of face that would be distinctive as he aged—broad forehead, a fine straight nose, and an expansive smile. He wore his thin blond hair cut slightly longer than Fred's generation ever considered, and his hazel eyes always carried a warm gleam of welcome. His skin had a slight olive tint, the kind that tanned easily winter or summer and made him look healthy year-round. His voice bore just the softest trace of an accent, an almost imperceptible *V* where a *W* should have been, scarcely noticeable to those who'd known him long. Once in a while Fred heard someone ask Albán where he'd been born, and the question always took Fred by surprise.

Albán tugged open the heavy door. "Are you here for lunch?"

"No."

"I didn't think so. We got the new dining room finished yesterday—let me show it off a little and I'll buy you a cup of coffee. Then you can tell me why you're here."

Leading the way through the main dining room, Albán talked quickly, tossing directions to members of his staff, pointing out a new vase here, a newly acquired antique there. Albán loved fine things, appreciated food and wine, art and music. He'd have been as genuinely pleased to see a fine piece of art in Fred's home as his own, and his habit of showing friends his latest acquisition stemmed from a desire to share his pleasure, not to show off his good fortune.

Albán ordered a tray sent into his office, then paused at a panel of sliding doors. Smiling broadly, he pushed them open with a flourish. "What do you think?"

He had removed the back wall and replaced it with huge windows so that the entire restaurant felt as if it floated on water. Behind the glassy gray surface of the lake, the Rocky Mountains shot to the sky, layers of granite unsoftened by foliage.

"Magnificent—huh?"

"To say the least."

Albán smiled. "I'm glad you like it. It cost me a fortune." He turned and put a hand on Fred's shoulder. "But enough of that. You want to talk about Doug."

"Yes."

"We'll do it in my office. There's enough gossip without my adding to it." Albán closed the doors and led Fred down a narrow corridor to a large room with windows framing a miniaturized version of the same view. "You know how bad I feel about all of this." The look on his face showed vividly how true this was.

"I know." Fred lowered himself into a comfortable chair and accepted coffee.

"I wish I'd known why they were asking—" Albán broke off and smiled grimly. "But then, my answer would have been the same anyway."

"I know that, too. Listen, Albán, I wouldn't want you to tell Enos anything but the truth. Douglas *was* there, but Garrett was still alive when he left. What I want to know is whether you saw or heard anything else—any*one* else— that night."

Albán's brow furrowed and he closed his eyes as if he were replaying the scene in his mind. Finally, regretfully, he shook his head. "If there was anyone else around, I didn't see them. But I was on my way to the Copper Penny to close out the till, and I'll admit I wasn't paying much attention to what was going on around me."

"So someone could have been there."

"Could have been, I guess. I was upset. I was thinking about that fight Doug and Garrett had. To tell you the truth, I'd had it with Garrett. It was the second argument he brought into one of my places that day. I was trying to figure out how to eighty-six him without alienating the entire town. I suppose I might have missed something, but I saw Doug plain enough. If anyone else had been around, I probably would have noticed them, too." He spread a cracker with something creamy and passed it to Fred. "Try this. You'll love it."

Fred took a bite, and a fishy taste exploded in his mouth. He had nothing against fish—in its place. But its place was *not* in cheese. Choking the tidbit down, he shook his head at Albán's offer of another. "Tell me what you saw."

"That night?" Albán perched comfortably on the edge of his desk. "I was heading down Main Street when I saw him. I'd come up the highway and turned onto Main by the sheriff's office. I saw someone running down the street and figured he'd probably stayed at the bar too late and was hurrying home before he got into trouble. But after a few minutes I realized he wasn't running easily. You know what I mean? He was . . . stumbling, I guess."

"Doug?"

Albán nodded. "Like he was tired or hurt or something. Anyway, I didn't see who it was until I got even with him, and I still wouldn't have known except he ran past the laundromat and the lights were still on, so of course I saw his face. I pulled over to offer him a ride, but he ducked between a couple of buildings before I could say anything. I don't know where he went after that."

For the hundredth time Fred reminded himself that whether or not Albán saw Douglas on Main Street didn't matter. Douglas admitted that. "And you didn't see anyone else?"

"No one. I wish I could say I had."

Fred pushed himself up and patted the younger man's shoulder. "I know. And that means a lot." He turned and walked away slowly, almost reaching the door before he turned back to clarify one of Albán's previous statements. "You said it was Garrett's *second* argument in here?"

"Not in here. But he had one in the Copper Penny earlier that night."

"With who?"

Albán looked up and frowned. "With Rusty Kinsella."

"Did you overhear any of it?"

"No. That place gets pretty noisy when we've got a crowd. Rusty was already there when Garrett came in. He'd been looking upset anyway, drinking more than usual, that sort of thing. Rusty's a pretty mild guy, so I was surprised when they started arguing."

"What happened?"

"It calmed down quickly enough—it was over before I even got around the end of the bar. Rusty took off almost immediately after that, but Garrett stayed a while longer and looked pretty pleased with himself. I figured he must have won."

"And this was the night he died?"

"That evening. Probably right around six after Garrett closed his store."

"Albán, my friend, thank you." Slipping through the door, Fred hurried to his car. Rusty Kinsella had argued with Garrett Locke the evening of his murder, and he found his body the morning after.

Fred liked Rusty. He didn't want him to be involved in Garrett's murder. But he couldn't allow personal preference to steer him in the wrong direction. Another visit to Rusty Kinsella was definitely in order.

Fred drove slowly past Locke's Fine Furnishings and surveyed the lay of the land. It didn't look busy. It didn't even look open. But the OPEN sign was in the window and Rusty Kinsella's beat-up old station wagon was in its usual place at the end of the block.

After pulling into a parking spot half a block away, Fred took his time walking back. Talking with Rusty again might upset Enos, but he had to take the chance. It might have been wishful thinking on Fred's part, but Rusty's argument with Garrett was too convenient to be coincidental.

Wriggling his fingers into his pockets, he tried for an aimless look and whistled a little ditty his father taught him long ago. When he reached Locke's, he glanced around quickly and stepped into the recessed doorway.

Rusty had been working at a small desk near the front of the store, but he stood up the minute Fred entered and closed the book he'd been writing in. "I wasn't expecting to see you this afternoon."

"I wasn't planning to stop by until a few minutes ago."

"I heard about Doug. How's he doing?"

"About as well as you'd expect."

Rusty ran his fingers over his chin and stared out the window. "This whole thing is so unbelievable. You know, I keep expecting Garrett to walk through the back door or call me back into his office—" He broke off and sent Fred an embarrassed look. "I'm sorry."

"Don't be sorry on my account. Douglas is innocent."

Rusty busied himself straightening the papers on the desk. "Yes, well, I—"

Fred lowered himself into a low chair by the desk and watched, silently, until Rusty fumbled with a stack of papers and Fred knew his interest made the other man uneasy. "I wanted to ask you about something."

"Really? What?" Rusty picked up the paper clip dispenser and studied the desktop as if debating where to put it.

"Tell me about the argument you had with Garrett at the Copper Penny the night he was killed." For just a second Fred thought Rusty would drop the paper clips.

Instead, he sct down the dispenser with studied casualness and tried to look confused. "Argument?"

"Just after closing, wasn't it?"

Rusty tried even harder to look confused. "I saw Garrett after work, but we didn't have any disagreement."

"Think about it again. I heard from a pretty reliable source that you'd been drinking more than usual before Garrett arrived and that you left right after the argument."

A laugh escaped Rusty's tight lips. "I don't remember anything like that."

"You don't remember." Sarcasm bit at the edges of Fred's words. "How can you not remember? There are witnesses who saw it . . ." He paused, letting his implication sink in, and waiting for Rusty to reconsider.

After a lengthy pause, Rusty shrugged. "I guess I do remember."

"What did you argue about?"

"Business. Nothing important."

Fred leaned forward and placed his palms down on the desk. "Now listen, Rusty. My son is sitting in jail right now waiting for Ivan to get back with a warrant for his arrest. He's going to be charged with murder. But I don't intend to let that happen. I intend to find out what really led to Garrett's murder, and right now you're my prime suspect. I know you argued with Garrett the evening he was killed. I know that after you left the Copper Penny, Garrett looked smug and satisfied. He obviously thought he'd won. So tell me what it was about."

Rusty stiffened for a second, then seemed to collapse in on himself. His face paled and when he tried to rub his chin again, his fingers shook. "Who saw us?"

"I'm not naming names. What was it about?"

"Business. He . . . um . . ." Rusty lowered himself into his chair and made a visible attempt to pull himself together. "He found some discrepancies in the books and he thought I might know something about them."

"And did you?"

"Yes."

"You were stealing from Garrett?"

Rusty's head snapped up and his eyes widened. "Don't say it like that."

"Were you?"

He folded in on himself again. "Yes."

"For Pete's sake, Rusty. Why? This job was the first thing you had going your way in a long time."

"He was paying me a lousy eight bucks an hour. Eight bucks! You ever try making ends meet on that? With a family my size? You don't know what it's like. I go home every night and they're all staring at me, expecting me to take care of them. Six of them. And in a few months, it'll be seven. And with the added medical expenses for the baby, and the doctor insisting on a deposit up front—"

"Doc Huggins?"

Rusty deflated even further. "No. A specialist Eileen's mother found for her. Eileen had trouble when Mackenzie was born, and her mother didn't want us taking any chances this time."

"So you skimmed money off the top of the books and Garrett found out?"

Rusty nodded. "I wasn't going to keep it—I just needed a loan for a little while. I would have put it back."

On eight dollars an hour? With six, soon to be seven children? Wishful thinking, if you asked Fred. And Garrett had probably seen it that way, too. "What happened when he found out?"

"He fired me." Rusty looked away, unable to even meet Fred's eyes. Defeat hung heavily on his shoulders and reflected from his face. "He fired me," he repeated dully. "I came in early the next morning to talk with him before the rest of the crew got here and that's when I found him. Dead."

"If he fired you, what are you doing here now?"

"I figured if nobody knew—" He broke off and shook his head.

"—you'd just go on as if nothing ever happened," Fred finished. "I take it Garrett never told anyone else?"

"I don't think so. At least, nobody's said anything yet. And I figure they would have by now." He met Fred's eyes and kept his steady, as if he were pleading. "I didn't kill him. I swear," he moaned, then buried his face in his hands. "Oh, God, what have I done? This is going to destroy Eileen. And my kids—" He choked off the rest of his sentence.

Those poor kids. They'd suffer the most, paying triple any penalty Rusty would earn for such a stupid act.

Fred rubbed the palm of his hand across his forehead, as if he could soothe the pounding that had started there. He should take this straight to Enos. But he wouldn't—not yet. For some reason, he believed Rusty's story. Right down to the part where Rusty said he didn't kill Garrett. And until something else came along to convince him otherwise, or until he could reconcile his conscience with the faces of those six Kinsella kids and the unborn baby, he wouldn't say anything.

It was always the same old story—children paying for the sins of their fathers. Even Alison, who had suffered enough already because of her parents' divorce. Now gossip and accusations would demand an even bigger price of her.

He pushed himself to his feet and placed a hand on Rusty's shoulder. "Give those kids an extra big hug when you get home."

Rusty looked up, disbelief written all over his face. "You're not going to turn me in?"

"I've got two reasons. First, I don't think you did it out of greed. It was a damned stupid thing to do, but you don't need me to tell you that. And I don't think you're stupid enough to do it again. And second, those kids of yours."

Rusty's eyes filled with tears again. "I don't know how to thank you."

Fred patted his shoulder and started for the door. "Well, don't thank me yet. If it turns out you had anything to do with Garrett's murder, I won't keep any secrets from Enos."

He turned back at the door and took one last look at Rusty. The man had certainly made a mess of things, and Fred could only hope he'd find a way to fix it—for the sake of his kids.

Once outside, he looked toward the lake and almost started home. But after taking only a couple of steps, he turned in his tracks and walked quickly toward Estes Street, giving in to the almost overwhelming urge to see Alison.

twelve

Fred reached Celeste's house just as fingers of early evening shadows stretched across the brown lawn and the setting sun painted the windows gold. He knocked and waited. No response. He was just about to knock again when the door creaked open a few inches and Alison peeked up at him.

"Hi, Grandpa." She made no move to open the door wider.

"Hi, sweetheart. Got a hug for me?"

She hesitated for only a second before she threw the door open and fell against him. She'd grown tall enough to hit him mid-section, but before he could even tighten his arms around her she'd backed away again.

Fred struggled to paste a smile on his lips. "How are you, Alison?"

She lifted her shoulders. "Okay, I guess."

"I thought I'd stop by and see you for a minute, if that's okay. Is your mother here?"

Alison shook her head.

"What are you doing here all alone?"

"I was at Ashley's, but I came home. Maybe they went to the store."

"You don't think she'd mind if I came in, do you?"

Another shrug. "I guess it'll be okay." She led him into the living room, her hands tightly clenched, shoulders tensed. Not like Alison at all.

Fred wanted her to run to him when she saw him, to pull him too quickly by the hand, to smile up at him with her honey-brown eyes. He longed to hear her talk too fast and

giggle when she tripped over a word. Instead, she perched
on the edge of one of Celeste's flimsy chairs and tried to
avoid making eye contact.

He hated the divorce for doing this to her. Her parents had
been wrapped up in their own hurt and anger so long they
couldn't see what was happening to Alison. Multiply all of
her frustrations over the divorce by the violent murder of a
family friend, Suzanne's wild accusations, and Douglas's
arrest, and you ended up with one very disturbed little girl.

He took a seat across from her, holding his breath until he
satisfied himself the chair would actually hold him. "Did
you go to school today?"

She nodded.

"How was it?"

"Not very good."

"Why?"

"Because."

"I guess there must be lots of talk—"

She flicked a brief glance at him and nodded again.

"So you've probably heard about your dad."

This time her eyes met his and she looked a little
surprised. "Mom doesn't want me to hear about it, but
everybody's talking about it."

Foolish. What good would it do to shield Alison? Better
to be open with her, tell her everything, and prepare her to
handle it all. But if that's what Suzanne wanted, he'd better
watch his step or he'd ruin his chances to have any
influence. He smiled. "Well, then, if that's what your mom
wants, maybe we'd better talk about other things. But you
know your dad is innocent, don't you?"

She lowered her head and nodded. "I don't like it when
everybody stops talking just because I come in. I can tell
what they're talking about, but they think I don't know."

"Maybe they're embarrassed that you've caught them."

She almost smiled. "Maybe."

Pleased by that tentative smile, Fred leaned back in his
seat, aware for the first time how quickly twilight had
descended and how dark the room was. Half lifting himself

out of the chair, he reached for the table lamp beside him and flicked it on just as the front door burst open.

Celeste stood framed in the open doorway, with her arms full of brown paper bags. The sudden glare from the lamp seemed to startle her and she stopped in her tracks. "Alison?" She squinted into the light and stretched her glossy pink lips into a wide smile. "What are you doing home?" When she saw Fred, the smile slid from her lips. "What's going on here?"

"I stopped in to see Alison." Fred pushed himself off the chair and started across the room to help Celeste with her bags.

"Why?" Celeste's voice stopped him.

But before he could answer, Suzanne came inside, stomping her feet and exclaiming about the cold. She ran into Celeste and looked up. "Alison, honey, I thought you were at Ashley's. Fred? I didn't know you were here."

He went the rest of the distance and reached for some of Celeste's bags. Old habit, he guessed. "It was a spur of the moment decision."

Celeste relinquished two of her bags to him, but she seemed almost reluctant. "You frightened me to death. What are you doing here?"

After the way he'd spurned her the night before, Fred didn't blame her for being suspicious.

Suzanne stepped around them and headed for the kitchen. "Well, I think it's wonderful. Alison needs a good relationship with her grandpa."

Her words sounded like music to his ears, and he suddenly realized how worried he'd been that Suzanne would try to keep him away. He turned back to Alison. But almost as if she didn't want to talk to him around her mother, she abandoned her chair, pressed a delicate kiss to his cheek, and disappeared into her bedroom at the end of the hall.

Fred watched her go, then followed Suzanne into the kitchen and waited for her to tell him where she wanted the bags.

Celeste wandered in a second or two later and leaned

against the counter. She waved toward an empty spot. "Just put those anywhere. We can take care of them."

Fred complied eagerly. He'd never had any intention of unpacking them.

"I'm sorry I snapped at you when I came in," Celeste said. "I was surprised to see Alison had company."

Suzanne stretched to put two cans on an upper shelf and spoke over her shoulder. "Fred's not company, Celeste. He's family. And I'm thrilled that he was here with Alison." She turned and smiled up at him. "I hope you'll come and see her again. It'll be good for her to have you around."

He liked the sound of this. Suzanne's new attitude boded well for Alison—and for Douglas. Maybe she'd finally come to her senses. "Does this mean you've changed your mind?"

She turned to face him. "About what?"

"Douglas."

Her smile faded. "I haven't changed my mind about anything. But there's no reason Alison has to lose you as well as her father."

"Now, Suzanne—"

"Don't, Fred."

Celeste rattled one of the paper bags and sent Suzanne a look Fred couldn't interpret. "I told you what *I* think," she said.

Suzanne nodded, but she didn't look inclined to discuss it.

And if it was the same claim she had made last night, Fred didn't either. "All of this is disturbing Alison—"

"Of course it's disturbing her," Suzanne interrupted. "Her father's in jail for murder."

"He's innocent."

"*Is* he?"

"Of *course* he is, Suzanne," Celeste insisted. "Your trouble is that you don't know the difference between a good man and a *bad* one. Now, if *I'd* ever been lucky enough to get a good one, you can bet I wouldn't have thrown him away."

Scowling at her, Suzanne turned away. "You two go right

ahead and believe that if you want to. I know how angry he was. I know—"

"You know Douglas couldn't possibly have murdered Garrett. He doesn't have it in him," Fred insisted.

Celeste's mouth pinched into a grim smile. "*Everybody* has it in them if they're pushed far enough."

"Maybe," Fred agreed. "But it'd take more than a little jealousy over Suzanne's choice of dinner companions to do that."

"People have been known to commit murder over *stranger* things. Why, half the murders you read about are over really *silly* things." Celeste's eyes glinted and tiny lines formed around her mouth.

Maybe in books, Fred thought, but this was real life. And Fred didn't need Celeste's interference. "This isn't getting us anywhere, Suzanne. I didn't come here to argue. Look, I know you and Douglas still have bad feelings about the divorce, but please don't let that distort reality," he said softly. "Please don't accuse Douglas out of spite."

Suzanne ran her fingers across her brow. "This has nothing to do with the divorce."

"Well, of *course* it does, darling," Celeste interrupted. "If you weren't still so upset—"

"Please, Celeste. Not now." Suzanne held up a hand to ward off her aunt's next words.

But Fred didn't want to drop the subject. "Why do you think Douglas killed Garrett? Was it because the two of you were serious?"

"Serious?" She chuckled without humor. "I wouldn't say that."

"They *weren't* serious," Celeste insisted.

"Why did Douglas feel so threatened by it, then?"

She looked suspicious. "By what? Garrett?"

Fred nodded. "And by your dinner together—your relationship."

"They did *not* have a relationship." Celeste shoved a carton of milk into the refrigerator. "Garrett still saw Suzanne as the prize he never won. *Douglas* won her twenty years ago and Garrett never got over it."

Fred tried to ignore her. "Do you know whether Garrett planned to meet anyone else that night?"

"How would I know?" Suzanne dropped onto a chair and propped up her forehead with the palm of her hand.

"I thought he might tell you—"

"We didn't have that kind of relationship."

"But you were seeing each other."

"Once in a while," she conceded.

"Did he ever confide in you?"

"Garrett never confided in anyone. He was a closed book."

"Please, Suzanne. I'm trying to find something that will help Douglas, and I think you know more than you're telling me."

She looked up at him from under her fringe of hair and shook her head. "Everything I know can only make it worse for him, Fred. I wish you'd just let it drop."

He didn't even give that suggestion serious consideration. Frustrated by her refusal to help, he asked, "Did Garrett bring you straight back here after dinner? What time did he leave? When did you last see him alive? And what did you do after he left?"

Celeste slammed the refrigerator shut and glared at him. "Are you asking her for an *alibi*?"

"I guess I am."

Suspicion colored Suzanne's features. "Does Enos know you're doing this?"

"What? Visiting my daughter-in-law?"

"You're not going to give up, are you?"

He shook his head.

"If you must know, I was here, asleep, when he was killed. He dropped me off right after our little scene at the restaurant and then he left. I didn't invite him in. And I don't know where he went or what happened after he left me." She folded her arms on the table and faced him with a look of determination written across her face. "And I don't know why I'm even bothering to tell you all of this. I've already told Enos, and I'm not going to discuss it with anybody else, even you."

He could see that he'd pushed her far enough—for now. "I'd better not stay any longer. Wouldn't want to wear out my welcome."

Suzanne nodded.

Some other emotion flooded Celeste's features. "Don't leave on an angry note."

This time he knew he saw the interest in her eyes and he didn't like it one bit. "It's time I got home."

"Oh, but you *must* stay. Tell him, Suzanne." Her eyes darted back and forth between them, pleading.

Fred expected Suzanne to argue. Instead, she unfolded her arms and attacked another sack of groceries. "There is one thing I'd like to discuss with you before you go."

"All right." Anything she said might help him.

"If Doug gets out on bail, I want you to convince him to stay away from Alison."

"You're not serious?" How on earth did she expect him to do that?

"She's been upset enough by everything with the divorce and moving back here. It's been hard enough on me, and she's only seven. She doesn't need *this* on top of everything else."

This, she said. As if saying Douglas's name was distasteful. "He's her father."

"That's why. Can you imagine how difficult it will be for her to go to school every day with this hanging over her? Can you imagine what the other kids are saying to her— about her? At least Ashley's still her friend. But even with Ashley on her side, she came home from school this afternoon in tears. And it's only going to get worse. I want to keep all of this ugliness as far away from her as I can. But if Doug comes around, he'll make it impossible. He'll make it worse for her."

Fred didn't agree for a minute, and he hated the idea of telling Douglas he couldn't visit his own daughter. But he understood Suzanne's concerns. "Maybe she'd feel better if she saw him."

"No."

"It might be just what she needs. If she could see him, see that he doesn't look any different, that he's not evil—"

"I don't want him around her."

"Suzanne, honey, listen to Fred—" Celeste began.

Suzanne's face tightened. "I'm her mother. I have to do what I believe is right for her. And if I have to, I'll get a restraining order. I'd hoped you'd want to avoid that."

Of course he wanted to avoid that. If he sided with Suzanne, he'd hurt Douglas. If he refused Suzanne's request, he'd inadvertently hurt Alison by escalating the hostilities between Douglas and Suzanne. He didn't want to do either, but he nodded his agreement. "I'll do what I can, but only until Douglas is cleared. After that—"

"You have to convince him," Suzanne insisted. "Doug never stops to think about what he does. He just acts. I can't let Alison be the victim of his impulsive behavior this time."

Fred didn't say anything. He wanted to get his coat and hat and leave before Suzanne said something else he didn't want to hear. She followed him into the living room and walked him to the door.

He pulled it open and met her hard gaze. "Tell Alison good night for me. I'll come again soon." He ducked back into the cold and started down the sidewalk. But even the frigid air didn't match the cold surrounding his heart.

He'd only walked a few feet when he heard Celeste calling out to him. She ran after him, waving her hands, glancing back toward the house as if she feared discovery. Drawing abreast of him, she hooked his arm with hers. "I just wanted to thank you for coming. I think that went *fairly* well, don't you? Can you see what I mean about Suzanne and Douglas? Can't you just *feel* it?"

"No, I can't." He tried to tug his arm away.

But she held fast. "You're so good for her. I just *know* having you around is going to help her see reason. And you'll be *wonderful* for Alison, too. I hope we see *much* more of you."

He mumbled something noncommittal.

"In fact," Celeste said, and her eyes brightened considerably, "why don't you have dinner with us tomorrow night?"

Fred shook his head and tried to back away. "I can't."

"Can't you see? It would be *perfect*! You could spend time with Alison, talk with Suzanne, put in a good word for Douglas—Oh, it's a *splendid* idea."

"No, I—"

"We'd just love to have you. *I'd* really enjoy your company." Her eyes glittered with a look he hadn't seen since he'd been courting Phoebe.

With renewed determination, he yanked his arm from her grasp and turned away. "I don't think so."

"Now, Fred, there's no sense in being shy. We're both adults. We're both lonely. What's the harm in sharing a little companionship?"

He stopped and whirled to face her. "I don't need companionship."

"Now, Fred—" She pouted at him and tried to look beguiling.

No doubt Phoebe would have found this amusing. She'd always maintained that jealousy was a lowly emotion, and that if another woman found him attractive, it merely validated her own good taste. And she'd had complete trust in him. Well, we wouldn't violate it now. Especially for someone like Celeste Devereaux. "I'm not available for dinner tomorrow night."

"Then Friday?"

"No." He took a few quick steps away. Glancing over his shoulder, he breathed a sigh of relief to see that she hadn't come after him. She looked disappointed. Well, he couldn't help that. He just counted himself lucky to get away.

thirteen

Fred scrunched his pillow under his neck and stared at the ceiling where stray moonbeams danced in little patterns through the shadows of trees. His back hurt. His neck hurt. His head pounded.

He closed his eyes, but Alison's face and her sad eyes loomed large in his imagination. He rolled onto his side and tried to ignore the twinge of pain in his knees.

Reaching out one hand, he touched Phoebe's pillow, imagining her beside him and fighting back the familiar ache in his heart. He forced his eyes closed again, and saw Douglas with his back against the cell wall, his head down, his skin pasty. The boy's despair made Fred's eyes fly open again.

This had happened often enough in seventy-two years for Fred to recognize it for what it was—insomnia. But he fought against it. Just before the ten o'clock news, Enos had called to let him know the arraignment was scheduled for nine o'clock the next morning. If all went well, Fred could get Douglas out on bail. It should have made him feel better, but it didn't.

Releasing Douglas on bail wouldn't clear him of the murder charges. He wouldn't be free. He wouldn't be able to get on with his life. The whole family would still be under this cloud until the real murderer was caught.

A vision of Rusty Kinsella, wife and children at his feet, appeared before Fred's eyes. He shook his head to rid himself of it and sat up and squinted at the clock beside his bed. Two-thirty. With a groan, he fell back onto his pillow.

He tried to sleep for a few more minutes, but finally

abandoned his efforts as a lost cause. He climbed out of bed, slipped into his robe, and stuffed his feet into his slippers. At times like this the house felt empty. Used to be it carried its own set of noises at night, comforting sounds of children asleep, Phoebe's light rhythmic snoring—all of which had soothed him. Now there was nothing but silence as he walked toward the kitchen.

Retrieving a pad of paper and a pen from the miscellaneous drawer in the kitchen, he put on a pot of coffee and settled himself at the table to wait for it to percolate. "Here's the deal," he said aloud to the empty kitchen. "Somebody killed Garrett Locke. I'm not going to sleep until Enos arrests whoever did it. And if that's the case, I'd better make myself a plan, or I'll never sleep again." He smiled a little at that.

Once the coffee was done percolating, he pushed himself away from the table and poured out a cup for himself. Pacing the floor, he started trying to pull the loose strands together, to make sense of the puzzle surrounding Garrett's murder. What facts did he have?

Garrett was murdered. Hit in the head with a blunt instrument—an oak table leg. And it happened at about midnight. What else?

Douglas admitted to being in the store that night. He admitted arguing with Garrett, but claimed Garrett was still alive when he left. Fred believed that, so he chalked it up with the other facts. Douglas was innocent—absolutely.

But who else had reason to kill Garrett? In his favorite television shows, where did the police look first? Family? The only family Garrett had was a sister down in Granby and an ex-wife and daughter somewhere between Cutler and Denver. What about Olivia?

She'd married Dan Simms several years ago—a man who was a real parasite, if you asked Fred. He knew their marriage had ended a little while back. And since her marriage, Olivia's lifestyle had never been on a parallel with Garrett's. Money as a motive? A definite possibility.

But money brought him right back to Rusty Kinsella. He believed Rusty's pathetic story, and his heart went out to the man. But the threat of ruin to himself and his family might have pushed him over the edge. Fred wouldn't exclude him from the list.

Were there any other employees with a grudge against Garrett? Fred couldn't think of more than a handful of people who worked there, but he ought to check them out. And women. Garrett had never lacked female companionship. Fred put down his coffee and wrote for a few minutes. Leaning back, he surveyed the list again and smiled.

Who else? He drew a blank. But who knew what a few well-phrased questions might turn up? He rewarded himself with a bowl of almond toffee crunch ice cream from the Tupperware container hidden underneath the frozen rhubarb, grabbed his new Deloy Barnes Western from the bookshelf, and headed back to bed.

He might not be able to sleep tonight, but at least he had a plan for tomorrow. And having a plan made him feel a whole lot better.

Fred escorted Douglas out the front door of the narrow brick county building and out onto the sidewalk. He'd arrived a few minutes early, hoping for a chance to say something to Douglas before they went into the courtroom. But Enos had brought Douglas in the back way, cutting across the alley that separated the buildings, and Fred hadn't even seen his son until the boy entered the courtroom between Enos and Grady.

The way things had gone the last few days, Fred had half expected Judge White to deny bail. But after rambling on about justice and equity for an unnecessary fifteen minutes, he'd finally set an amount.

They stopped for a minute outside the courthouse to let Douglas pull himself together. Enos and Grady had already disappeared, and for a few blessed moments no one else approached. Douglas breathed deeply, as if he were inhaling freedom. The sun brought out the golden highlights in his hair, but his skin looked pasty and his eyes were dull. These last few days had been rough.

With the arraignment behind them and bail now posted, Fred hoped things would calm down for a little while. His first order of business was to get Douglas settled at home and to put a little color back into his cheeks. After that, he'd try to explain Suzanne's request that he keep Douglas away from Alison. But it would be a sight easier to do if he understood it himself.

Deciding they'd waited long enough, and wanting to avoid the most curious of local residents, Fred led Douglas away. "How do you feel?"

"Better."

"Get some rest today and a good night's sleep and by tomorrow you'll feel better still."

"I'm sure I will. In fact, I think I'll run over to Suzanne's before I go home. That ought to help."

Fred looked at Douglas quickly to see if he was serious. He was. "I don't think that's a good idea."

"Why not? I've got to talk with her."

"No, you don't."

Douglas gestured broadly, signaling his displeasure. "She's the only one who can help. I've got to talk with her. I've got to see Alison."

"She doesn't want to talk with you, and she's not going to help you."

"You don't know that."

"I saw her yesterday, son. She doesn't know anything."

"Yes, she does."

A bud of hope sprang to life. "She does? What?"

"I don't know. But she *must* know something. She was with Garrett that night."

Fred swallowed his disappointment. Douglas didn't have anything new to add. "I've already asked her. She doesn't know anything."

"Then I'll talk to her."

"You can't do that, son." They rounded a curve in the road and Fred squinted into the sunlight.

"Why not?"

He didn't like being in the middle of this argument. He tried to think of a tactful way to phrase it, but couldn't. "She asked me to keep you away."

Douglas stopped in his tracks. "That's ridiculous. How

does she think she can get away without talking to me? How does she think—"

"Calm down. Getting all riled up isn't going to do any good. First, let's get you settled at home. Then we can talk about all this other business."

"I don't want to go home. I want to see my daughter. I want to see my wife."

Fred couldn't remember when he'd last seen someone who could match Douglas for stubbornness. But he wouldn't let Douglas push him into changing his mind. "I'm not letting you go over there."

"You can't stop me."

"Now listen, Douglas. I'm just going to say this one time. You're out of jail because I paid your bail. You were released into my custody. That mean's I'm responsible if you get yourself into trouble. Do you understand that? That means I call the shots. You're not going anywhere near Suzanne or Alison unless I give you the okay."

"Dammit, Dad."

"I don't want to hear another word."

Douglas threw his arms in the air in a gesture of futility and started walking again. "I can't *believe* this."

"I'm doing everything I can to help you out, son."

"I can see that." Bitterness tinged Douglas's voice.

Fred didn't respond to it. He didn't like this situation any more than Douglas did, but if Douglas went anywhere near Suzanne, she'd make trouble. And Douglas didn't need any more trouble.

Nobody understood Douglas's fears better than Fred. Nobody wanted the answers more than he did, but he wasn't convinced Suzanne had them.

Douglas lapsed into self-pity, and they walked the rest of the way home without breaking the silence. Fred couldn't say surely that he would act differently if he were Douglas, and he believed Alison would benefit from the interaction with her father, but he could also see the wisdom of keeping Douglas and Suzanne apart.

Letting Douglas rush over to Suzanne's wouldn't solve anything. Fred had already covered that and learned absolutely nothing. It was time to move on. And he'd made up his mind to visit Olivia Simms next.

Money had to be the key. If Olivia was a beneficiary under Garrett's will—and Fred couldn't see why she wouldn't be—she would have had a motive for wanting him out of the way. Olivia had been struggling financially for years while Garrett's style of living had been improving. And people often did strange things because of money.

Fred rounded the last curve before his house and noticed Margaret's car in the driveway behind Douglas's. She'd been waiting on the porch in Phoebe's favorite chair, and she stood to greet them, smoothing the legs of her jeans and tugging her sweatshirt over her hips. She strode across the deep lawn toward them with the same easy grace Phoebe'd had in her youth. For a moment she looked enough like her mother to take Fred's breath away.

When Douglas pushed past Margaret on his way to the house, her smile faded. She said something to him that Fred couldn't hear, but Douglas kept going. He walked quickly across the deep lawn that separated the house from the street and stormed up the steps to the front door, apparently forgetting Fred locked the house these days as a precaution against Margaret's unannounced raids on his kitchen.

Fred hid a smile at the petulant look Douglas sent him and brushed a kiss on Margaret's cheek. "How are you, sweetheart?"

"Is he all right?"

He waved a hand toward Douglas, dismissing the boy's anger. "He's upset."

She squinted into the sun as she looked at Douglas. "Well, he has a reason to be, but why is he angry with you?"

"He wanted to go see Suzanne and Alison after we left the courthouse, and I told him he couldn't." Fred touched her arm to keep her from rushing after her brother. "He'll get over it. He's upset about a lot of things right now, and if he needs to take a little of it out on me, that's all right."

"It most certainly is not."

"You're not trying to protect me again, are you?"

She paused, considered, and shook her head. "That's not it. He makes me angry, but I'm not protecting you."

"What's he done to make you angry?"

"He's still trying to get back with Suzanne."

"Seems to me that's his business."

"But he's angry with you for trouble he's brought on himself—" She broke off and looked at him, her eyes dark and wide.

Fred put his arm around her shoulder and led her across the driveway, but he didn't see any need to belabor a point well made. "What brings you out this morning?"

She looked toward the house as if she wanted to be sure they were still out of Douglas's earshot and kept her voice low. "I wanted to make sure he was all right."

"He's doing as well as can be expected, I guess. This isn't easy for him."

They reached the sidewalk that cut from the top of the driveway to the front door and Fred gave her shoulder a squeeze before pulling his arm away to search for the key.

Douglas watched with barely concealed impatience until the door opened, then he brushed past Fred in his hurry to get inside.

"You want some breakfast, son?"

Douglas disappeared into his bedroom and slammed his door as an answer.

Obviously trying hard not to react, Margaret busied herself tidying the living room. She adjusted the crocheted doilies on the back of the couch, straightened the conglomeration of pictures on the old oak dining table Fred and Phoebe had never once used for a meal, and started on the pile of newspapers at the foot of Fred's rocking chair.

Fred waved her away and picked up the morning paper as he dropped into his rocking chair. Margaret obviously had something on her mind, but it looked like she'd have to let her thoughts stew for a while before she'd tell him what it was.

She moved back to the couch and twice plumped the cushions.

Fred turned the page and scanned the stories there.

"Looks like we're supposed to have nice weather the rest of the week."

"Really?" She didn't look up and she didn't sound particularly interested. She crossed to Fred's bookcase and started pushing and pulling books until their spines lined up exactly.

Fred picked up another section of the paper and shook it out. "It says here the Nuggets will probably be going to the playoffs this year."

She didn't respond, but made quite a production of dusting the tops of the books.

He let several minutes tick by, waiting for her to speak. But she remained silent, and after what seemed an eternity, he couldn't wait any longer.

"I thought I'd go over and pay my respects to Olivia Simms in a little bit." He watched Margaret over the top of the newspaper, waiting for her inevitable reaction. This time he got what he wanted.

"Why?"

He shrugged and gave the paper his attention. "There's been a death in the family. Seems like the decent thing to do."

She propped herself against the back of the couch and looked at him with narrowed eyes. "How well do you know Olivia?"

"Well enough, I suppose." He folded the sports section and laid the paper on the floor.

"Well enough to pay her a personal visit?"

"Why not?"

"Because, Dad, you can't."

"I don't see why not."

"First of all, you're not concerned about Olivia and you don't want to pay your respects. You just want to worm information out of her. Second—"

"What's wrong with that?"

"You're not supposed to do that. You're supposed to leave everything to Enos."

"Enos's son hasn't been accused of murder."

"But Enos is a trained law enforcement official—"

"Poppycock." Fred set the rocker in motion and stared out the window.

"—and he's warned you once already to stay out of this investigation—"

"Which I'd do if he'd get himself in gear."

"He'll find the murderer, Dad."

"When?" He stopped rocking and faced her.

"Soon."

"Not soon enough. Did you get a good look at your brother? This is destroying him."

"Your getting involved isn't going to help him."

"It'll help him a damn sight more than sitting here waiting for Enos to get around to it."

Margaret crossed to him, sat on the ottoman at his feet, and took his hands in hers. "Promise me you'll stay out of it. Don't go see Olivia."

"I can't promise that."

"Did Douglas ask you to do this?"

"No."

She looked skeptical. "You swear?"

"Of course."

"Then let him fight his own battles."

"This isn't a battle. This is his life. I'd do the same thing for any of my children."

Margaret dropped his hands, but left her own, palms down, on his knees. "You've bailed Douglas out of every scrape he's ever been in. This is just one more in a long string of rescues."

He turned away so she couldn't see the pain her words caused. He knew how troublesome Douglas had been over the years, and he knew how often Phoebe had urged him to step in between Douglas and disaster. He'd done it willingly every time, even when he questioned the wisdom of his actions. But this situation was different, and he could distinguish between the annoyance of boyhood scrapes and the threat of a murder charge, even if Margaret couldn't.

Pushing himself out of his chair, he took a few steps away. "I didn't know you felt that way."

"We all feel that way. Joseph called me just last night—"

"And the two of you decided I shouldn't help my own son?"

"We didn't decide anything except that I needed to talk

with you. You're not being rational, Dad. We all want to help Douglas, but investigating Garrett's murder yourself is ridiculous."

He snorted, and would have protested, but she held up her hand and continued.

"I know—you got involved in the Cavanaugh murders and you came out of that okay. But it was luck. You don't have the skills or the training—"

"How much skill does it take to ask a few questions?"

"Joseph says you might make matters worse. He thinks you should leave this to professionals."

Fred thought Joseph had turned into a stuffed shirt, but he didn't voice his opinion. If Margaret couldn't see how important this was, he wouldn't stay here and listen to any more. He picked up his jacket and shoved his arms into it.

Margaret stopped. "Where are you going?"

"Out."

"Out where?"

He shrugged. "The Bluebird, I guess."

"Not to see Olivia?"

"No." Not yet, anyway. He'd let Margaret calm down a little first, or she'd be over there after him.

Margaret planted her fists on her hips. "What about Douglas?"

With his hand on the knob, he turned to her. "I'm not forgetting him."

"I can't stay here with him."

"I don't remember asking you to." He stepped through the door, closed it behind him, and pulled in a deep lungful of air. After walking two blocks he began to feel better, and by the time he reached the Bluebird, he'd almost managed to put Margaret's attitude behind him.

He didn't blame her. Joseph could always sway any of his siblings to his view within minutes—it's what made him such a good attorney, but after she had some time to think about it, Margaret's scales would tip back into balance and she'd see reason again. In the meantime, he'd sit in his favorite booth and enjoy the kind of peace and quiet he hadn't found at home since Douglas arrived.

fourteen

Fred pushed open the door to the Bluebird and glanced around. George Newman took up his usual stool at the counter, and he greeted Fred with a slight incline of his head. "Got your boy out of jail this morning, I heard."

"Sure did." Fred turned away quickly. He didn't want to discuss Douglas or Garrett Locke with anyone, especially George.

But George picked up his coffee cup and followed. "Heard he was looking a little peaked."

"I suppose anybody would after a night or two in jail." Fred slipped out of his jacket, tossed it onto one cracked Naugahyde-covered bench at the corner booth, and slid onto the other.

George shoved Fred's jacket out of the way and took a seat. "Got yourselves a good attorney?"

"Not yet."

"You'll want to talk to my boy David. He's an attorney down in Aurora now, you know."

"I didn't know David handled this kind of thing."

George shrugged. "He doesn't usually, but he'd do you a good job, since he knows you and all. You want his number?"

If it would get George to leave him alone, Fred would take it willingly. "Might as well, I guess."

George dug out his wallet and pulled out a business card from on top. He'd obviously come prepared. "I talked to him about your boy last night, just in case you were interested. He'll be expecting your call."

Fred had no intention of calling David Newman, but he

took the card and tucked it into his shirt pocket. As he remembered, David had been a stuffy-headed little boy who'd spent most of his childhood throwing rocks through other peoples' windows.

"I heard Albán Toth is going to testify that he saw Doug leaving Locke's the night of the murder." George's lips curved in a sympathetic smile.

Fred didn't want George's sympathy, his son's telephone number, or his company right now. He wanted George to go away or be quiet, but he'd known George all his life and he knew better than to expect either.

So he turned his thoughts back to his children. He decided he'd ignore Joseph. It didn't do to give Joseph too much attention when he started spouting off ideas, and arguing with him never accomplished anything.

George leaned back in his seat. "But I wouldn't worry about it if I was you. I learned a long time ago we can't live our kids' lives for 'em . . ."

If Fred gave Margaret time to calm down, she'd come to her senses. But he didn't like thinking she'd been harboring bad feelings about Douglas all this time.

". . . do our best, that's all we can do. After that, it's up to them. Nobody's going to blame you for what Doug's done . . ."

As for Jeffrey . . . well, Jeffrey hadn't said anything yet, and he probably wouldn't. He didn't tend to get as irrational as the other two.

". . . not your fault, that's what I say. Not your fault at all."

Fred's thoughts ground to a halt and he looked into George's watery blue eyes. "What's my fault?"

George blinked in surprise. "Nothing. That's what I'm saying. Can't hold a man responsible for the things his kids do after they're raised."

"None of my kids has done anything."

George's gaze faltered. "Well . . . no. What I mean is—"

"What you mean is that people think Douglas is guilty?"

"I didn't say that." George looked uneasy.

"You didn't have to."

"Now, don't go taking offense at something I didn't mean. That's a weak spot with you, Fred—taking offense. People can have the best intentions, but if you think they're saying something—even if they're not—you take offense."

Whether or not he did it often, Fred was taking offense now. Weak spot. Believing Douglas was guilty. Blaming *him* for something Douglas hadn't even done. He didn't want to hear another word or he'd say something that would make George take offense—on purpose.

Fred pushed himself out of the booth just as Lizzie approached with a coffeepot in hand. It must have been the look on his face that made her turn on her heel and walk away.

George got to his feet. "You call my boy David. He'll be glad to help out." Then with a nod and an injured look he turned away.

Fred sat back down. Peace and quiet, that's all he wanted. And a chance to sort through his jumbled thoughts. He caught Lizzie's eye and beckoned her back.

She filled his cup and pulled out her order pad.

"Nothing for me this morning, Lizzie. Just coffee."

She nodded and turned to go.

"Lizzie? Is that what everybody in town thinks—that Douglas is guilty?"

"Not everybody."

"Most folks?"

"A few." She stuffed the order pad into her apron pocket. "Just a few."

Knowing even a few believed it made him angry. Realizing some absolved *him* of nonexistent guilt rankled. And he knew others probably blamed him for childhood experiences or neglect that somehow drove Douglas to crime.

"Have you heard anything you think I ought to know?"

Lizzie shook her head. "Nothing. Grady isn't even talking about it." Someone at the counter called out, and with a last glance at him, she left.

This kind of unnatural quiet from the sheriff's office

made Fred uneasy. Grady never kept anything from his mother, unless it was something serious.

Lizzie dropped a few quarters into the jukebox as she passed, and seconds later Elvis began to sing "Kentucky Rain." It didn't help. Fred nursed his coffee, wishing he could find some solitude at home, and wondering how he'd ever find a way to help Douglas when the door opened and Celeste Devereaux stepped inside.

Of all the people in town, Fred wanted to see her less than anyone. Wishing he could make himself invisible, he hunched into the corner of the booth, but she spied him immediately and clinked her way toward him. Damn.

"This is *incredible*!" she gushed as she stuffed herself into the seat across from him, sitting on his jacket. "Imagine running into you of all people."

Imagine.

"It's a sign, that's what it is."

He would have called it something else.

Celeste waved at Lizzie and searched neighboring tables for another cup. "You'll never *believe* where I've been." She spied one and lunged out of her seat to snag it. "Summer Dey's. Can you believe it?" She lowered her voice and stage-whispered, "I've just had a *reading* done."

Summer Dey, Cutler's resident nutcase, ran the Cosmic Tradition, a New Age art and bookstore. She claimed to be psychic, but Fred thought it was all a lot of nonsense and he avoided her whenever he could. He didn't have a clue what Celeste was talking about, but knowing Summer, he didn't think he wanted one.

Celeste patted her red hair, smiled with pink lips up at Lizzie, and turned her attention back to Fred only when Lizzie walked away again. "Aren't you going to ask me what she said?"

"Who?"

"Summer! In my reading."

Something in the glitter of her eyes and the wide smile warned him not to ask.

But Celeste didn't seem to notice. "There's a new man in my life. It was all right there in the cards. I cut them and there he was—the King of Hearts!" She sipped heartily and looked at Fred from under her lashes in a way that made his heart sink. He'd seen that look in a few movies and he knew what it meant. But if she imagined him as the King of Hearts, she'd have to start playing with a new deck.

"And she said I should use it for my next book—that I'd make a million. My heroine, Gazelle Leone, returns to her hometown after her husband leaves her and—just *guess* what happens?"

Elvis changed moods and started singing "Burning Love." Good Lord. Fred had to get out of here.

"Rafe Hunter, her true love, still lives there, but his wife has died! And from the minute she sees him again, Gazelle *knows* they're destined to be together. It's going to be absolutely beautiful." She reached a hand toward him and her eyes glittered with unshed tears.

Fred jerked his hand away and considered the wisdom of abandoning his jacket to its place beneath her. No question, the jacket would have to go. He slid toward the edge of the booth and almost made his escape when her mood suddenly shifted, her eyes dulled and her face lost its dreaminess.

"Don't go."

He mumbled something about having lots of things to do and stood.

"There's something important I need to talk with you about."

"Another time, maybe." He didn't intend to stay here another minute.

"It's about Suzanne—"

All the more reason to get away.

"—and Garrett." She reached for his arm and held. "I've just heard the most disturbing news."

He hesitated, then sat back down. No matter the source, he couldn't ignore anything that might help Douglas. "What is it?"

She looked around, as if making sure they couldn't be overheard, then mouthed, "Olivia."

"Olivia?"

Holding one finger over her lips, she checked the area

again, then whispered, "I heard she was very angry with Garrett for dating Suzanne again. So angry, in fact, she might have done *anything* to put a stop to it."

"Where did you hear that?"

She shook her head, refusing to divulge her source. "I think you ought to talk with her."

At last. Something about which he could agree with her. He'd waited long enough to pay that condolence call on Olivia Simms.

He got back up, glanced quickly at the seat, and decided he'd retrieve his jacket later. Lizzie would keep it for him. "I appreciate your telling me, Celeste."

She struggled to her feet and followed him to the door. "Don't you want me to go with you?"

"No." Not if his life depended on it.

"But—"

"No." He wrenched open the door, stepped through, and let it slam behind him.

Glowering across the street at the deceptively innocent-looking windows of Summer's store, The Cosmic Tradition, he stormed down the sidewalk. Later he'd pay Summer a little visit and let her know how much he resented her interference. But that would have to wait. He needed to get to his car and then head down to Olivia's before Celeste decided to follow him.

If Olivia profited financially from Garrett's death, or if she *was* angry over his relationship with Suzanne, he might have found the missing link. And that would give him something he could take to Enos.

He walked quickly, reaching home in under fifteen minutes in spite of the persistent ache in his knees. But the instant he came around the corner, he smelled trouble. Margaret's car was still there. So was Douglas's. But Fred's Buick was suspiciously absent.

Margaret met him coming up the walk. "I don't imagine you'll do anything about this."

"Where's my car?"

"Ask your son."

His shoulders drooped, as if a heavy weight had settled on them. "Is *my son* home?"

She gave him a piteous look and spoke slowly, as if he were too old to understand. "No, he's with your car."

"Do you know where he is?"

"No." She turned back toward the house.

"And I don't suppose you feel like telling me what happened after I left."

"I know what you're thinking, but we didn't argue. He waited until I went out back, then he took your car. I didn't even notice he was gone until I came back inside."

Fred didn't have to think very hard to imagine where Douglas had gone. He might be old, but he wasn't stupid.

Margaret's eyes narrowed. "You know where he's gone, don't you? Suzanne's." She spat out the name as if it left a bad taste in her mouth.

Fred opened the front door and held it until she passed through. "Maybe. We don't know that for sure."

"What is he thinking of?"

"Now, Margaret—"

"Can't he see what he's doing? Can't he see how much worse he's making it for himself?" Her voice kept its hard edge, but tears pooled in her eyes. She wiped them away with the back of her hand and turned toward the window.

Fred lowered himself into his rocking chair, wincing when his knees twinged in protest. Maybe it was just as well he didn't have his car. It might do him good to rest a bit before he drove down to see Olivia.

"So what are you going to do?" Margaret demanded.

"What would you suggest?"

"Call him. Go get him and make him come home. I'll even take you over there."

If he thought it might work, he'd do it in a second. But starting an argument between his kids in public would only make matters worse. He sighed and leaned his head against the back of his chair. "Are you under some kind of delusion that my word carries more weight with Douglas than it does with you? You don't really think he's going to turn around and come home because I go after him, do you?"

Margaret hesitated. "You can't let him run off like this—"

"I don't see that I can do anything about it."

"You've got to *try*."

"Unless Suzanne gets a restraining order, there's no reason except common sense why Douglas shouldn't go over there. I said I'd *try* to convince him to stay away, but I can't lock him up."

Margaret opened her mouth, a protest at the tip of her tongue, when the telephone rang. Expelling her breath loudly, she grabbed up the receiver. "Hello? . . . Oh, Webb." She turned away and lowered her voice, probably to keep Fred from hearing the exchange with her husband. Webb must be unhappy to find her gone. She checked the time on her watch and spoke again, too softly for Fred to hear.

Just about lunchtime. In nearly thirty years Webb still hadn't learned how to fix his own lunch. The man would wither to nothing without Margaret.

". . . in a few minutes. Yes." Margaret straightened her shoulders and turned halfway back, then paused. At Webb's next words, she darted a glance at Fred. "You saw Dad's car where? At Suzanne's? And what else?" She spoke loudly, obviously wanting Fred to hear this part. "Enos's truck? Really—"

She turned and gave Fred an "I told you so" look. "Isn't that interesting? I'll be sure and tell him. No, Dad's here. *Douglas* took his car."

Enos's truck and Douglas in the same three-block radius? Not a good sign. Fred pushed himself out of his chair as Margaret replaced the receiver. Holding up one hand, he motioned for her not to speak. He didn't want to hear it.

But that didn't stop her. "So?" she demanded.

"So I guess maybe you ought to take me over there."

Nodding in a self-satisfied way, she grabbed up her keys and opened the door. But her face froze in a look of disbelief, and she half-turned back toward Fred just as Douglas appeared in the doorway. This time Fred gave her a look of "I told you so."

Whistling, Douglas dropped Fred's keys onto a table and slipped out of his jacket.

"Where have you been?" Margaret demanded.

Douglas tossed his jacket over the back of the sofa. "Out."

"You've been at Suzanne's, haven't you?" Margaret pushed the front door closed and threw her keys down beside Fred's.

"What if I was?" Douglas dropped onto the sofa and stretched his arms across its back.

"Webb just called. He said he saw Dad's car there—and Enos's truck."

"Yeah, Enos was there for a second."

Fred lowered himself back into his rocking chair. "There wasn't any trouble?"

"No trouble." Douglas's mouth stretched wide in a yawn. "I didn't get to see Alison, tough. She wasn't home."

Perching on the arm of the sofa, Margaret asked, "Why did you try to see Alison after Suzanne asked you to stay away and Dad told you not to?"

"She's my daughter." Obviously unwilling to offer further explanation, Douglas picked up the newspaper and unfolded a section.

Margaret yanked the paper from his hands. "I'm not through."

"I am." He picked up another section of the paper and held it in front of his face.

Margaret flushed with anger and Fred groaned silently. He loved his children dearly, but at this moment he wished he could turn them both out of the house for a while.

Growing up, these two had been closer to each other than to either of the other boys. Douglas had consistently turned Margaret's intensity to laughter, and Margaret had taken Douglas's dreams seriously when no one else had.

Of all his children, Fred had expected Margaret to give Douglas the support he needed. Instead, she was being unreasonably hard on her brother. And Fred hated to see it, though he understood her frustration—Douglas's stubborn refusal to listen to reason even grated on *his* nerves.

Margaret turned to Fred, pleading silently for his help, and he didn't know what to do. Douglas yawned again and folded the newspaper, and Fred felt a faint hope stir. "Tired, son?"

Douglas nodded and rubbed his eyes. "Very. I haven't slept very well the last few nights." He leaned his head against the back of the sofa and let his eyes close.

"Maybe you ought to lie down for a while."

Douglas reared up, looking suspicious. "Why?"

"For Pete's sake, what's gotten into this family? I suggested that you lie down because you've been locked up in jail, and you act like I'm trying to pull something on you. And you"—he turned to Margaret—"I don't know why you've been acting the way you have, but I'm warning you—this constant bickering has got to stop. I won't tolerate another minute of it in my house."

Douglas jumped up and faced him, but Margaret stepped in front of her brother. "Now look what you've done. You know Dad's not supposed to get upset. You know—"

"You act like I'm the only one upsetting him," Douglas shouted. "Why don't you get off my back and look what *you're* doing to him?"

"That's it—pass the blame on to somebody else, just like you've always done."

"The blame for what? Upsetting Dad? I'm not the one who's charging around here acting holier than thou—"

"—so now it's all *my* fault?" Margaret's face turned a dangerous shade of red.

Douglas pushed his fingers through his hair and leaned over his sister. "I won't take the blame for something I didn't do—"

"Margaret. Douglas. That's enough."

"—nothing but trouble ever since you came back home. And poor Dad—"

Had they even heard a word he said?

"Dad's upset because somebody murdered Garrett. Well, it wasn't me. Or are you going to blame me for that, too?"

Fred walked slowly to the table and picked up his keys. He wanted Phoebe here. She would have known what to do.

She'd have known what to say that would calm them both down and restore harmony.

"There you go, twisting everything around just like you always do," Margaret said.

Forcing his aching knees to turn him, Fred faced his children. "Stop!" he thundered in a voice he hadn't used with any of his children for a good thirty years. They both stopped speaking and turned toward him, eyes wide. Well, well, well. Look at that. It worked.

"Both of you listen to me. I don't understand what's going on here, and I don't know that I want to. But I'll tell you this just once more—I won't tolerate this sort of behavior in my house. *Do you understand?*"

Margaret nodded. Douglas raked his fingers through his hair again and let his shoulders sag.

"I'm going out for a little while. Douglas, you stay here."

Douglas nodded.

"I mean it. You step one foot outside this house and I'll let Enos take you back to jail. I won't put up with you hotfooting it all over town. You got that?"

Douglas nodded again.

"Margaret, come with me." Fred started toward the door.

"Where?"

"To see Olivia Simms."

fifteen

"*Olivia?*"

Fred stopped and faced Margaret with his hand on the doorknob. "Yes, Olivia. Whether you like it or not, I'm going to talk with her. She likes you, and I figure I can use your help." Margaret would argue with him, of course, and he steeled himself for it.

But to his surprise, she said, "What about Webb?"

"Tell him to add a little mayonnaise to some tuna and put it on bread. It's not that difficult. I'll wait for you in the car." He opened the door and nearly stepped outside, but instead looked back over his shoulder to make sure she wouldn't launch into the argument with Douglas again. But Douglas had already started toward his bedroom and Margaret had the receiver in hand.

Less than five minutes later, Margaret slid into the front seat beside him and strapped herself in with the seat belt. She didn't look happy, but she didn't speak until long after they'd left Cutler's city limits.

Granby was less than fifteen miles away. In bad weather, the drive on the narrow, winding highway could be treacherous, but on a good day like today they had an easy drive. Fred let a little air in through an open window and looked at the remains of snow in the shadows of the trees, wondering how many weeks it would be before it all melted.

"Dad? I'm sorry."

He saw no need to carry on about it, so he merely nodded.

She stared out the window and sighed, silent for several minutes before she spoke again. "Sometimes I wonder why the boys all left Cutler."

"Their careers, for one thing. A small town doesn't offer the same opportunities a city does. But their personalities had a lot to do with it, too. Joseph would have been miserable here. You know Jeffrey—he could survive anywhere, but he's happier away. Douglas would have gone crazy."

"I'm not sorry I stayed. I wouldn't give up the years I had with you and Mom for anything, but sometimes I resent it when the boys come back home. Every time I talk to Joseph he tells me everything I've done wrong and what changes I should make—how I should treat you, what I should have done for Mom." She put her chin in her hand. "Now all of a sudden Douglas quits another job and shows up on your doorstep expecting to be treated like the prodigal son. And all he does is make trouble for everybody."

"Douglas didn't make the trouble."

"If he hadn't argued with Garrett over Suzanne, nobody would have accused him of murder."

"But he *didn't* commit the murder."

Weariness seemed to settle over her. "I know. I'm not saying he did." She shifted in her seat until she faced him. "I'm so angry with him I can hardly think straight, and I'm not even sure why."

He patted her knee but didn't bother offering meaningless platitudes. If she'd been content in her own life she wouldn't have felt this way. Her anger at Douglas—at all her brothers—was a symptom of her own unhappiness.

She touched his hand and sighed deeply. "Maybe I'm just tired of having to be everybody's mother. Ever since Mom died it seems like I have to take care of everyone."

"Well, you can stop mothering *me*."

She hesitated only a second before she laughed.

"I'm serious, Margaret. I don't need you to take care of me and neither do the boys. You've got enough on your plate without taking extras."

She shook her head. "I don't—"

"Don't tell me that's not what you mean." He decreased the speed of the car as they entered Granby's city limits.

"We never talk about your marriage, but I know there are times when you're unhappy."

She didn't answer, but he didn't expect her to. She rarely discussed Webb with him.

"I just wish you could have found the kind of partner I found in your mother."

"You and Mom were special. Not many people have the kind of marriage you had."

He waited for a white pickup truck to pass before he turned left onto Sycamore. "Well, you're right about that. But good marriages are possible."

She turned away again and straightened her shoulders, studying the houses as he drove slowly down the narrow street. When she spoke again her voice was all business. "Olivia's place is about two blocks east, but I still think you're making a mistake coming to see her."

"I'd be making a mistake if I didn't."

"Enos is going to have your hide."

He nodded his agreement. "I know it. But I can't worry about Enos. Douglas is my first concern."

They drove the rest of the way in silence, not breaking it even as Fred pulled up in front of Olivia's small-frame house. It hadn't been painted in a while, and the yard looked in need of attention. In front, a patchy winter-brown lawn straggled across a plot of dirt enclosed within a sagging chain-link fence. A blue Toyota shared driveway space with an orange Pinto station wagon that didn't look road worthy. When Dan Simms bailed out on Olivia last year, he obviously didn't leave her with much.

Olivia answered the door almost immediately, and Fred suspected she'd watched them arrive. Of medium height with a medium build and medium coloring, Olivia wouldn't stand out in a crowd. She wore faded jeans, battered tennis shoes, and a T-shirt with wording that had long since worn away. But let her open her mouth and you'd never forget her.

"What do you want?" Her voice was husky, as if she'd smoked too many cigarettes or shouted too much.

"We came by to pay our respects." Fred took a step toward the open door, intending to finagle his way inside.

But Olivia blocked him. "Well, that's kind of you, but I'm not up to having company just now." Olivia never was one to beat around the bush.

Fred decided on a more direct approach. "I wanted to ask you a few questions."

"Questions?" She looked from him to Margaret and back. "What kind of questions? And who said you could ask questions?"

"You know they arrested my son Douglas—"

"Yeah. So?"

"I need to prove Douglas didn't do it." He hated to sound desperate, but he was beginning to lose hope.

Olivia barked a laugh. "How are you going to do that?"

"That's what I'm hoping you'll help me with."

"As far as I'm concerned, they've caught my brother's killer. You want my honest opinion, I'm disgusted they'd let Doug out on bail. *Everybody* remembers how much Doug and Garrett hated each other, and obviously nothing's changed."

If Fred kept running into that attitude, Douglas wouldn't stand a chance.

Olivia stepped back and would have slammed shut the door, but Margaret pushed her way forward and held it open. "Olivia, please—"

Shaking her head, Olivia tried again to close the door.

This time Margaret used more force and managed to open it a little further. "Just let us talk with you for a minute. We know how it must look to you, but Douglas didn't do it and you're our only hope."

Fred groaned inwardly. She shouldn't have said that. He didn't want to give Olivia that kind of power against them.

But Olivia hesitated and an interested look crossed her face. With an elaborate shrug, she moved away from the door. "I guess it can't hurt."

On the other hand, it might be better not to question Margaret's tactics.

They followed Olivia into a narrow living room with

inadequate lighting. Fred perched on the edge of a gold and green crushed velvet sofa probably left over from the early seventies. Margaret settled herself beside him and Olivia chose a blue leather recliner close to her ashtray and cigarettes. The room smelled of stale tobacco smoke and something else he couldn't immediately identify.

Olivia pulled a cigarette from the pack and dragged deeply as she lit it. "So what did you want?"

Fred resisted the urge to wave away the smoke she blew toward him. "Tell me how you and Garrett got along."

"Why?"

Wrong question. "What I mean is, who do you know that might have been angry with him?"

"Angry enough to kill him? *Besides* Doug?" She exhaled heavily again and shook her head. "No one."

"And were you close? Would you have known if Garrett had an enemy?"

She narrowed her eyes and studied him. "Yes."

Well, that told him a lot. "What did you think of him dating Suzanne again?"

"What?" She looked surprised. "Why do you ask?"

"I heard you weren't happy about it."

"Who told you that?"

He shook his head and shrugged. "My source heard it from someone else."

She snorted a laugh and smoke escaped her nostrils. "Your *source*. That's really cute, Fred."

Settling back into her chair, she studied the ceiling. After a few seconds, he realized she wasn't going to say anything else.

Margaret put one hand on his arm and leaned forward slightly. "After everything that happened in high school between the three of them, I wouldn't have blamed you if you were upset."

Olivia crossed her legs and smiled. "You want to know the truth—I couldn't have cared less *who* Garrett was seeing. He was a grown man. He didn't need me to approve or disapprove of the women in his life."

"So it didn't bother you that Suzanne and Garrett were back together?"

"I'm not even sure they were 'back together.' I know they saw each other a couple of times, and I think Garrett wanted something to come of it, but I'm not sure Suzanne was as gung ho as he was. He probably would have been able to talk her into it eventually. He usually got what he wanted." Bitterness edged her voice.

Margaret sighed and nodded and made sympathetic noises, and Fred decided to let her take over.

"That's probably why he and Douglas never got along," she said softly. "Douglas is exactly the same way. But I thought Suzanne *was* interested—"

Olivia shook her head and rolled her eyes. "I didn't say she wasn't interested. I said she wasn't *as* interested as Garrett. But when it comes right down to it, Suzanne would have been a lot better for him than that Paula ever was. I wasn't sorry he gave her the brush-off when Suzanne came around."

"Paula who?"

Olivia looked wary for half a second, then shrugged. "Guess it doesn't matter if I say. Paula Franklin, from down in Winter Park. You might not know her, she hasn't lived up here long."

Paula Franklin. The name didn't sound familiar to him, but he'd find her soon enough. A scorned love interest might just bear looking into.

Margaret led the conversation off track, discussing funeral arrangements, flowers, and the after-service family meal, which seemed a moot point since Olivia was all the family Garrett had.

He let them wander for a minute or two, then said, "Do you know what you're going to do with the store?"

Olivia blinked her surprise. "The store? I don't think that will be up to me."

"I thought maybe you'd inherit from him—?"

She lit another cigarette, her brows knit in concentration, her forehead furrowed. "I assume everything will go to

Jenny, but I guess we'll find out after she and her mother get here, won't we?"

Margaret looked confused. "I didn't realize Yvonne would come back for the funeral."

Olivia waved her cigarette in the air and sent smoke drifting toward them. "I don't think she *wants* to. But he *was* Jenny's father, after all."

"Yes, but—"

"I'd do the same thing if I had kids and Dan keeled over. I'd lug them to the funeral, let them say good-bye—all that stuff."

Margaret smiled. "Well, it will be good to see her again. I always liked Yvonne."

Surprisingly, Olivia's face softened. "So did I. Sorriest thing that ever happened to Garrett was when she left him. He brought it all on himself—I'm not excusing him for one minute—but I don't think he ever really got over her." Without warning, her face crumpled and tears leaked from the corners of her eyes. Burying her face in her hands, she gave reign to her grief.

Margaret crossed to her and perched on the arm of her chair. She wrapped her arms around Olivia's shaking shoulders and murmured soothing words. They sat like that for several minutes while Olivia sobbed silently.

When Olivia lifted her face again, anguish contorted her features. "Oh, Maggie, I just can't believe he's gone."

Fred watched, helpless and uncertain. He'd been convinced he'd find answers here. Instead, he'd found more confusion. Even stretching his imagination to its limit, he couldn't picture Olivia as Garrett's killer.

Each turn he took led to a dead end, and all the trails led back to Douglas.

sixteen

Fred pushed the shovel into the soft earth beneath Phoebe's lilac bush in the corner of his yard. He turned the soil the way he always had every spring—and missed his wife.

Each year, the pain in his soul diminished a little more. Each season passed easier than the last. But with spring, her memory always returned sharply, probably because it had been her favorite season. Everything about it made him think of her—the texture of the air, the spongy soil underfoot, the first blossoms in the garden—and the lilacs.

He mopped his brow with the sleeve of his light jacket and watched Douglas on his hands and knees pulling dead weeds from between the bleeding hearts near the front walk. It was hard now for Fred to do the low work. His knees bothered him too much, and a morning spent weeding could make him ache for a week afterward. Last year his grandson Benjamin had helped out. This year, the basketball team claimed too much of Benjamin's attention.

Fred watched Douglas, glad of his company but aware that half the reason he found such pleasure in it this morning was because Douglas's mood suited his own.

Margaret had endured the visit to Olivia Simms yesterday, but by this morning she'd have regained her equilibrium and she'd be ready to fight him on the subject of a visit to Paula Franklin. When she dropped by and found him innocently working in the yard, she'd relax. He could slip away later and drive down to Winter Park.

As if he felt himself being watched, Douglas raised to his knees and looked around. His face flushed with exertion, he smiled easily. "Maybe I'll mow the lawn for you this afternoon."

"That would be fine."

"Have you serviced the mower yet?"

"Not yet." Fred plunged the shovel back into the earth and turned another load of soil.

Douglas watched him for a second, then turned back to the weeds, speaking over his shoulder and trying to sound nonchalant. "I called Margaret this morning."

"Oh?"

"I thought maybe we should talk."

Fred kept working and tried to match Douglas's easygoing tone. He didn't want to put Douglas off the idea by sounding too eager. "Good idea."

"I feel kind of bad for the way we've been acting—" Douglas sat back on his heels and rested his hands on his thighs.

Kind of bad? Well, it was better than nothing, Fred supposed. "Did you tell *her* that?"

"Sort of. But I could hear Webb in the background and the kids getting off to school. We couldn't talk long."

Fred leaned on the handle of the shovel. "Well, it's a start. Maybe you can talk again later."

"Yeah, sure." But Douglas didn't sound convinced, and he turned back to the flower bed too quickly to persuade his father.

Well, Fred wouldn't push it. Hard as it was to keep to himself, he wouldn't interfere unless they started bickering again. He needed to stay focused on solving Douglas's real problem.

Mopping his brow again, he asked, "Do you know anything about Garrett and a woman named Paula Franklin?"

Douglas dropped a handful of weeds and looked back over his shoulder. "*Should* I?"

"Does the name sound familiar to you?"

"No."

"I was hoping maybe Suzanne had mentioned it."

Douglas frowned. "Suzanne isn't speaking to me, remember?" He got to his feet and brushed off his knees. "Who's Paula Franklin?"

"An old flame of Garrett's. Sounds to me like he gave her the push when Suzanne came back to town, and it could be that she was upset about it."

"Have you told Enos?"

Fred turned back to his shovel. "No."

"Don't you think you ought to?"

"Eventually."

"*Eventually?*" Douglas shook his head and rolled his eyes and tried to look outraged. "You really are as bad as they say!"

Fred opened his mouth to make an appropriate response, but the sound of rapid footsteps made him keep quiet. He didn't want to discuss this in front of anyone else.

A second or two later Celeste Devereaux rounded the corner, waving her arms excitedly as she approached. Dressed in a bright green pantsuit with a pink and blue scarf knotted at her neck, her clothes clashed violently with her too-red hair. She clutched Fred's jacket in one hand. The instant she spied Fred, she increased her pace and waggled the jacket at him.

"I saw this at the Bluebird this morning," she cooed. "And I told Lizzie I'd be happy to bring it over to you."

Fred barely suppressed a groan. He made a mental note to discuss the return of his lost property with Lizzie sometime soon.

She dragged her fingers along his as she released the jacket and leaned in close to him. "You just have to tell me, Fred. Did you see Olivia? Was she there? What did she say? I've been *dying* of curiosity. In fact, I barely slept all night." She looped her arm with his and smiled at him with brilliant pink lips. "You *must* tell me *all* about it, I can't wait another minute."

What was she doing here? Didn't she have books to write? She tried to tug him away from his shovel, but Fred held his ground. "I saw her."

"*And—?*"

"And nothing. She's upset about her brother's death—"

"Well, of course she'd *say* that." Celeste's face puckered in thought; then she brightened again. "Anyway, I don't think she's the one you want, after all. I heard that Garrett was dating some woman down in Winter Park before Suzanne came back."

She was quick, he'd grant her that. "I know." He tried to pull his arm away from her grasp, but she wouldn't release it.

"Oh." She looked flustered, but she recovered in a heartbeat. "So you know that Garrett dumped her for Suzanne?"

"That's what I heard."

"You're going to talk to her, I guess?"

"Maybe."

"Oh, we *must*. And we'd better get started right away."

"We?" This time he managed to disentangle himself and took a few steps away for good measure.

"You're *not* leaving me behind this time, Fred Vickery."

"I'm not going now. I might not even go later."

Celeste stopped, eyed him suspiciously, and broke into a pleased grin. "But we *have* to go now if we want to catch her when her *husband* isn't home."

"Her husband?"

Celeste took advantage of his confusion to lunge at him and grab his arm again. "You didn't know that? You didn't know what kind of man Garrett was?" She shook her head and sent a soft look in Douglas's direction. "Garrett was the *worst* sort, Fred. *No* morals, if you know what I mean." She leered meaningfully and tugged at his arm again. "Now *come on*, let's get started."

Douglas strolled toward them, his smile reaching his eyes for the first time in days. He obviously found this all very amusing. "Go on, Dad. I'll stay here, I promise."

Celeste raised a hand toward Douglas, as if she intended to pinch his cheek or something else equally inappropriate. "You dear, *dear* boy. I can't tell you how *terrible* I feel. When this is over—" She broke off and lowered her head and for a moment Fred feared she might start crying. But she recovered almost immediately and sent Douglas a dazzling pink smile. "Don't you worry about your father, I'll take good care of him."

When she pulled at him again Fred backed away, shaking his head. "I'm busy right now, Celeste."

"Oh, come on, Dad." Douglas put an arm around Celeste and looked at him expectantly.

Celeste's eyes glinted. "I let you slip away yesterday, but I'm *not* going to do it again. I'll stay right here until you agree to let me go."

"It won't do you any good." Fred turned back to the lilac bush just as Margaret's car pulled into the driveway.

Squealing her delight, Celeste tottered across the lawn toward the car as Margaret climbed out. "Maggie, you absolutely *must* make your father stop being so *mean* to me. He's refusing to let me go."

"Go where?" Margaret spoke to Celeste, but her eyes locked on Fred.

"To question Paula Franklin. I have the most *brilliant* idea for how we could handle the investigation. You know how they do it on *television*? Good cop, bad cop? I thought *I* could be the bad cop—"

With her long legs Margaret could have outpaced Celeste easily, but she strolled toward Fred slowly. "I didn't realize you were going to visit Paula Franklin today, Dad."

"I'm not."

"Then when are you going?"

Fred leaned on the shovel. "I didn't say I was, did I? This is all her idea." He flipped a hand in Celeste's direction.

"Really?" Margaret tilted her head in Douglas's direction. "Really?"

Douglas battled the smile that tugged at his mouth, managed to get it under control, and faced Margaret squarely. "It was. All Celeste's idea. Dad and I are working in the yard." He gestured toward the tools and the flower beds and looked back at her innocently. Good boy, Fred thought.

Margaret half-turned away, tilted her head at an angle a little like a cat waiting to pounce on an unsuspecting mouse, and took a few steps toward the house. "Don't even think about it."

Fred raised his hands and put on an innocent expression of his own. "I wouldn't dream of it."

Fred dug out from his pocket the address for Roger and Paula Franklin, and he slowed his car for the first stoplight in Winter Park. He'd scrawled the address on the back of a deposit slip, and in the dim interior of the car he had to squint a little to see it. Number A–51, The Overlook, on Silver Hill.

Fred drove until he found the cluster of roughwood condominiums crawling up the side of Silver Hill on the south end of town. They cut into the stands of aspen and spruce and tried hard to look like they belonged there. Fred knew the builders went for this look on purpose, but he didn't like it. It seemed to him they could at least sand down the rough spots and paint.

He followed the winding road to the top of the hill and then pulled into an unnumbered parking space in front of the building marked *A*. He found number 51 on the ground floor, nearly concealed behind a clump of aspen trees.

He rang the bell, and a tall, dark man of about thirty-five with thick black eyebrows and deep-set eyes that squinted out of a suspicious face came to the door. "Yeah?"

The husband. Fred froze in place, trying to think of a reasonable explanation for his visit.

"Is this the Franklin residence?"

"Yes."

"Is Mrs. Franklin in?"

"She's at work. What do you want?"

That was a million-dollar question. Maybe he could act vague enough to throw him off. "I was hoping to catch her. Any idea when might be a good time to find her home?"

"Why?"

Vague might not work. "I had a few questions to ask her."

Roger's eyebrows melded together. "For what? A survey?"

That sounded good. Fred nodded.

"Since when do they let old folks do surveys?"

"It's not a survey exactly . . ."

"Who did you say you were?"

Fred had hoped to avoid that. He tried to think of a clever answer. "My name's Fred."

"And what did you say you wanted with my wife, Fred?"

"A few minutes of her time, that's all." Fred turned to go. "I'll try her again some other time."

"What company are you with? You aren't one of those door-to-door salesmen, are you?"

"Nothing like that."

Roger nodded in satisfaction. "You got a business card? Maybe I could leave it for her."

Fred shook his head. "I'll just check back."

Roger pulled himself back inside and almost shut the door, but he yanked it open again and shouted, "I know where I've seen you before. Don't you live up in Cutler?"

"Yes, that's right."

"So who are you, anyway?"

Fred shivered in the light breeze. He didn't see any way to avoid the truth any longer. "My name's Fred Vickery. Please tell Mrs. Franklin—"

Roger's posture didn't change, but his face snapped to the alert and his eyes glinted. "Vickery? Any relation to the guy who killed Garrett Locke?"

"My son was accused of murdering Garrett, but he didn't do it."

"Too bad. Some people might think he did the world a favor. So, what do you really want with my wife?"

"I'm trying to talk with everyone who knew Garrett—"

"What makes you think *she* knew him?"

"She didn't?"

Roger shrugged a little too casually. "No telling who she knew, but I never met him."

"But you didn't like him."

"I didn't say that."

"You said that whoever killed Garrett did the world a favor."

Roger gave him a tight smile and leaned against the door.

"I said *some* people might think so. I've heard about him, but I never met the man."

"Well, then, I don't think I need to disturb you any longer."

"Who told you my wife knew him?"

"I don't remember," Fred lied.

"Well, she didn't know him and I don't want anybody spreading rumors that she did. You got that?"

"Sure." Unnerved by Roger Franklin's hostility, Fred took a few more steps away, and Roger gave the door a shove so it slammed shut with a bang.

Roger Franklin was an angry, hostile man. So much so that Fred couldn't help whistling as he walked back to his car. No matter how hard Roger Franklin tried to convince him that he'd missed the target, Fred believed he'd just scored a direct hit.

seventeen

When the Bluebird Cafe appeared to Fred's line of vision, he decided he needed coffee—lots of it. He pulled into the nearly empty parking lot and found a spot by a huge Englemann spruce. He didn't see George Newman's battered gray pickup anywhere, and he breathed a sigh of relief. He didn't think he could handle George just now.

Inside, he claimed a seat at his favorite corner booth and signaled Lizzie. He wondered whether Roger Franklin would warn his wife he'd been asking about her. He hoped not. He wanted to get her honest reaction to his questions. But he couldn't do that until he figured a way to talk with her when her husband wasn't around, and that might be difficult. Roger might not warn Paula, but he wouldn't make it easy for Fred to reach her.

Through the window that overlooked Main Street, Fred saw Enos drive slowly past in his truck, stop, survey the parking lot, and pull to the side of the road. Jamming his battered black hat over his thinning hair, Enos climbed out of the cab, looked both ways for traffic, and then jogged across the street.

He soon burst through the door and headed straight for Fred's table. His face showed creases of anxiety that weren't normally there. Narrow slits appeared where his eyes usually were and his lips compressed to form a thin line.

Without a word of greeting, he slid onto the seat across from Fred and leaned his arms on the table. "What the hell do you think you're doing?"

"Having coffee. Want to join me?"

"I know you've been talking to people about the Locke case."

He couldn't deny it, so he shrugged and tried to look unconcerned. "One or two."

"Didn't I warn you about this? Didn't I specifically say—"

"You said you were doing everything you could to find Garrett's murderer. Instead, you arrested my son and kept him locked up. What were you doing to investigate other witnesses while you had him in jail? Nothing."

"That doesn't give you the right to take the law into your own hands."

"I have every right to help my son prove he's innocent."

"Not if it interferes with an official investigation."

"If you were conducting an investigation, I wouldn't have to do it myself, would I?"

Enos snapped his gaze away and stared out the window, but his jaw worked and Fred could sense his tension. After a lengthy silence, Enos asked, "Does Douglas have an attorney yet?"

Fred hesitated. He didn't want to actually *lie*.

Enos turned back to Fred and shook his head like a parent might over an unruly child. "Do you realize how strong the case is against him? We found the murder weapon with his fingerprints on it, for tar sakes. We've got half a dozen witnesses who saw Douglas fighting with Garrett and heard him shout a threat at him. And we've got one who puts him at the murder scene. Good billy hell, Fred—"

"I know."

"You don't have the kind of skill it's going to take to get Douglas out of this mess. Unless he finds a miracle, he's probably going to take the rap for this."

"He's not going to prison." Fred sounded more confident than he felt, but he refused to grant the idea any chance to take root.

Enos rubbed his palm across his face. He looked worn out, and Fred wondered how long it had been since he'd had a good night's sleep.

Fred pulled his cup back in front of him. He still needed coffee. "Have a cup with me. You'll feel better."

Enos's face relaxed slightly and a tiny smile tugged at the corners of his mouth. "I hope that's decaf."

"That's what I'm supposed to have, isn't it?"

The smile grew. "Yeah. And we all know how you do what you're supposed to."

Fred lifted his cup in a salute and let himself return the smile. He nearly had the cup to his lips when something across the street caught his eye. From the recessed doorway of the Cosmic Tradition a figure emerged—a woman, but not Summer Dey.

She looked up and down the boardwalk, as if checking to see if she'd been seen. Apparently satisfied, she pulled the collar of a jacket up around her ears and hurried away in the opposite direction from the Bluebird; but Fred thought he recognized her. And when she stopped after a few feet to light a cigarette, his suspicions were confirmed. But what was Olivia Simms doing in the Cosmic Tradition? She didn't seem the type to go in for all that mystical, magical baloney. She crossed the street and disappeared from his view.

As he turned back, another person near the Cosmic Tradition caught his eye. Standing on the sidewalk, looking after Olivia, Summer Dey stood with set shoulders and rigid body. She held that pose for a moment, relaxing and turning away only after Olivia had been out of sight for several seconds. Something about Olivia's visit had disturbed her.

He hated to do it, but maybe next he ought to pay a little visit to Summer's store. If there was even a remote possibility of her helping Douglas, he'd willingly seek her out. But he probably ought to wait until Enos left.

He must have given himself away, because Enos followed his gaze. "What are you looking at over there?"

"Nothing."

Enos looked suspicious. "Something going on I should know about?"

Summer had vacated her post and Olivia had disappeared, so Fred shook his head. "Nothing at all. Look for yourself."

Enos looked over his shoulder, but when he turned back he still looked skeptical. "You're sure?"

"Absolutely. You going to join me for a cup?"

Settling his hat in place, Enos shook his head. "Can't. Some other time." He lightly slapped the palm of his hand on the table and slid out of the booth.

"Try to get some rest," Fred counseled.

Enos gave a sharp laugh. "Sure." His face sobered and he pointed one finger at Fred. "Promise me you'll stay out of trouble."

Fred wished he could. "Are you going to find Garrett's killer?"

"I'm doing what I can." Turning on his heel, Enos worked his way across the room, waving at Lizzie, patting Bill Lacey on the shoulder, sparing a word or two for people at the counter. Once outside, he sprinted across the road and climbed into the cab of his truck.

Tossing a dollar bill on the table, Fred made his own way to the door. He checked first to make certain Enos had pulled away, then crossed the street as quickly as he could and stepped onto the boardwalk.

Remembering the last time he tried to question Summer, Fred almost changed his mind. She couldn't have been old enough to take an active part in the sixties, but she looked like a flower child with long, straight hair and beads— and had a convoluted philosophy of life Fred would never understand.

Hesitating for a moment at the door, he had to remind himself that she might have information he needed. But even with that in mind, he had to force himself to step inside.

She'd been lighting a candle at a low table across the room, and when the bell over the door tinkled to announce him, she whipped her head up, almost as if she were afraid of something. But when she saw him, the fear left her eyes. "Fred?"

She crossed to him and gauzy black material billowed around her ankles. She wore only a thin skirt and a sleeveless T-shirt with a scooped neck that would never keep her warm in the early spring weather. But on her feet she wore thick-soled, hightop boots, the likes of which Fred hadn't seen since World War II.

Rumor had it that Summer believed she couldn't paint unless she was depressed. So she surrounded herself with black to keep her spirits down and her creative genius in high gear. In over fifteen years, Fred had never seen her wear any other color.

"You've finally come," Summer said. "Are you seeking direction? Counsel? Are you looking for your spirit guides?" A wistful smile played on her lips and her eyes looked unfocused.

He tried to ignore the sickly sweet smell that seemed to be coming from either the candle or a piece of something smoldering in a silver tray near the cash register. "I came to ask you a few questions."

"Questions. Seek the answers within your own soul, Fred. Search for peace and you will find it."

The bell over the door sounded again and Fred snapped his mouth shut on his next words. Heavy footsteps alerted him as to who he'd see when he turned around. Enos.

"Mornin' Summer." Enos pulled off his hat and nodded. His lips twitched. "Fred. Hope I'm not interrupting something."

Fred moved down the nearest aisle and picked up a book. "Not a thing," he lied, "just browsing."

Enos leaned his arm on the counter by the smelly stuff and looked around with interest. "You don't mind if I cut in front of you then?"

"Not a bit." He opened the book and pretended to scan a few pages, but he kept his eyes on Enos and Summer.

"Mind if I ask you a question or two, Summer?"

Summer shook her head, but her shoulders tightened again.

"I happened to be sitting over at the Bluebird a few minutes ago and noticed Olivia Simms coming out of your store."

So, he'd seen Olivia after all.

Summer nodded slowly. "Olivia is a client of mine."

"She shops here often?"

"Shops, yes. Occasionally."

"Is this the first time she's been in here since Garrett was murdered?"

Summer shook her head.

"What'd she buy?"

"Nothing."

Enos looked confused. "She just came in to look?"

"She came in for a reading."

"And she's been in before?"

"I've been giving Olivia readings for several years, ever since she and Garrett had all that trouble."

Fred lowered the book to its shelf. Trouble between Garrett and Olivia? Then he'd been right, after all.

Enos nodded as if he'd heard about it before.

Summer flipped a lock of hair over her shoulder and looked to where Fred still stood. Almost too quietly for Fred to hear, she said, "She wanted to find a way to forgive her brother."

"And did she find it?"

"Of course. She came to understand Garrett's obsession with her share of the family business and her need to lose it to him as karma. Because she robbed and cheated so many in one of her previous incarnations, she *had* to allow Garrett to cheat her in this life or she would have carried that karmic debt with her."

Here she went again, spouting all that nonsense. Why couldn't she just give a straight answer?

Enos nodded and looked serious. "I see. And after she came to terms with Garrett—?"

"There are many who seek direction and insight into their futures. Olivia is one."

It sounded to Fred like Olivia used Summer as a fortune-teller. Suddenly Celeste's enthusiasm over her anticipated love interest and the plot for her next book made sense to him.

"Can you tell me about her last few readings?" Enos asked.

But Summer's face closed and she shook her head rapidly. "Absolutely not."

"Look, Summer, I'm investigating the murder of her brother. Any information you can give me—"

"I mean I can't, Enos," Summer interrupted, turning and putting a few feet between them. "I don't remember. When I give a reading, it's like I'm in a trance. The information is strictly between the client and my guide. I can't remember a thing afterward."

Enos scratched his head and shifted position. "Nothing?"

Summer tried to look sorry. "Nothing. And even if I could remember, I couldn't share any specific details with you unless my client agreed, the same way lawyers and priests can't talk about what somebody tells them."

Fred bit back a smile at the look that crossed Enos's face.

Enos raked his fingers through his hair and replaced his hat. "If you think of anything else you *can* tell me, let me know." He took a step or two away, then looked back at Fred with a grin. "Did I ask her everything you wanted to know, Fred?"

Very funny. Fred snagged a book from the shelf and walked toward the front of the store. "I told you, I came in to browse."

Enos chuckled.

"How much for this book, Summer?" He'd be damned if he'd let Enos laugh at him.

"Twenty-three ninety-five." She crossed to the counter and pulled out a receipt book. "Do you want it?"

Fred slapped it on the counter. "Ring it up."

Enos pulled open the door. "You'll have to tell me whether it's any good." Laughing to himself, he stepped outside and let the door close behind him.

Summer added tax and quoted him the total. Fishing in his pocket for his wallet, Fred glanced at his latest acquisition and noticed the title for the first time—*Past Loves, A Study of Karma and Human Sexuality.*

eighteen

Fred tucked his book under his arm and turned his face into the sun as he started for home. Summer's words replayed endlessly through his head. He didn't believe her psychic mumbo jumbo, but there might be something to her ideas about Olivia's relationship with Garrett.

He wanted to talk to Olivia again. And this time he'd find out the truth. He scanned the street looking for her blue Toyota, but without luck. It hadn't been more than half an hour since he'd seen her coming out of Summer's place, but even if he couldn't find her in Cutler, he had plenty of time to drive back to Granby before dinner.

Crossing Main Street, he tried not to notice Webb's truck parked near the door to the Copper Penny. He never said much to Margaret about her husband—she'd make up her own mind, anyway—but he had his opinion.

Two women at the back of the parking lot caught his eye—one petite and dark, the other medium height and coloring. He slowed his step, studying them as he passed. Suzanne and Olivia. Now what were they doing together?

Olivia gestured with one hand, leaving a trail of smoke from the cigarette between her fingers. Suzanne shook her head fiercely, but Olivia didn't seem phased by it. She jabbed one finger toward Suzanne's chest as if punctuating her words.

Brushing away Olivia's hand, Suzanne turned to leave. But Olivia grabbed her arm and spun her back around.

Fred stopped near the corner of the building. He wished he could hear them, but if he moved any closer they'd probably catch sight of him.

Releasing herself from Olivia's grasp, Suzanne then backed away. Olivia tossed her cigarette to the ground and mashed it underfoot, waving her hands to emphasize her words. Suzanne shook her head once more and yanked open the door to her car. She slid into the seat and slammed the door, pressing on the lock when Olivia reached for the handle.

The engine roared to life, and Fred ducked into the doorway of the Bureau of Land Management's satellite office just as Suzanne roared past. He hurried back to the parking lot to find Olivia, but she'd disappeared. She hadn't passed him, and he recognized her car in the lot, so he decided she must have gone inside the Copper Penny.

Shoving his hands into his pockets, he allowed himself a little smile. He knew he was onto the scent of a secret, and he wouldn't rest until he learned it.

Stepping into the Copper Penny, Fred felt as if he'd gone from day into the dead of night. Albán kept the place clean, but to Fred the atmosphere left much to be desired.

As the door creaked shut behind him, Fred hesitated and let his eyes adjust to the dim light. Neon beer signs glowed from the walls and candles flickered at each of the tables placed around what appeared to be a dance floor. Smoke rose from ashtrays on some of the tables and formed a heavy cloud at ceiling level. But a clear light behind the bar dispelled some of the gloom.

Albán leaned against the counter, talking with a customer. A burst of laughter he recognized as Webb's erupted from the back corner near a pool table. Fred pushed aside his irritation and scanned the room for Olivia. The lunch crowd had thinned out and it was too early for those who stopped in after work, so the bar wasn't crowded, yet still he couldn't see her. He crossed the room and hoisted himself onto a stool. She *must* have come in here. Where else could she have gone?

Fred hadn't been inside this place for years, but some things never changed. Someone, perhaps the original owner way back when, had covered the bar with pennies and shellacked them in place. Must have been thousands of them. He traced his finger in a figure-8 over those closest to him and waited for Albán to finish. He didn't have to wait long.

Tossing a towel over his shoulder, Albán worked his way down the bar. "We don't usually see you in here, Fred. What's up?"

"Did Olivia Simms come in here?"

Albán nodded toward an empty seat at the other end. "A few minutes ago. I guess she went to the ladies' room or something."

"I'll wait."

"Can I get you a drink?"

Fred shook his head. "Nothing, thanks."

"I didn't think so." Albán half-turned away, then stopped and pointed at Fred. "Hey, you've never had my *lecsó*, have you? You've got to try some." He busied himself over a large pot and returned with a steaming bowl of chunky red-colored soup with tiny noodles floating at the surface.

Placing it in front of Fred with a flourish, Albán hurried away and returned with a thick slice of crusty bread and a glass of ice water.

He leaned against the bar and folded his arms across his chest. "So, what do you think?"

Fred stirred the mixture and winced at its spicy smell.

"It's my mother's recipe. One of my biggest sellers."

If Albán hadn't been watching him so closely, Fred would have pushed it away. But the eagerness in Albán's eyes forced Fred to lift the spoon to his lips.

Fire erupted in his mouth the second the soup touched his tongue. Tears flooded his eyes, his nose began to run, and he could feel heartburn already. He swallowed quickly and shoved the bread into his mouth. "What the hell's in that?" he finally managed to say.

Albán shrugged. "Onions, tomatoes, yellow peppers— hot ones—paprika and kolbász—Hungarian sausage. It's great, isn't it?"

Fred gulped water and prayed for Olivia's return so he could avoid eating more.

Albán pulled the towel from his shoulder and wiped the counter. "How's Doug doing?"

"He's all right." Fred filled his mouth with water again and waited for it to cool his tortured tongue. It didn't help.

"Are the rest of you doing all right? Do you need anything?"

Fred swallowed quickly. "No, we're doing okay. But thanks."

"If you *do* need anything, give me a call."

Before Fred could respond, Olivia Simms came around the corner. When she saw him sitting there, her eyes narrowed and her footsteps faltered. But she recovered nicely.

"Well, how ya doin', Fred?" She patted his shoulder, but didn't stop as she passed. "Can I get a bowl of that lay-cho, Albán? And a beer?" She perched on a stool at the end of the bar and dug a cigarette out of her purse.

Fred followed her. "Mind if I join you?"

She shrugged and exhaled in his direction. "Plenty of room, I guess."

Albán settled Olivia's food in front of her, walked back to Fred's place, and returned with his bowl. Criminy—he thought he'd escaped it.

Olivia stubbed out her cigarette. Ladling an oversized spoon through the red soup, she took a huge bite and spoke with her mouth full. "This is wonderful, as usual. When are you going to give me the recipe?"

Albán smiled. "When you learn how to pronounce it."

She raised her spoon toward Fred. "Great, isn't it?"

Great—for paint thinner, that is. He moved his head in a way he hoped Albán would take as a nod. It must have worked because Albán grinned and pushed through the swinging doors into the kitchen.

Fred leaned toward her. "I met Roger Franklin the other day," he said casually. "You didn't mention that Paula Franklin was married."

"You didn't ask."

"What do you know about her?"

Olivia eyed him suspiciously. "You still playing Sam

Spade?" She gulped beer from the bottle, ignoring the glass Albán had given her, and used the back of her hand to wipe her mouth.

But Fred didn't intend to let her off the hook. "What can you tell me about her relationship with Garrett?"

"Nothing." She scooped up another bite of *lecsó*.

"How long did they know each other?"

Olivia shrugged. "Who knows? A few months maybe. Garrett never lasted very long with anybody."

"Was Paula in love with him? Was she upset when he started seeing Suzanne again?"

"How would I know that? We weren't friends. She didn't confide in me. Why don't you ask her that?"

"I will." He stirred his *lecsó*, but he didn't make the mistake of eating any. "I couldn't help but notice you and Suzanne in the parking lot a few minutes ago."

She lowered her spoon. "Really?"

"What were you arguing about?"

"For hell's sake, Fred—"

"What were you arguing with Suzanne about?"

"What makes you think we were arguing?"

"Don't beat around the bush, Olivia—you never have before, and I don't have time for you to start now."

She shrugged. "Okay. We were arguing, but why is none of your damned business."

She tried to look nonchalant, but her eyes flashed and her shoulders tensed, and Fred knew that if he pushed any harder he'd lose her. But somehow this was all connected to Garrett. And everything about Garrett was his business as long as Douglas was accused of murder.

Wanting her to relax a little, he slid from his stool and made a few adjustments to his clothing, as if he intended to leave. "Maybe you're right," he said. "Maybe it isn't any of my business."

Her eyes cleared a little and her shoulders straightened as if she'd been vindicated. She spooned a chunk of tomato into her mouth.

"And it might not even come up when I'm talking to Enos."

She stopped chewing and looked at him warily.

He patted his pockets, pulled out his wallet and extracted a bill, smiling at her. "He probably won't even think it's important—the sister and girlfriend of a murder victim having an argument."

She carefully placed her spoon on the counter and leaned one elbow on the bar.

"You're right not to give it a second thought," he said.

She studied him and brushed a stray lock of hair away from her mouth. "Where'd you learn to do that? Your kids must have a hell of a time getting away with anything around you."

"Will you tell me what you were arguing about?"

Olivia didn't speak for what seemed like a very long time. So long that Fred nearly gave up hope. But just before he turned away, she cleared her throat and said, "Suzanne called me this afternoon and asked me to meet her here. I was curious, so I came. When I got here, she was all wigged out about Garrett. She feels responsible for his death."

His heart gave a little jump. "*Suzanne* feels responsible?"

"Yeah. But that's ridiculous. Like I told her, she can't blame herself for anything that happened."

"Why did she think she was responsible?"

Olivia shrugged and looked away. She picked at the label on her beer bottle for a few seconds before she spoke again. "Because of the whole thing with Doug. If Doug hadn't seen her with Garrett, Garrett might still be alive."

His elation faded.

Olivia looked up and flicked pieces of the torn label onto the bar. "You and Maggie are probably the only ones in town who don't believe Doug's guilty. I feel sort of bad for you, Fred. You guys shouldn't have to pay the price for his mistakes."

He opened his mouth to protest, but stopped himself. He sounded like a broken record lately, and words alone weren't going to help Douglas. "Why didn't you tell me the truth about your relationship with Garrett?"

"Ex*cuse* me?" Her face hardened.

"Why didn't you tell me about the hard feelings between you and Garrett over the store?"

"Because there weren't any."

"Not even when he cheated you out of your share?"

She pushed her bowl away, and lit a cigarette. "Garrett didn't cheat me out of anything."

"What happened?"

"Family business. Certainly not any of yours." Her voice sounded calm, but the cigarette trembled slightly in her fingers.

"Why did Garrett end up with the store, a big house, and a pile of money, while you got nothing?"

"I got my share."

"You're still part owner in the business?"

"No."

"Nothing?"

She took one last pull from the beer bottle and slid off her stool. Digging a bill out of the pocket of her jeans, she dropped it on the counter beside her empty bowl and headed for the door.

But Fred didn't intend to let her get away so easily. He followed her outside and stayed behind her as she started through the parking lot. "I figure you just might wind up with a bundle now that he's gone. And for a woman who's been on the low end of the stick as long as you have, that must look pretty good."

She didn't respond.

"I imagine Enos will figure it out soon enough."

She increased her pace.

It hurt his knees to do so, but he kept up with her. "I don't suppose you want to tell me where you were the night he was killed?" She stopped suddenly, and he had to brace himself to keep from plowing into her.

"Are you suggesting that *I* killed him?"

"Stranger things have happened . . ."

"Don't be stupid!" Contempt filled her voice. She took two steps away, changed her mind and whirled back, her face flushed and angry. "When Garrett bought me out, it was the best thing that ever happened to me. Sure, he ended up with the business, but he deserved it. That worthless son of a bitch I married gambled away everything I owned— *everything*. I'd already lost my car, and the bank was ready to foreclose on my house. I know it doesn't look like much to you, but it's all I had. Garrett offered to give me the money, but I wouldn't let him. So he bought me out—gave me cash. If it hadn't been for him, I'd be on the streets." With trembling fingers she found a cigarette, lit it, and seemed to draw strength from it as she inhaled. "You want to help Doug, look somewhere else. But leave me alone."

This time he made no move to stop her when she walked away. Part of him wanted to believe her, but part of him resisted. Olivia had been down for a long time. Garrett might have helped her once, but it hadn't been enough to lift her to another style of living. And considering the difference in their life-styles, Fred doubted Garrett's help equaled Olivia's half of their father's estate.

He'd let her cool off a little before he approached her again. In the meantime, maybe he could check with Rusty Kinsella to see if Garrett had kept any personal records at the store. If he could find a record of Garrett's transaction with Olivia, he might be able to convince Enos how much she had to gain from Garrett's death.

Turning toward home once more, Fred battled a sudden weariness. Olivia Simms and Rusty Kinsella. He didn't want to believe either of them guilty of murder. But who else could have done it? Roger Franklin? Or Paula? Maybe. He hoped so. He didn't like thinking the murderer was somebody he'd known forever. He didn't like thinking that at all.

nineteen

Morning sunlight streamed through the branches of trees as Fred walked slowly along the lake path. He'd gotten a later start on the day than usual. Yesterday had worn him out more than he liked to admit. But nothing, not even tired bones, would keep him away from Garrett's funeral this morning.

He planned to get to the church early and find the best seat in the house. He'd watch everybody who came in and study their reactions. Somebody somewhere had to slip up sometime.

He rounded a curve in the path at the southern tip of the lake and stopped in his tracks. Alison sat at the water's edge, head lowered, shoulders slumped.

"Alison?"

She whipped her head up and surprise flicked across her features. "Grandpa?"

"What on earth are you doing out here alone?"

She shrugged. "Just thinking."

"About what?"

"Stuff."

"Stuff, huh? Stuff like dolls? Or more serious stuff?"

"Just stuff."

Gritting his teeth against the stiffness in his knees, Fred hunkered down beside her, then gave a little laugh. "This was probably a foolish thing to do. You might have to help me up."

She tried to smile, but her face wouldn't cooperate.

"What's wrong, sweetheart?"

"Nothing."

"I might be an old man, but I can still recognize a sad young girl when I see one."

She didn't respond.

"Something so bad you can't even tell Grandpa about it?" He touched his fingertips to her chin and tilted her head up until her eyes met his. "I hope nothing's ever so wrong in your life that you can't talk to me."

This time she smiled a little. "I'm just confused, Grandpa."

He stretched out his legs and sat on the cold ground beside her. He'd worry about stiff joints later. "Maybe I can help."

She looked out over the lake, but didn't say anything for several minutes. Fred forced himself to wait, knowing that if he pushed, she'd back off.

After a long pause she sighed and lowered her head again. "Everything's gone wrong."

"Like what?" He didn't want to just assume she meant the divorce and the rift between her parents.

"Like coming here and leaving all my friends behind in Seattle. Like living in Aunt Celeste's yucky old house and going to this dumb old school. Like having my mom go on dates with other men. And having my dad thrown in jail. And listening to my mom say awful things about him all the time." The words tumbled out of her mouth so fast he knew they'd been dammed up for a long time.

Fred waited a few seconds before asking, "Anything else?"

"Why doesn't my dad come to see me?" Her voice quivered and tears pooled in her eyes.

"Your mom asked him not to."

"Why?"

"She doesn't want you upset."

Alison made a derisive sound and looked away. "She doesn't care whether I'm upset."

"Of course she does, sweetheart. You know, the saddest part of growing up is finding out that your parents aren't perfect. They're human and they make mistakes—"

"If my dad cared about me, he'd come to see me."

"He's respecting your mother's wishes."

"If he loved me, he'd come and see me anyway. He'd find a way, and he wouldn't care what she said." She jumped up and took a few steps away from him.

Groaning a little in spite of his best efforts not to, Fred worked his way back to his feet. "When this is over, when Enos finds the real killer, things will get back to normal."

She met his gaze steadily for half a second before she looked away again. "No, they won't."

"Okay, maybe not normal. But you'll be able to see your dad again, and after a little while, we'll all get used to the way things are. I understand how you feel, sweetheart, but sometimes when parents get divorced, they're so hurt and angry themselves they don't realize how bad their kids feel—"

"They know," she shouted and moved away from him again. "They both know, but they don't care. Now my mom's talking about moving again. And you know what? I don't care, either."

Fred reached for her, wanting to offer comfort. "Alison—"

"Don't," she sobbed and twisted away. "I *don't* care. I hate it here."

Before he could do anything else, she turned away and ran down the path toward town. He watched her disappear, unable to move quickly enough to catch her, unsure whether he'd try even if he could.

She needed attention from her parents. This self-indulgent battle they'd been fighting had to come to an end. No matter what they thought of each other, Douglas and Suzanne had to work together to help Alison.

Fred knew Suzanne feared some harmful side effect to Alison because of Douglas's arrest. But the separation from her father was causing Alison very real damage, and Suzanne needed to learn to tell reality from fantasy.

Was Suzanne really talking about moving again? What good did she think that would do? She'd run here after the divorce, and now that trouble arose, she wanted to run away. Well, she couldn't spend the rest of her life running from her problems. And Fred didn't want her to teach Alison to do it, either.

Suzanne had to put her grievances with Douglas aside and help her daughter through this. And as Alison's grandfather, he had to make Suzanne see that.

He turned away on the now empty path and continued his walk. Going back wouldn't accomplish anything. Alison was far away by now, and if he stopped walking too soon after sitting on the cold ground he wouldn't move for days. He had a funeral to go to and a puzzle to solve. He couldn't afford to be laid up in bed.

Fred shifted the flowers in his hand and stepped carefully between the headstones as he made his way down the hill to the place he hated more than any other—Phoebe's grave. Within that cold earth lay the remains of his beloved. The remains—what an insufficient term.

He forced back the tears that always burned the back of his eyes when he came here and he bent stiffly over the flat headstone to wipe away a couple of moldy leaves from the carved letters.

PHOEBE COOPER VICKERY
1925–1991

He came on her birthday every year—September 19. He came on Memorial Day because she'd made him promise once, when they were young and carefree, that he wouldn't let a year go by without putting lilacs on her grave. But that was in the days when neither of them thought they'd ever die. Back when they were immortal. He couldn't stand to come any more often than that. Phoebe wasn't here, and he derived no particular comfort from visiting her grave.

But he'd come today, because after seeing Alison at the lake, he'd been overcome by the need to bring Phoebe flowers. He placed them carefully beside her name and pushed against his knees with his palms to straighten his back. He'd have to head over to the church soon, but he still had a few minutes before the funeral.

He looked at the flowers he'd brought. They weren't much—a couple of carnations he'd found in the cooler at Lacey's. But Phoebe'd always told him she'd rather have him give her a scraggly old tulip because he wanted to than a dozen roses because he felt he had to. And she'd meant it.

He cleared his throat and almost turned away, but a gentle breeze shifted along the ground and ruffled the petals of the flowers. And for an instant, he thought he felt Phoebe here.

He waited, letting the feeling warm him, wanting it to go on for a while. "We got us a little girl in trouble, sweetheart. And our boy . . . I'm doing my best to get him out of this mess, but I don't know what to do for Alison. You'd have known, though. You always knew." He looked around, suddenly conscious of how funny he must look talking to no one, but the cemetery was still empty.

He lingered, but the breeze faded away and left him alone. He didn't know what he expected—maybe some fanciful bit of nonsense like Phoebe sending him a message on the wind. But he didn't get one. And when a car pulled up in front of the cemetery and the Laceys spilled out of it, he decided he ought to go. His being here would only ignite Janice's imagination. She'd whisper to everyone that he was beside himself because of Douglas's trouble. That he'd taken to coming to church for comfort in this time of travail. She'd used that word, too—*travail*.

He climbed the hill and crossed the street to the little white church. Choosing a pew in back, he planted himself in the corner, where he could have a clear view, and waited. Within minutes, the spectators—no stretch of his imagination allowed him to think of them as mourners—began to stream into the small chapel in small groups. Subdued conversation hummed almost too low for him to hear, and the occasional, almost irreverent, burst of laughter was quickly stifled.

Most everyone in Cutler turned out for weddings and funerals. And Garrett's proved to be no exception. With less than five minutes to go before the service, the pews at back had nearly filled, but the one in front reserved for the family remained conspicuously empty. Fred shifted himself on the hard wooden bench, trying to find a more comfortable position.

Emma Brumbaugh started playing something soft and soothing on the organ. A few minutes later, Olivia appeared in an almost concealed doorway at the front of the chapel. She wore a wrinkled black dress that looked as if it had been stuffed into the back of her closet. But other than the color of her clothes, she gave no obvious signs of mourning. Her expression looked more like someone conducting a business meeting than burying her brother.

She passed Garrett's coffin, barely sparing him a glance, and took her place alone in the front pew. The organ music swelled around them, and a few last-minute arrivals scurried up the aisles to their seats. As the music stopped and Reverend Simper took his place at the pulpit, someone slipped into the pew beside Fred.

It was Suzanne. She smiled at him and Fred nodded back, bracing himself for Celeste to come next, while looking for Alison.

Suzanne leaned toward him and whispered, "Celeste didn't come—she hates funerals. But she said to tell you hello."

Well, that was the best news he'd heard in a long time. "Where's Alison?"

"She's at home. With Celeste. Everything's been so hard on her." She said no more and looked back toward the front of the church.

Reverend Simper's long face was cast in its most somber expression, and his eyes looked out over the congregation with deep sympathy. "Dearly beloved," he began. "We are gathered here today on this most solemn occasion to pay tribute to our friend and neighbor, Garrett Locke."

Fred scanned the crowd. Two rows in front of him, Rusty Kinsella sat stiffly beside his wife Eileen. Beside them, one dark head and five red ones were staggered in a row to the end of the pew.

Janice Lacey's eager eyes darted around the room, and Bill leaned forward slightly in a posture that told Fred he'd soon be asleep. Enos and Jessica had seats directly behind Olivia. George Newman sat in the same pew as Lizzie Hatch, and Grady had worked his long body into the corner, ready for a nap.

Reverend Simper droned on in that church monotone that always lulled Fred to sleep. ". . . so sad when a life ends so abruptly. A man with so much to give, such a contribution to make . . ." Funny, the reverend's dull cadence wasn't having its usual effect on Fred today.

Albán Toth. Ivan Neeley and his young, pregnant wife. Doc and Velma Huggins. Margaret must have come in late. She sat with Sara, Benjamin, and Deborah in the pew directly across from Fred's. No Webb—as usual.

Fred had hoped for some sort of breakthrough in finding Garrett's killer. But it didn't look like he'd get it. He scanned the crowd once more, and this time he noticed a petite blond woman with shoulder-length hair sobbing quietly into a handkerchief. He'd never seen her before, but he'd bet money he knew who she was—Paula Franklin. Had to be. He'd catch her after the service and talk to her—it might be his only chance.

The reverend continued, extolling Garrett's virtues, quoting Bible passages, sharing anecdotes from Garrett's life. Devoted son. Hardworking businessman. Thoughtful and generous employer.

Grady slipped a little lower in his seat. Janice Lacey fanned herself with the program. Margaret slid an arm around Deborah's shoulders.

". . . such a shame," Reverend Simper said, "that Garrett's lovely daughter couldn't be here today." And for the first time a trace of sympathy moved Fred. If Douglas died tomorrow, Suzanne probably wouldn't allow Alison to attend the funeral.

Olivia sat in the front pew, her shoulders rigid, her face unmoving. One of the youngest Kinsella children started to cry. Rusty scooped her up and hurried to the back of the chapel. And the blond woman dabbed at her eyes with her handkerchief.

Out of a chapel full of people, only the blond woman

looked upset. But surely the death of a young man cut down in the prime of his life ought to inspire more than this almost sterile acceptance of his passing. Shouldn't it?

At last the reverend ran out of virtuous things to say, and Loralee Kirkham moved to the front of the chapel, beaming benignly upon the congregation. Emma Brumbaugh worked her way through a musical introduction, and Loralee, hands clasped together in front of her, began to warble, "The Lord is my shepherd. I shall not want . . ."

And then, at last, it was over. Fred watched Paula Franklin pull herself together. He wanted to talk to her, but he needed to talk to Suzanne about Alison. He hesitated, uncertain which woman to approach first.

He watched Paula dab at her eyes again and decided she'd probably stay for the graveside service. But when Suzanne opened her purse and took out her keys, he made his decision.

Fred placed a hand on Suzanne's arm to keep her from leaving. "Can I talk with you for a minute?"

She pulled away from him a little. "What about?"

"I saw Alison this morning. I'd like to talk to you about her."

Her eyes narrowed skeptically, but she nodded. "Outside."

Now that the funeral was over, the crowd seemed almost festive. Groups had formed all over the church lawn and down the sidewalk to the street. Fred followed Suzanne through several clusters of people to the end of the parking lot where she'd left her car. She leaned against it and folded her arms across her chest. "What about Alison?"

"I found her by the lake when I went out this morning. She's very upset, Suzanne."

"You think I don't know how upset she is?"

He didn't let her harsh tone stop him. "She tells me you're talking about moving again."

"As a matter of fact, I am. Coming back here wasn't a good idea. I need to take her someplace—"

"You need to let her stay right here and work out the things that are bothering her. She doesn't want to go."

"She's seven years old. She doesn't know what's best for her."

"Maybe not, but she thinks you don't care about her. That Douglas doesn't care. You can't run away every time the going gets rough."

Suzanne stared at him for one long moment, her eyes filled with loathing, or something awfully close to it. "I'm not running away."

Gently he placed a hand on her shoulder. "Don't get upset with me. I don't want to argue, but I am concerned about Alison."

"Well, so am I. And I'll decide what's best for her. Staying in Cutler is out of the question."

"I think you're making a mistake. Make sure you're not putting your own desires before Alison's needs."

He meant the words to sound mild, but Suzanne's temper flared. "*I'm* not the one putting my desires first. *You're* the one doing that. You're afraid that if Alison moves away, you'll never see her again. And you don't want to lose her." She turned away from him, yanked open the car door, and dropped into her seat. "I've never tried to keep Alison from you, Fred. You know that. But don't interfere with my decision. And don't you dare go behind my back where Alison is concerned again." Slamming the car door between them, she ignited the engine and shifted the car into reverse so quickly Fred had to skip backward to keep his feet from being crushed by the tires.

He stared after her, stunned by her reaction. He'd obviously gone about the situation the wrong way. He hadn't intended to make her so angry.

She rounded the corner and disappeared from view. He'd certainly have to watch his step in the future. Only a slender thread tied Alison to the family now, and he couldn't afford to let it snap. He'd have to wait and hope Enos could find the murderer and calm everybody down before Suzanne took Alison outside his reach.

He walked slowly back to the church, trying to buoy his spirits. At least he'd found Paula Franklin. He wanted to talk to her before she disappeared.

He spent the next ten minutes looking for her, but with no luck. He'd lost her. She must have slipped away while he was talking with Suzanne. Swallowing his disappointment, he decided he'd have to go to Winter Park, again. Her obvious grief over Garrett convinced him she had a story to tell—one he was sure he wanted to hear.

twenty

Fred stopped on the sidewalk in front of the church the second he saw Janice Lacey bouncing down the steps toward him, but he didn't get turned around in time to escape.

"Fred? Wait. Fred?"

He pretended he hadn't heard her. He just couldn't deal with her. Not right now.

But she grabbed his arm and pulled him to a stop. "Wasn't the service lovely? Doesn't the reverend do a wonderful job? And I thought the flowers were just beautiful. I've told Becky Grimes a thousand times if I've told her once—she ought to set up a shop. Don't you think she ought to set up a shop?"

Maybe if he just agreed with her she'd leave him alone. "The flowers were lovely."

"And such a wonderful service. Wasn't it?"

"Wonderful."

"But I think it's so sad that Garrett's daughter couldn't be here. It's such a shame—don't you think so? Why in the world didn't Yvonne bring her?"

He didn't answer. The minute Janice started speculating, she strayed into territory Fred wanted to avoid. He scanned the crowd for Paula Franklin, but he couldn't see her anywhere.

"Of course, the divorce probably left them with some bad feelings—don't divorces always?—but don't you think she could at least have brought Jenny back for the funeral?"

He did, but he didn't want to encourage Janice's vivid

imagination. He checked behind him, hoping he'd see Paula still in the parking lot, but there was no one.

Janice's eyes brightened suddenly and she waved to someone behind him. "Enos, Jessica! Over here." She lunged at them and dragged Enos into their circle. "I was just saying to Fred what a shame it is that Yvonne didn't bring Jenny back for the funeral. Don't you think it's sad when parents let their own feelings take over like that?"

Jessica tugged at her blouse and leaned into the fray eagerly. "Oh, my, yes—" And the two women were off and running.

Fred met Enos's eyes and smiled. Enos smiled back, but Fred sensed immediately that a level of unease lay behind it. "What's wrong?"

Enos led him a few steps away. "I got a call from the county attorney's office this morning."

A chill streaked down Fred's spine. "What did they say?"

"The judge has set a date for the trial—May second. And they want to get some pretrial motions heard before that. They'll have to serve Doug with notice of everything, of course . . ."

The mental image of Douglas going to trial blocked out the sun, the sound of the women's voices, the chattering of chipmunks in trees overhead—everything.

"You've got to hire an attorney," Enos insisted. "Get somebody on board now before your deadlines lapse and you can't get a continuance."

Nausea welled up in Fred's throat. He couldn't speak.

"I'm serious, Fred."

"I know. Thanks."

Enos put a hand on Fred's shoulder and squeezed gently. "I wish I could help."

"You can find the killer."

"We're still looking into it as much as we can, but the county attorney is satisfied with the case he's got, and we're not getting backup on any further investigation. I've got limits on how far I can go officially."

"That's ridiculous."

"You know that, and so do I. But my hands are tied."

"Tell me something, then. Was that blond lady at the funeral Paula Franklin?"

"Why do you want to know?"

"For my diary. Why on earth do you think I want to know? Was that her?"

Enos hesitated for a second, then nodded once.

Fred patted his arm. "Thanks, son."

He'd taken several steps away before Enos called out. "You be careful, you hear?"

He looked back. "I hear."

Enos pushed his hat back and scratched the top of his head. "Why doesn't that make me feel better?"

"I can't imagine."

"You find out *anything*, you bring it straight to me. I don't want you playing hero this time."

Fred gestured a quick salute but didn't bother to answer. Being a hero was the furthest thing from his mind.

Fred rang the Franklins' doorbell three times before the fragile-looking blond woman from the funeral yanked open the door and stared up at him. "Oh! I thought you were my husband."

"Sorry, I didn't mean to disappoint you."

"I'm not disappointed." She flicked her eyes over him. "What can I do for you?"

"I'd like to ask you some questions about Garrett Locke." Paula scowled. "Why?"

"My son has been accused of murder and I'm trying to help clear him."

"You're Douglas Vickery's father?" She looked him up and down, no doubt making calculations about his age. "How do you expect to do that?"

"By finding Garrett's real killer."

She laughed shortly. "The sheriff seems to think he's found the killer already."

"He hasn't."

She hesitated, but kept herself firmly planted in the doorway. "What do you think I can tell you about Garrett?"

"You knew him well." It wasn't a question.

"Yes, I suppose."

"You were seeing him romantically?"

She didn't answer, but her eyes narrowed. "Why do you think that?"

"You looked pretty upset at the funeral."

"Funerals make me cry."

"You were the only one who did."

Her shoulders sagged and she looked down at her feet. "Garrett and I were friends."

"You were more than friends."

"Even if we were, it's none of your business."

He ignored her. "You were seeing each other right up until the day he was murdered, weren't you?"

This time she shook her head. "No."

"I understood you were."

She seemed to take his measure and to find something she liked in him. "If I tell you what I know, will you go away and leave me alone?"

"If I can."

"You have to promise."

"If you didn't kill Garrett, you don't have anything to be afraid of. I'm not going to tell your husband about the affair—"

She laughed bitterly. "Roger's already heard all the gossip. When he finds out I went to the funeral today—" She broke off quickly when fresh tears wet her eyes.

Fred didn't prod her, he just waited for her to regain control.

"I didn't kill him," she said at last. "I hadn't even seen him in weeks."

"Why did you stop seeing him?"

"He changed. Overnight."

"Changed how?" Fred asked.

"Lack of interest."

"Oh."

"It was your daughter-in-law. She came back and Garrett forgot about me completely—acted like I didn't even exist. We'd been meeting a couple times a week before that. Then all of a sudden, nothing." She wiped her tears away with the back of her hand. "He made excuses the first couple of times he stood me up, but after a while he stopped doing even that."

"And you believed they were having a . . . relationship?" He hesitated over the word and felt his face grow warm.

"Of course they were! Garrett was a very passionate man. If he was spending time with Suzanne, it was only for one reason."

Fred hated to admit it, but maybe Douglas was right. In *his* day, dinner between a man and a woman meant only that. But maybe now it symbolized something deeper. "Suzanne claims she wasn't in love with him."

"I never said she was in love with him. I know she wasn't, and that made it worse somehow, knowing she didn't even really want him." She twisted her wedding ring and looked away. "I *was* hurt. Of course I still had Roger, but there hasn't been anything between Roger and me for so long. We're more like an old habit than anything else."

"How long ago did your husband find out about your affair?" Fred asked.

Paula didn't respond.

He tried again. "How long did Roger know about you and Garrett?"

Paula blinked at him. "I don't know."

"You must have some idea."

"A while." She shook her head and looked vague. "A month before Suzanne came back, maybe less."

Well, that wasn't what he wanted to hear. The county attorney would argue there was too much water under the bridge for Roger to still be angry enough to commit murder. "And how long had you and Garrett been seeing each other?"

"Six months or so."

"How did Roger react when he found out?"

"He was furious. He told me flat out to stop seeing Garrett and, of course, I said I would."

"But you didn't."

"I intended to, I really did. But the night I decided to tell

Garrett, he got some bad news. I just couldn't tell him then, so I decided to wait. And then it just got harder and harder . . ." Tears pooled in her eyes and she tried unsuccessfully to blink them away.

Sympathy tugged at Fred's heart. "Maybe we ought to step inside."

But she recoiled, horrified. "Roger would blow up if he found you in here."

Fred gave her a second to pull herself together before he asked, "What was Garrett upset about?"

"Yvonne—his ex-wife. He'd called her because he wanted to see Jenny, but Yvonne refused to let Jenny come. He even offered to drive down to see her—stay in a hotel and everything—but Yvonne wouldn't even discuss it. I just *couldn't* tell him what Roger said that night. He needed me. He told me I was the only one who made him feel better, and I believed him. But he didn't have any trouble dumping me the minute Suzanne came back." This time she made no effort to stop her tears.

Again, Fred gave her a minute to compose herself before he asked, "Did he have much contact with Yvonne and Jenny?"

Paula shook her head. "Hardly any. Yvonne was so unreasonable about his visitation rights after the divorce that I think he gave up even trying for a while. But for the last little while, I think he wanted to make things right with Jenny."

"Where are they living now?"

"Just down in Idaho Springs. Not far."

"Yvonne didn't bring Jenny back for the funeral. Any idea why?"

"She hated him. She'd do anything to spite him—even now."

"Why?"

She gave the question a little thought. "He never really talked about what happened between them. Funny, isn't it? Most people can't wait to tell their divorce stories, but Garrett never talked about his."

Fred didn't hear the footsteps until they were too close to

react, and he knew Paula hadn't heard them either. A second later, Roger Franklin came through the trees and stopped dead in his tracks when he saw them standing at the door.

"What the hell's going on here? I thought I told you we didn't know that son of a bitch."

Anxiety flickered across Paula's face, but she replaced it immediately with a stoic expression. "It's all right, Roger. Mr. Vickery just stopped by to ask me a couple of questions."

"I already answered every question either one of us is going to. Now, get out of here."

Fred thought that might be a good idea—just as soon as he asked one more thing. "Where you were the night Garrett was killed?"

Paula's eyes widened and her face seemed to pale a little. "Here."

"All night?"

"Yes."

"Both of you?"

Roger's face darkened like a thundercloud. "That's none of your damn business."

Fred lifted his shoulders, hoping he looked casual, and started to turn away. "It doesn't really matter, I guess. You can answer when you get the subpoena from our attorney."

"You can't do that," Roger shouted.

"You go right on believing that, Mr. Franklin. I'll see you in the courtroom." He took several steps away.

"Hold on a second." Roger's voice dropped about an octave. "Look, I'm sorry. This whole thing has me really upset. The gossip and all." He draped an arm around Paula's shoulder and Fred saw the effort she used to not pull away. "I wasn't here that night—I'll admit it. I was at a meeting."

"Where?"

"In Cutler. Look"—he held out his free hand in an almost pleading gesture—"I know what people were saying about Paula and that dirt bag. I figured if they knew I was anywhere near by, they'd start to wonder."

"What kind of meeting?"

"Rocky Mountain Fly Fishers. We meet once a month at the Copper Penny."

"What time did the meeting get over?"

"Ten-thirty or so. But I usually stay a while and have a couple of drinks with some of the guys."

"How long?"

Roger shrugged and looked down at Paula. "Till the bar closes." He then looked at Fred. "Look, you want to subpoena me? Go right ahead. That's exactly what I'll tell your lawyer and anybody else who asks. And Paula was here asleep when I got home." He gave her shoulders a squeeze. "Don't get me wrong, I hated that jerk, but I didn't kill him. And I think your son deserves a medal for what he did."

twenty-one

Fred knew he could make it to Idaho Springs in a little over an hour if he didn't drive all the way back to Cutler. But he'd already been gone all day, and he felt a little guilty about leaving Douglas locked up at home with nothing to do. With Douglas's impulsive nature, he must be climbing out of his skin by now.

But he couldn't take Douglas with him. On the one hand, Yvonne might not open up with Douglas there. On the other hand, she might. And Fred didn't want Douglas to hear the type of sentiments about the murder and Douglas's part in it Fred had been exposed to the last couple of days.

Figuring a phone call might be a fair compromise, he stopped at the strip mall in the center of town and found a pay phone. But when Douglas hadn't picked up after eight rings, he started getting a little nervous. He tried to convince himself the boy was outside working in the yard. And the story worked long enough for him to get back to the car. But by the time he climbed inside and started the engine, he knew he didn't believe it.

He dug another quarter from his pocket, returned to the phone, and punched in Margaret's number. She answered almost immediately.

"Dad? Where are you? You disappeared so fast after the funeral I didn't even get a chance to invite you for supper."

"I'm running a couple of errands, sweetheart. I'll probably just eat something while I'm out."

"What kind of errands?"

"This and that. Little stuff." He purposely kept the answer vague. Margaret wouldn't like the truth.

"Just come here after you're through. We can wait a little for you."

He glanced at his watch. After two-thirty. If everything went according to plan, he could make it. If not . . . "Better not count on me," he said. "I'll just grab something—"

"—at the Bluebird. I know," said Margaret, interrupting him. "You're making up excuses."

Yes, but not for the reasons she suspected. "Have you talked to Douglas today?"

Margaret's voice dropped. "Yes. Earlier."

"I just called home, but I didn't get an answer."

"No, you wouldn't. He's gone to the Copper Penny with Webb."

In the years since Webb had started frequenting the Copper Penny, Fred had never found one good thing about it. Until now. Webb would keep Douglas busy all afternoon, and Fred could head to Idaho Springs with a clear conscience.

He made a noise of disgust—the one he knew Margaret would expect from him—but his heart wasn't in it. "Hope he doesn't do anything foolish."

"You and me both."

"Nothing I can do about it, I suppose."

"I suppose not."

Fred knew Margaret wouldn't risk upsetting Webb by going after Douglas. He couldn't have asked for a more perfect setup.

"We'll eat at seven. Try to get here." She tried to sound stern, but concern crept out around the edges of her voice.

"Don't wait for me."

"I don't want you eating at Lizzie's. I'll save you a plate."

He groused for a second or two, mentally patting himself on the back for the skillful way he'd handled the conversation without arousing Margaret's suspicions.

But just as he was ready to hang up, Margaret asked, "So, did you find her?"

"What? Who?"

"Paula Franklin. Did she tell you anything helpful?"

"What makes you think—"

"Enos called."

He should have expected it.

"Did she tell you anything?"

"Not really. Nothing I didn't already know." He hesitated. Could she handle the truth? "I'm just going to run down to Idaho Springs and talk to Yvonne before I come back home."

Silence hung between them for a minute before she said, "Be careful, okay?"

"I will."

"Because I love you."

"I love you, too."

"I asked Enos to stop you, you know."

"I figured you might."

"He says he can't keep you from helping Douglas."

"That's right."

"I worry about you and I want you home in one piece. You're too bullheaded to listen to reason, but if you let anything happen to yourself, I'll never forgive you."

Before he could utter a sound, she broke the connection. He replaced the receiver slowly and shook his head all the way back to his car. Imagine *Margaret* calling *him* bullheaded.

Come to think of it, Phoebe had used that expression for him a few times.

Once inside his car, he put it into gear and pulled out onto the highway, smiling to himself. He really didn't mind being called bullheaded. It sure beat being called old.

Yvonne and Jenny Locke lived in an old Victorian-style house backed up against the mountain on a piece of property too steep to call a yard. A narrow set of steps climbed from the road to the house, and Fred's breath came in shallow intakes and his knees ached by the time he had climbed to the top.

Only the sound of a radio playing inside made him feel better, because at least he knew someone was home.

He knocked, and someone lowered the radio's volume. A

second later the door opened. He remembered Yvonne
Locke as a thin, mousy woman with vapid blue eyes and
nondescript hair. He recognized her face, but the resemblance ended there. He didn't recall her being so tall. Or so
thin. Or so self-assured.

Her eyes, no longer dull, burned with life. Her hair had
been cropped in a style so short that only an extremely
confident woman would wear it. She wore a red suit with a
skirt that stopped several inches above her knees, and high
heels. She'd probably just come from work. Even so, Fred
thought she was a little overdressed, but attractive.

He must have looked surprised because she laughed, a
very pleasant sort of laugh, and her eyes danced with
merriment. "Fred Vickery? Is that you?"

"Yvonne Locke? Is that you?"

She laughed again. "Come in. What brings you here?"
She stopped suddenly as realization dawned. "It's about
Garrett."

"Yes."

"Come in." But this time her voice held no hint of her
earlier delight. "Can I get you something to drink?"

"Nothing, thanks."

She led him through the entryway into a sensible-looking
living room and settled into a wingback chair near the
fireplace. Fred chose its mate and leaned back into the
chair's thankfully firm form. It was good, solid furniture.
He liked this.

Yvonne let him get comfortable before she asked, "So,
what can I do for you?"

"I suppose you've heard that Douglas was arrested for the
murder?"

She nodded. "Yes. I can't believe it."

"He's innocent."

"I have a hard time imagining him guilty," she admitted.

"I want you to tell me anything you can about Garrett that
might help my son."

She chuckled, but her laughter held no amusement this time.
"I'm not the best person to ask for a character reference."

"I don't want a character reference. I want the truth about
him."

She studied him for a long moment, then rubbed her forehead with long fingers and looked out the window through its lace curtain. "What do you want to know?"

"You didn't bring Jenny back for the funeral. A lot of people are speculating about why."

"Are they? And what do they say?"

"I haven't heard any answers yet—just the questions."

"Jenny didn't want to go, it's that simple."

"Why?"

"She didn't like her father."

"Why?"

Yvonne stopped rubbing her forehead and met his gaze. "Because he was a despicable man."

"Tell me about your divorce."

"What does all this have to do with his murder?"

"I don't know," he admitted. "Maybe nothing. Maybe everything."

She crossed her legs and rested both of her arms on those of the chair, as if seeking its support. "What's the rumor going around Cutler about that?"

"There isn't one. At least not that I've heard. Listen, Yvonne, I know it's probably all very personal and hard to talk about, but my son's life is on the line here . . ."

"It's not that hard to talk about. I stopped playing victim several years ago." She gave him a thin-lipped smile. "What do you want to know?"

"Why did you get divorced?" he asked again.

"Because I had to get my daughter out of there."

"You denied visitation—"

"I had to, for Jenny's sake."

Fred shifted in his seat, not liking the similarities between Suzanne's protests and Yvonne's, and growing impatient with her game of twenty questions. "You heard that Douglas and Suzanne got divorced? And their daughter—"

Yvonne's expression tightened. "Is she all right?"

"Who? Alison?"

"Their daughter. Is she all right? I've thought about her a lot since Suzanne called."

"When did Suzanne call you?"

Yvonne shrugged and tried to look casual, but her upper foot jiggled rapidly in agitation. "A few days ago."

"I didn't know you and Suzanne kept in touch."

She stopped jiggling the foot and crossed her legs the opposite way, but the left foot started jiggling almost immediately. "We didn't."

He waited for her to explain, but she just smiled and said nothing. Fred had the definite impression they were dancing circles around each other, and he didn't like it. "What is it you're not telling me?"

She smiled a little wider. "Am I that obvious?"

"Or I'm extrasensitive."

Her smile faded and her face grew serious. "Suzanne obviously hasn't told you."

"Told me what?"

"She called me a few days before Garrett died and asked me the same sorts of questions you're asking now."

"Why?"

"Because she was worried about Alison."

His patience strained against the pace she set, and he leaned forward, eager for the answers. "You're working awfully hard at not telling me something. Why don't you just spit it out?"

She stood and crossed to the window, pulling back the lace curtain and staring outside for several long seconds. "I divorced Garrett when I found out that he'd been molesting Jenny."

Fred's heart fell to the ground somewhere near his feet and Alison's sweet, sad face floated in front of his eyes. He blinked back tears and worked to control his nausea. "Alison?" he croaked.

"Suzanne suspected it. Alison had been acting strangely for several weeks, and then I guess Suzanne's aunt came home early one day and found Garrett alone in the house with Alison." Yvonne turned back to him and her eyes blazed with anger. "I told Suzanne everything, of course. I have no reason to hide it. If I had my way, it would have been tattooed on his forehead so there'd never be any question about what kind of man he was."

"Who else knew?"

"Garrett convinced me to keep it quiet—and for Jenny's sake, I agreed. I saw later what a mistake I made. Other than his family, I'm not sure anyone else ever heard anything about it."

"But his family knew?"

"Yes."

"And Suzanne found out before he was murdered?"

Yvonne nodded. "I urged her to take Alison in for counseling. To make absolutely sure. If it happened, Alison needs help dealing with it."

He knew that. He'd sensed Alison's desperate need for help, but he'd blamed it all on the divorce. "How long before Garrett's murder did Suzanne call you?"

She thought about this briefly. "Not more than a day or two."

"Did she tell Douglas?" Fred didn't realize he'd spoken aloud until she answered.

"I don't know what she planned to do. She reacted like we all do—we want to hide it, sweep it under the rug, pretend it never happened. It's an ugly, horrible thing to admit, but that kind of thinking is so destructive."

Suzanne knew. The words echoed in his head, bounced off the walls, and hit him over and over again. Suzanne knew.

"Are you all right, Fred?"

He met Yvonne's clear blue eyes and nodded.

"Are you sure? Can I get you something?"

With some effort he pulled himself together and nodded again. "How is Jenny doing now?"

"She was doing a lot better. Garrett's murder has set her back a little, as you can imagine. But that's what it's like. Good days and bad days. We try not to let the setbacks get us down."

"Someone told me Garrett had been trying to see Jenny again just before he died . . ."

To his surprise, Yvonne laughed. "It must have been a woman. He got a lot of mileage from the women in his life that way. Poor misunderstood Garrett and mean old Yvonne." She laughed again. "If he'd ever asked, I would have refused."

"And he never asked?"

"He was sick, not stupid. He'd never take a chance on me going public."

Fred pushed himself to his feet and crossed the room to her. "Who do you think killed him?"

She shook her head vaguely. "I don't know. There are so many possibilities. Garrett made enemies like some people make promises. He couldn't even maintain a good relationship with his family."

"What about Olivia?"

"They hadn't spoken to each other in over a year when we got divorced. She got into a tight spot once when her husband gambled heavily in Central City. Garrett made a big deal about bailing her out, but he really took her to the cleaners. He bought her out, but at about fifty cents on the dollar. She was pathetically grateful at first, but after she figured out what he'd done, she got angry."

"Was there anyone else who hated him?"

"Other than the women he dated, the parents of young girls, and his family?" A ghost of a smile flashed up at him. "No. Other than that, he was a swell guy."

Fred patted her arm. "Thanks for talking to me."

"It's all right." She struggled to put on a confident expression. "It just stirs up some bad memories."

She walked with him to the front door, but when he touched the doorknob, she covered his hand with hers. "You make sure Doug and Suzanne get that little girl some counseling. And Fred—talk to Alison about it, even when you don't think you can stand to hear what she has to say. Don't make her hold it inside." Her eyes brimmed with tears, and Fred could feel his own eyes stinging.

He nodded, but he couldn't trust his voice to speak. He felt her watching him as he worked his way back down the steep stairs. But when he looked back at the house, the lace curtains hid her from view. Still, he waved to her, certain she was watching, before he reached his car and slid behind the wheel of the Buick.

twenty-two

Fred had to get home. A million and one questions plucked at him, demanding answers. Why did Suzanne have dinner with Garrett that night if she knew what he'd done? He couldn't imagine Suzanne willingly dating the guy if she even suspected him of molesting her daughter. So why was she at the Four Seasons with him?

Driving as quickly as he dared, he followed the narrow road through the twisting canyon, but the thought taunted him. Suzanne knew, but she never told him. Had she told Douglas? Or did she think she could hide the truth away like some shameful secret?

Fred brought the car around a curve and found himself driving directly into the sun. He let off the accelerator a little, but the need to get back home outweighed his usual caution, and the minute he drove out of the sun's glare, he speeded up again.

Douglas couldn't have known. He would have said something. But Suzanne knew.

Tears flooded Fred's eyes when he thought of Alison. He pictured her laughing and running and talking too fast and dancing around, and he let the tears pour down his face. But when he remembered the changes in her, his tears stopped forming. His hands gripped tighter the steering wheel, and his grief burned out and rage ignited from the ashes.

Suzanne knew, and she'd gone out with Garrett anyway. Why? There could be only one reason. She'd protected her daughter the only way she knew how—by killing Garrett. But afterward, anxious to protect herself, she'd been willing—

eager—to let Douglas go to prison for her. And Douglas had no idea why.

Fred waited in the green rocking chair by his front window for Douglas to come home. Too agitated to rock, too nervous to sleep, too angry to even pretend to read a book, he stared at his reflection in the glass and thought of Phoebe and what a thing like this would have done to her. He thought of Alison, and of the countless innocent children abused by sick adults.

Here in his house, memories of his own children danced around him. He remembered their blind faith in him, and he raged silently because he knew how horrible the betrayal of that trust would have been. It had happened to Alison, and now Fred had to break the news to Douglas.

When Douglas's footsteps sounded on the front walk, Fred pushed himself up and crossed to the door. He opened it before Douglas even reached the porch.

Douglas had been drinking, but he wasn't drunk. He blinked his surprise and smiled as he passed Fred and came into the house. "I haven't had anybody wait up for me since I was a kid."

"I need to talk to you." Even to Fred's ears his voice sounded angry.

Douglas's smile disappeared. "What's up?"

"I went down to Idaho Springs this afternoon, to visit Yvonne Locke."

"What? Why?"

"Because I'm trying to help you."

"How? By visiting Yvonne?"

"Why I went there isn't important, Douglas. What I learned there is—"

"Does Enos have any idea what you've been up to?" Douglas demanded.

Fred snapped his mouth shut in confusion. He hadn't expected this reaction. "Do you want to hear what I found out?"

Douglas flushed an angry shade of red and turned away from him.

"You know, don't you?" The words fell like an accusation between them.

Douglas's shoulders slumped.

"You know about Alison?"

Douglas nodded.

"Why in blazes didn't you tell me?"

"We didn't want to upset you—"

"Upset me? What do you think this has done? How would telling me the truth upset me?"

"Suzanne and I thought it would be best."

"You were wrong." Fred turned away and struggled to pull himself together. "Why didn't you tell Enos?"

"We can't tell Enos. Can you imagine what it would do to Alison to have this whole thing come out? To have people like Janice Lacey talking about her, or her friends whispering about her at school? She's in second grade, Dad—"

Fred whipped back around. "What do you think hiding the truth is going to do for her?"

"You don't understand how these things are—"

"You're acting like this is some shameful secret of Alison's. She's the victim, Douglas. She has nothing to be ashamed of. Don't make her think she has."

Douglas didn't respond.

Fred didn't want to ask the next question, but he had to. The bottom had fallen out of his world and he needed to find solid ground again.

"Is it true, then? Did he really hurt her?"

Douglas nodded, but he didn't speak.

"Did you kill him?"

When Douglas looked up agony filled his eyes, but he shook his head. "No."

"Tell me what happened that night. And tell me everything. I want the truth this time."

"I went to see Suzanne after I left here. I didn't know about Alison then, I was just crazy jealous. I wanted her back so bad I thought I'd die. We argued, and that's when she told me about Garrett. She wasn't positive then. She suspected him of molesting Alison. She said she agreed to have dinner with him so she could find out for sure."

"Did you believe that?"

Douglas nodded. "At the time. I was so mad I couldn't see straight. I was on my way to Garrett's house when I saw the light on at the store. I confronted him and we fought. He came at me with that table leg and I grabbed it—I guess that's why my fingerprints are all over it." Douglas shuddered and met Fred's eyes. "I wanted to kill him, Dad. I *wanted* to kill him. But I didn't. Leaving him alive when I left that place was the hardest thing I've ever done in my life."

Fred closed his eyes and silently thanked God. "What did you do then?"

"Then I ran out. That's when Albán saw me, I guess. I went back to Suzanne's house, but she wasn't there. Celeste was outside looking for her—she'd heard us arguing and she'd seen Suzanne run off after me. Celeste was frantic. I told her I'd try to find Suzanne. I tried, but I never did. The next morning, Doc came over to tell us about Garrett."

"And you realized Suzanne did it."

Douglas nodded.

"You were willing to go to prison to protect her?"

Another nod. "I love her."

"I loved your mother, but I'm not sure I would have gone to prison for her if I thought she'd murdered someone."

Douglas smiled bitterly. "Mother wouldn't have let you. Suzanne's not only willing to let me go, she's been trying to get me there since the first day."

"Well, thank the good Lord you've finally realized that."

"Yeah, well, I didn't come to it on my own. Webb's the one who finally talked sense into me."

Two things Fred had to be grateful to Webb for in one day? He didn't know if he could stand it. "You realize we're going to have to tell Enos what we know . . ."

Douglas nodded. "This is going to kill Alison."

"Alison's a survivor. She'll be all right—if you'll stop treating her like she's going to break."

Douglas nodded, but his eyes held a terrible sadness. "I'll go with you tomorrow."

*   *   *

Just after two o'clock the next afternoon, Fred pushed open the door to the sheriff's office, relieved to find it unlocked. Enos spent every Thursday morning cruising the highway between Cutler and Grand Lake, so they hadn't been able to come any earlier than this. He often went home for lunch and stayed there to read while Jessica watched her favorite game show. He believed it helped their marriage, and since everyone in town knew where he lived, he didn't feel any special urgency to hurry back. By two-thirty he'd be having coffee at the Bluebird, but Fred wanted to talk to him now—alone, not in front of half the town.

Enos looked up when the door opened and pushed away a package of Twinkies he'd been studying.

"Have you got a minute?" Fred asked. "It's important."

"Sure. Any time." But he checked his watch as if he had somewhere important to go. "What's up?"

"We know who killed Garrett."

"You what?"

"I said, we know who killed Garrett."

Tilting back in his chair, Enos eyed Fred as if he'd grown something foreign where his head used to be. "Who?"

"Suzanne."

Enos froze for half a second, then turned to Douglas. "Is he serious?"

"I'm afraid so."

"Maybe you'd better fill me in."

With his face pale, his eyes dark-rimmed, and his hair standing up from his forehead like he'd just pushed his fingers through it, Douglas spoke softly, hesitant to share his story. "Garrett was molesting Alison. Suzanne knew about it—she's the one who told me. Apparently, he molested his own daughter. That's why he and Yvonne divorced."

Enos's face lost its color. "Are you sure?"

Douglas nodded and tears filled his eyes. "That's what we fought about when I found Garrett at the store that night. He came after me with that table leg, and I wrestled it away from him. But I swear I didn't kill him." He blinked his eyes clear and looked down at his hands. "I went back to Suzanne's afterward, but she wasn't there."

Enos rubbed one trembling hand across his chin. "Good billy hell," he whispered. "Why didn't you tell me earlier?"

Suddenly too weary to stand any longer, Fred lowered himself into one of the battered chairs in front of Enos's desk. "They didn't want any talk."

"Talk? That piece of scum was molesting girls and you wanted to avoid talk?"

"For Alison's sake," Douglas insisted. "We just wanted to keep it quiet—"

But Enos didn't look convinced. "This happened to Alison because they kept it quiet after it happened to Jenny."

"I never thought—" Douglas began.

"And chances are, Alison's not the only girl he got to. Did you think of that? Who knows how many other girls he's hurt?"

Other girls? An unwelcome prickle of anxiety ran up Fred's spine.

"Hell," Enos shouted, "we might not know for another twenty years how much damage he's done." He leaned over his desk dragging in deep breaths of air and struggling for control.

But Fred could only think of other parents.

"Where's Suzanne now?"

Douglas had been about to speak, but he snapped his mouth shut; then he ventured, "I don't know. Home?"

Maybe Fred should bring up the thought that had just occurred to him.

Enos grabbed the phone and punched in a number. "Grady? You got any idea what time it is? You planning to come back from lunch or stay home?"

On second thought, maybe Fred should wait until he had some kind of proof to back up this new idea. No sense upsetting Enos for nothing . . .

Enos's face colored and he gave the telephone receiver a disgusted look. "You do that," he snapped. "And while you're at it, I want you to find Suzanne Vickery and bring

her in . . . Now . . . No, for questioning. Criminy—"
He shook his head and rolled his eyes. "Are you going to
keep yapping at me, or are you going to do what I asked?"
He slammed down the receiver and glared at it for emphasis.

All at once, Enos's anger seemed to cave in on itself and
he looked up at Fred, his eyes bright with unshed tears.
"How's Alison doing?"

"Too quiet. Withdrawn. Afraid of her own shadow." Fred
hesitated, then added, "Ashamed."

"You going to get her some help?"

Douglas nodded eagerly. "Whatever it takes. We should
have come to you, Enos. We just didn't know . . ."

"You didn't know." Enos repeated softly. "Hell, I don't
know what I'd do if it were my daughter, either, Doug. I just
like to pretend I do. Get Alison professional help. I'll get
some names for you."

Douglas dropped into the seat beside Fred's. "I just want
what's best for her."

"We all do," Enos agreed.

"Then let's stop treating it like some sort of guilty secret,"
Fred insisted. "Alison has nothing to hide. Professional help
might be all right, but the way we react is even more
important to her."

Douglas put a hand on Fred's arm. "I agree with you,
Dad, but I don't see how telling the whole world the truth
will help her."

"If Garrett hurt anyone else around here, maybe the girls
could help each other. Admitting what happened to Alison
might encourage other girls to tell their parents, or their
parents to tell the truth." And maybe they'd find someone
else who had reason to want Garrett Locke dead. But Fred
didn't voice that thought. Instead, he asked, "What do we do
next?"

"*We* don't do anything," Enos said. "I'm going to have a
talk with Suzanne and I'll look into your allegations. But
from here on out, it's part of an official investigation. Here's
where you don't cross the line."

Fred nodded. He'd done what he could, he'd have to trust

Enos to take it the rest of the way. "I guess you'll be wanting us gone when Suzanne gets here."

Enos dropped heavily into his chair and formed a tepee with his fingers. "Actually, I'd like you to stay for a few minutes. I'd like to talk with Doug and Suzanne together. But when I tell you to go, I don't want any argument."

"Of course not." Fred tried not to resent Enos's suggestion that he made a habit of arguing.

Enos narrowed his eyes but nodded his acceptance, and silence fell between them. He tapped his fingers against his lips to a beat only he could hear and made occasional sounds with his tongue against his teeth.

Douglas managed to sit still for about three minutes before he jumped up and started pacing. He looked as if he'd aged ten years in the past week.

Fred watched them both and told himself he'd done the right thing. But he had to struggle to quiet the constant repetition of Enos's words in the back of his mind. *Other girls.*

twenty-three

Several minutes dragged by before Enos stopped tapping his finger tepee against his lips long enough to ask, "What did you do with the table leg after you got it away from Garrett?"

Douglas stopped in mid-stride. "I must have dropped it on the floor on my way out. To tell you the truth, I don't remember. I remember thinking Garrett could grab up another one and come after me again, so I held on to it for a while."

"Why didn't you just leave? Or call me?"

"I was too angry. I just kept picturing his filthy hands on Alison, and the only thing that made me feel better at all was smashing my fist into his face."

Fred digested Douglas's words slowly. "Then why did you stop?"

"What?"

"You were that angry. You were fighting the man. You had a weapon in your hand. What made you stop?"

Douglas shook his head as if to clear it. "I didn't want to kill him. I mean—" He broke off, looking confused.

"Maybe you heard something that made you stop. You were violently angry and you had Garrett down—or at least backing up. So what made you leave? Did you hear somebody else coming?"

Douglas considered that, his eyes trained on the ceiling as if he'd find the answer there. But after several seconds, he shook his head. "I don't know. Maybe. No. I don't know."

"Think back, son—"

"I am, but I can't remember. I wish I could."

Enos rose and put a hand on Douglas's shoulder. "I'm going to look into it. I'd give anything to prove you're innocent, but I don't want to find out Suzanne's guilty, either."

"None of us do," Fred agreed.

Enos checked his watch again and frowned. "You haven't told Suzanne what you suspect, have you?"

Fred shook his head. "We came straight to you."

"Then what's keeping them?" Enos crossed to the window and peered out.

"I guess this'll shoot any chance I had of reconciling with her down the tubes," Douglas said with a feeble attempt at humor.

Enos looked back at Douglas over his shoulder. "Don't try to hang on, Doug. She doesn't care about you anymore, and once a woman stops caring, it's time to give up." He stared out the window again.

Fred kept his mouth shut. He couldn't have said it better himself, but he couldn't help wondering whether Enos was thinking of Margaret or Jessica.

They stayed like that for several minutes until Enos turned back suddenly. "They're here."

Douglas's color rose and he looked toward the door.

Suddenly nervous, Fred couldn't sit any longer. He stood and took his place beside Douglas as the door opened.

Suzanne saw Fred and Douglas immediately, and with narrowed eyes she turned to Enos. "What's going on here?"

"Doug and Fred have told me something I want to check out with you." Suddenly all business, Enos turned away from the window and went back to his desk. He dropped into his chair and gestured to the one Fred had just vacated. "Why don't you have a seat? This should only take a few minutes."

She didn't move. "What did they tell you?"

"It concerns Alison."

Her face blanched. With wide, frantic eyes she turned to Douglas. "What did you tell him?"

"The truth," Douglas said.

Enos gestured again to the chair. "Sit down, Suzanne."

This time she took his advice and lowered herself into the chair.

"Is it true that Garrett molested Alison?"

Instead of answering, she glared at Fred. "I suppose this is your doing. You just can't leave well enough alone, can you?"

"Having Douglas go to trial for murder just doesn't sit well with me."

"Is it true, Suzanne?" Enos pressed.

She waited for several seconds, as if she hoped Enos would forget his question. But when he cleared his throat to speak again, she nodded and said, "I didn't want anyone to know."

"We can't keep it secret, Suzanne. Alison—" Douglas protested.

She bolted from the chair. "You promised me, Doug. If I'd had any idea what you were going to do, I never would have told you about it."

"How long have you known?" Enos asked, ignoring the interruption.

"I found out a few days before Garrett died."

"Did you confront Garrett with it?"

She shook her head and looked away. "I tried to deny it at first. I didn't want to believe it. But after a couple of days, I realized something was terribly wrong with Alison, and I decided to call Yvonne. When she told me about Jenny, I knew it was true."

Fred had intended to keep quiet, but he had to ask, "What happened to make you call Yvonne in the first place?"

"Alison didn't like Garrett. She didn't want him around and she avoided him whenever he came over. I thought she was having trouble adjusting to the divorce, that she hated seeing me with somebody besides Doug—that sort of thing. Anyway, one day Alison was home from school with the flu. I ran out for a few minutes, and Celeste ran up to Lacey's for something. She thought it would be all right to leave Alison alone, but when she got home, she found Garrett there. Alison started acting strangely soon after that—quiet, withdrawn, almost as if she was afraid of something. Celeste told me something was wrong. In fact, she suspected Garrett had upset Alison in some way, but I just kept insisting what a nice man he was and how sweet he'd been to check on her . . ." She broke off with a sob.

Fred fought the urge to put his arm around her shoulders for about a minute, then gave in to impulse. She stiffened when he touched her, but she eventually relaxed and leaned against him.

"I didn't want to believe it. I didn't want to think I could have been so stupid. I'd seen it before when it happened to my cousin, and I should have known. But I didn't want to believe it."

"Did you kill him, Suzanne?" Enos asked softly.

"No."

"Did you tell him what you knew?"

She shook her head. "I was going to ask him about it that night—that's why I went to dinner with him. But things got out of hand and I never got the chance."

"Don't blame me for that," Douglas protested. "I didn't stop you from confronting him."

"He was too upset when we left the Four Seasons. I couldn't confront him then. I decided to wait a day or two—"

"You believed the man had sexually molested Alison and you were worried about his feelings?" Fred didn't understand that reasoning at all.

Suzanne met his gaze with wide brown eyes. "I didn't want to believe it. I didn't want to hear him admit it. He just didn't seem the type . . ." Her words trailed away and she looked at each of them as if pleading for them to understand.

But Fred couldn't oblige her. He didn't understand at all.

Douglas didn't look inclined to accommodate her, either. "You haven't had the same kind of trouble believing I'm guilty of murder."

"I know how angry you were when I told you. And telling you was what made me realize the truth—hearing myself say it aloud, I guess. But you'd already gone after him. I waited a little while, and when you didn't come back, I went out to find you. I didn't want you to do something you'd regret. But the store was dark and nobody answered at Garrett's house, so I went back home. I guess you and Celeste were still out looking for me." She shuddered at the memory. "When I heard the next day that Garrett had been murdered, what else could I think?"

Douglas's face didn't soften. "Yeah. What else?" He turned away from her. "Do you need anything more from me right now, Enos? I'd like to get out of here."

Enos shook his head and nodded to Grady, who opened the door. With his head high, Douglas stepped outside into the sunshine, and Fred followed. They walked down the boardwalk, stepped off onto the pavement, and started across Main Street in silence. But Fred couldn't resist putting his arm around Douglas's shoulders as they walked away.

Douglas had finally put Suzanne behind him, and they'd raised significant doubt in Enos's mind about Douglas's guilt to prod further investigation into the murder. And he'd eventually clear Douglas. Fred should feel satisfied. But he couldn't push the thought of other girls—and other parents—from his mind.

From two blocks away, Janice Lacey stopped in the act of propping up the in-store special sign and waved energetically. Grateful they weren't any closer, Fred waved back. He'd have hated to get caught up in one of her gossip fests.

He almost rounded the corner onto Lake Front Drive when a particular thought pulled him up short. Janice Lacey. If anybody would know whether there were troubled children in Cutler, she would.

He patted Douglas's shoulder and pulled his arm away. "You go on home, son. I'll be there in a minute."

"I don't need to go home right now. I can come with you."

Fred shrugged casually. "Fine. I'm just running down to Lacey's for a few things.

Douglas stopped. "Lacey's?"

"I just want to pick up a few things."

Douglas shook his head and backed away a couple of steps.

"We'll be quick," Fred urged.

"I don't want to go there. That woman's the most god-awful gossip . . ."

Fred tried to look disappointed. "Are you sure? Look, we'll just ignore her—"

Douglas had already turned away, but he waved his hands over his head as if to ward off demon spirits. "No way. You go ahead. I'll see you at home."

Fred watched until Douglas had moved off several feet before he allowed himself to smile. Tucking his hands into his pockets and whistling his father's favorite tune, he set off in his own direction.

He could almost see Janice Lacey's nose twitching with excitement as he drew closer. Her gray curls bobbed in the sunlight as she struggled with the sign over a crack in the boardwalk.

If she had looked at her task instead of him, she'd have put it right in an instant. As it was, Fred had to help her position the sign's legs on two solid boards to keep it from tipping sideways.

"Gracious," Janice sputtered. "I don't know why I was having such a time with that sign today."

Fred bit his tongue to keep from pointing out the obvious. If he wanted Janice's informed opinion on disturbed young girls, he couldn't start off by antagonizing her. "I'm just glad I could help."

"Were you coming here? Didn't I see Douglas with you? I haven't seen much of him since he came back to town." She frowned for an instant, then replaced it with a sympathetic smile. "Of course, I know just how he must feel. Why, yesterday morning, Emma Brumbaugh brought up the murder again—you know what a busybody she can be. She had everybody in the store talking about it. And as long as people are going to talk about it, Douglas isn't going to want to show his face." She shook her head and pushed open the store's wide glass door.

Fred stepped inside and breathed the familiar cinnamon-spice scent Janice always used. He gave the place a quick once-over. Empty. Good. "It's been real hard on him," he admitted.

Janice's eyes lit up. "I can just imagine. That poor boy. Bill thinks—and Bill knew Garrett as well as anybody, I'd imagine, since they worked right here in town almost alongside of each other—anyway, Bill thinks it's tied up with the money somehow."

"Does he? Why?" Fred didn't need to pretend an interest in that.

"Have you seen Olivia lately? No? Well, she's turned herself into a new woman. Fancy new car, new clothes, had her hair cut. And"—Janice looked around and lowered her voice—"she told Bill that she's changing the name of the store . . ."

"Really?"

". . . to 'Olivia's.' Now why do you suppose she's doing that? Locke's isn't good enough for her, I suppose."

Fred glanced out the window to the storefront of Locke's across the street. "She inherited the store?"

"Lock, stock, and barrel." Janice bobbed her head up and down vigorously. "Garrett didn't leave one thing to that poor little girl of his. Not one thing. Tragic, that's what I call it. Parents get upset with each other and split up, and what happens to the kids?" She broke off and put her hand over her mouth. "I didn't mean anything personal by that."

Fred had no doubt just how close to home she'd intended the remark to hit. He dragged his eyes back from the front of Locke's and forced himself to smile while he guided the conversation closer to where he wanted it. "Kids seem to take the brunt of most everything these days. Seems like every time I pick up the newspaper some child or teenager's been hurt in some way—"

"Isn't that the truth?" Janice tied an apron around her ample middle and worked her way behind the cluttered front counter.

Fred picked up an issue of *Field and Stream* and thumbed idly through it. "And it's not just in the cities. Cutler isn't as quiet and safe as it used to be."

"Now that's for sure. It's getting so a body hardly feels safe in their own home anymore."

"There are a lot of angry people out there, and a lot of hurt kids."

"Yes, there are. I hate to say this, Fred, but just look at your own example—that poor child of Doug's."

He had to force himself not to snap at her. "The divorce has been hard on Alison. But I'd imagine there are other kids in Cutler who've been through rough times."

Janice nodded sadly, then snagged up a rag and flicked dust off the paperback display on the countertop. "There surely are."

"It must be heartbreaking to see some of the things they go through." Fred struggled not to sound more than mildly interested.

"Heartbreaking," Janice agreed. "And we're in a position to see so much of what goes on."

Fred held his breath, waiting for her to expound a little, but she just sighed heavily and worked her dust rag over the magazine rack.

She'd picked a devil of a time to start keeping her mouth shut. He closed the magazine he'd been looking at and replaced it. "Does it seem to you that girls have more trouble than boys?"

Janice looked thoughtful. "Nooo . . . not necessarily."

"It seems like my granddaughters have a more difficult time adjusting to things than the boys do—"

"That's an awfully sexist thing to say, Fred. Honestly—" Janice looked outraged.

"Maybe it's the hormones," he suggested, struggling not to smile at the look on her face.

"I can't believe I'm hearing this from you. Hormones, indeed." Janice turned away from him. "No matter what you men like to believe, you have hormones, too. And they're what cause you most of your trouble."

Fred picked up an issue of *Outdoor Life*. "Well, it just seems to me that young girls have trouble, that's all."

Janice looked back over her shoulder. "What's gotten into you, Fred? Just listen to you—" She broke off and snapped her mouth shut when the front door opened, but the look she sent him spoke volumes.

Fred looked up at Bill Lacey and nodded a greeting.

"Afternoon, Fred." Bill pulled off his cap and jacket and slipped into the white smock he always wore at work.

"Fred was just talking about the murder." Janice certainly had a talent for bringing newcomers up to speed. "Bill was practically there when it happened, weren't you, Bill?"

Bill concentrated on the buttons on his smock. "I was at the Copper Penny, Janice. That's a little different."

"If he'd stepped outside half an hour sooner, he would have seen the murderer. Or he might have been killed."

Bill looked up at Fred with an expression of well-worn patience mixed with exasperation. "I left about 12:30."

"You were in the Copper Penny the night of the murder?"

Janice nodded. "He could have been killed. Like I said, half an hour sooner—"

Fred tried to tune out the sound of her voice. "Why were you there?" He'd never known Bill to be a drinker, though heaven only knew he had enough provocation.

"My fishing club meets there once a month."

Janice snorted. "Fishing club! An excuse to imbibe, that's what I say. Nothing but an excuse . . ."

"The same one Roger Franklin belongs to?"

Bill adjusted his pocket protector. "Roger? Yes, he's in the group."

Well, imagine that. At least one alibi checked out.

". . . or he used to be, anyway." Bill looked up innocently. "But I haven't seen him for the past few months."

"Are you sure?"

Bill nodded and pushed his glasses up on his nose. "Positive. I've been wanting to ask him about the fly he used to get that six-pound rainbow trout last summer."

Fred had another question all ready to ask, but the front door opened again and Bill turned away, his expression suddenly the one he used for business. "Well, hello, Eileen. Children."

Fred inserted his magazine back into the rack and looked up at Eileen Kinsella. Short and round, with dark plain hair and a plain face, she always moved slowly, even more so when she was pregnant. She had half the brood with her today—the darkhaired boy and two redheaded girls.

While the boy and the older girl scampered around Eileen, reaching for things on the shelves, popping in front of her and back out of her way, the younger girl—the one about Alison's age—walked sedately, eyes down, at her mother's side.

Fred coughed, then gave his best grin when Eileen smiled at him in that ineffectual way she had. "Hello, Eileen."

"Hello."

"How are you? And how's the family?"

She hesitated as if she had to give it some thought. "Fine." She looked back at the bread.

She'd never been on Fred's list of people he'd most like to have a conversation with, and her lifeless responses this afternoon reminded him why. He didn't have the energy it took to pry words out of her.

He reached for the handle to the front door when Janice stopped him. "Weren't you going to buy something?"

"Not today."

"Then what did you come in here for?"

"To browse." He pushed open the door and looked back at the Kinsellas. Something about that quiet girl bothered him. Had she always been a replica of her mother? Or was her quiet the unnatural kind Alison suffered with? He watched her a second or two longer, but when he realized Janice, in turn, watched him, he let the door go.

Just before it closed he heard Janice say, "Men. And they try to claim women are gossips. You'd never imagine in a million years what he was just talking about—"

twenty-four

Old boards creaked underfoot as Fred walked away from Lacey's. Since Cutler's Main Street stretched only eight blocks from one end of town to the other, Fred often walked its length to stretch his legs or clear his mind. And today, he needed to do both.

He'd been so certain of Suzanne's guilt last night, but now everything jumbled together in his mind—Olivia's inheritance, Roger Franklin's broken alibi, Garrett's perversion . . . which trail was the right one? Or did the answer lie along some other path he hadn't even discovered yet?

When he reached the corner of Porter Street and had to step down to the road, he glanced down the block at Locke's Fine Furnishings—or maybe he should call it Olivia's now. Maybe he ought to talk with Rusty Kinsella again. Asking the questions that echoed through his mind would be a sight more productive than trying to walk them off.

He started across the street, but before he took half a dozen steps, Celeste stepped out of the trees on the side of the road. "Pssssst."

"Celeste? What in blazes—"

"Shhhh." She beckoned him urgently and her jewelry jingled furiously. "Come here. Please."

Good grief. He slipped closer to her hiding spot, taking care to keep several feet between them.

"I just came from the sheriff's office. Did you know they have Suzanne there?"

"Yes, I know."

"And do you know they're *questioning* her about Garrett's murder?"

"Yes." He carefully avoided revealing that he'd been the one to point the finger at her. The less said about that, the better.

"*How* are we going to get Douglas and Suzanne back together *now*?" She pressed the back of her hand to her forehead dramatically, exuding a fresh wave of perfume.

"Well, now . . . maybe getting them back together isn't the best thing."

"Don't be silly. Of *course* it is. Suzanne found herself a *good* man. A really *good* man. She can't lose him now."

Fred tried to push aside his irritation with her, but her fixation on mending the kids' broken relationship had gone far enough, and she needed to realize it. "Listen, Celeste. Douglas and Suzanne's marriage is over, and nothing you or I do is going to change that."

"How can you *say* that?"

"Because it's true. Leave it alone."

She blinked, obviously confused, and took a step toward him. "But—"

He held up his hands to keep her back. "I'm not going to do anything to get those two together again. I try really hard to keep my nose out of things that aren't any of my business—and this is one of them." Having made his point he strode away, but she ran after him.

"But you don't understand—"

"I understand more than you think I do."

She tugged at his arm. "Don't you even *care* what happens to Suzanne and Alison?"

"Of course I do."

"How many good men do you think there *are* out there? How many chances do you think Suzanne's going to *get*?"

He stopped and faced her, taking her by the shoulders as if by holding her still he could get through to her this time. "I know it's not easy to find the right person. Suzanne might be alone for a while. Douglas might, too. But in the end, they'll be all right."

She shook her head emphatically and whispered, "You don't understand."

"I know you'd like to see them work things out, but it's

ot going to happen. And with everything that's gone on the ast few days, maybe it's for the best."

"I will *never* believe that."

Fred dropped his hands. It was hopeless. He'd never find he words that would make her see reason. "Celeste, I'm ruly sorry it's so hard for you to accept their decision. But really need to go. I'm this close to figuring out who killed Garrett." He held up his thumb and forefinger a hair's readth apart.

"Who?"

"I'd rather not say anything until I know for sure."

"Do you know why he was killed?" Her eyes glittered.

"Not for sure."

She smiled up at him, though not her usual pink smile but hard-edged one he'd never seen before, and for the first ime Fred glimpsed a woman capable of parlaying her magination into a successful career. "Keeping secrets from ne?" she asked.

"They're not my secrets to share. Not unless it becomes absolutely necessary."

She stiffened and pulled away from him. "I see. And once you've found your murderer, what will you do?"

"Tell Enos. Whoever did this needs to pay. That's all I care about. And it's the only way Douglas—and Suzanne—will be able to get on with their lives."

"Well, I see you don't have the same hesitation about sticking your nose into the middle of *murder*. Maybe it's only affairs of the *heart* that frighten you."

She wore him out. She honestly did. And he didn't have what it took for him to deal with her now. "I've got to go, Celeste."

"You won't help Suzanne?"

"There's not a blasted thing I can do."

"Then you're *not* the kind of man I thought you were, Fred Vickery. Not at *all*."

"You're probably right," Fred admitted. But he didn't necessarily think of that as a bad thing. He turned from her and crossed the street, stepping onto the boardwalk at the corner. Almost afraid to look, he glanced back over his shoulder, but when he saw that Celeste had disappeared again, he breathed a sigh of relief.

He moved on past Silver City Bank and tried to calculate how long until Logan Ramsey finished his prison sentence for embezzlement, but gave up. His mind was too full of other things.

He'd just started across Porter Street when a door opened halfway down the next block and a woman stepped out onto the boardwalk. If she hadn't already seen him, he would have tried to avoid her. But she walked in his direction without taking her eyes from him.

When she drew abreast of him, she brushed stray hair from the corner of her mouth. "You came. I wondered how long it would take you."

"Hello, Summer."

"Did she find you?"

"Who?"

"Celeste. She was anxious to find you."

"Now look here, Summer. I've been meaning to talk with you about this Celeste business."

Summer cocked her head to one side and a curtain of pale hair slid from her shoulder and caught the sunlight. "It's not my doing. I'm only an instrument."

"Well, don't encourage her."

"I don't encourage or discourage. It's not my place to push people toward their destiny or to keep them from it."

He should have known talking with her would be as senseless as reasoning with Celeste. But he tried again. "I am not Celeste Devereaux's destiny, and it's exactly that kind of nonsense—"

"We can't always see our own destiny, Fred. But neither can we avoid it."

Her foolish talk made him uncomfortable. He stepped around her, intent on going his own way, but she followed. "I could give you a reading if you'd like."

"No."

"It might help."

"I don't want anything to do with that nonsense."

She fell into step beside him and brushed her hair back

out of her face. "Don't disregard an entire science because of some archaic belief from your past."

"A science? Biology is a science. Chemistry's a science. Telling fortunes is not a science."

She stopped suddenly and grabbed his arm. Tilting her head a little to one side, she looked like she was listening to something. After several seconds she nodded and loosened her grip. "You're deeply troubled, aren't you, Fred?"

And getting worse by the minute. First Celeste. Now Summer—how much more should a man have to tolerate in one day?"

"My guides can sense it. They want me to tell you how much you could gain from a reading."

"No."

"They could give you the answers you seek—"

He took several quick steps away. If she wanted to start talking to imaginary friends, she could do it when he wasn't anywhere near.

"You're skeptical," she called after him, "but sooner or later you'll come face to face with your destiny, and I only hope you recognize it before it's too late."

Ignoring her, he pushed open the door to Locke's. The bell over the door announced him, but the showroom stood empty. On first glance, the place looked no different. But he felt a difference in the atmosphere immediately.

It might have been the subtle aroma of cigarette smoke that indicated Olivia's presence. Or the sound of her throaty laughter coming from the back room. Or the evidence of take-out cartons from the Bluebird and ashtrays on the desk. But Garrett's stamp of ownership had disappeared and Olivia's had replaced it.

The bell on the door jingled again when the door closed, and this time Rusty Kinsella poked his head out of the back room. But when he saw Fred, his welcoming smile faded. "Fred? What the—Is anything wrong?"

"Have you got a minute?"

"Sure. I guess . . . Now?"

"If Olivia doesn't mind."

"I don't mind, Sherlock," Olivia called. "Just don't keep him too long. We've got a lot to do today."

Rusty glanced nervously over his shoulder, then joined Fred near the front of the store. "What's wrong?"

"Nothing. I just wanted to ask you a few more questions."

"Can't it wait? Olivia's in the back—" He spoke in a whisper and darted repeated looks at the door that concealed her.

But Fred didn't want to wait. He wanted answers. Now. "Tell me about that little girl of yours. The quiet one. What's her name?"

"Kayla? Why?"

"I just saw her at Lacey's with Eileen. Is she always that withdrawn?"

Rusty started to shake his head, then looked at Fred in confusion. "Just the last couple of months. Why?"

"Did she ever have anything to do with Garrett?"

"Not really. She came in here to see me after school once in a while, and I'm sure she ran into him from time to time, but nothing more than that."

"Did you ever come across Garrett alone with her?"

Rusty straightened his stance slightly but dropped his voice even lower. "What's going on, Fred? What are you trying to say?"

Fred had to force the words out. "I found out last night that Garrett molested my granddaughter Alison. And I'm told he molested his own daughter. Now I'm trying to figure out whether he bothered any other girls in the area."

Rusty's red coloring faded. "You're not serious?"

"I'm deadly serious. And I think someone found out and killed him."

"A parent?"

Fred nodded.

"Me?" Rusty's voice broke out of its whisper.

"I didn't say that."

"Because you think Kayla was one of his victims?" Rusty gulped in deep breaths of air and reached out for a nearby chair to steady himself.

"Look, Rusty, we're sure about Alison. I'm only guessing about your daughter."

Rusty didn't take much comfort in Fred's reassurances. His knuckles turned white from the effort he used to brace himself.

"It was just a guess," Fred repeated. "There was just something familiar about the way she was acting just now over at Lacey's. Something very like Alison. Is she always so withdrawn?"

"She's very much like her mother, if that's what you mean. But she has been quieter than usual lately. Eileen thought it was just one of the signs of growing up—" He broke off and colored brightly.

"There wasn't anything in particular that happened just before she changed?"

Rusty shook his head and would have spoken again if Olivia hadn't stepped out of the back room at that moment.

Like Janice said, she'd had her hair cut, and it looked a shade darker, but she didn't look like a new woman at all—just a more expensive version of the same old one. She still wore jeans, but they weren't old and faded. She still wore tennis shoes, but they had a brand name on them now. And she still wore a T-shirt, but Fred could read this one.

She raised a cigarette to her lips and inhaled deeply. "What are you two whispering about? I'm dying of curiosity and I can't hear a thing."

Rusty darted a warning look at Fred before he shook his head. "Nothing."

She glanced at Rusty, but dismissed him with a shrug. "Come on, Sherlock. Out with it. You're asking questions about Garrett again, I can feel it."

Fred thought about denying it for less than a second. Olivia would see right through him, and his conversation with Yvonne had left more holes in Olivia's story.

"I went to see Yvonne yesterday." He didn't say more— he knew he didn't need to.

Olivia's mouth tightened. "Really? You look like you learned something interesting there."

"Yes."

Olivia smirked. "She told you about the money, didn't she? All right, I confess. My brother screwed me out of a lot of money and we didn't exactly get along. Satisfied? But I didn't kill him over it. No matter what he did, he was my brother and I loved him." Her lips curved into a smile. "I just didn't like him a whole lot."

"Yvonne told me about Jenny."

Olivia's expression froze. "I might have known she'd say something eventually."

"You knew about Garrett, but you kept it quiet. Why?"

Rusty whipped around to face her. "You knew? And you didn't say anything?"

"He was my brother."

Fred pulled in a steadying breath, but the words came out easier this time. "He molested my granddaughter."

"Which one?"

Did it make a difference? "Alison. Douglas's daughter."

Olivia's eyes widened in horror an instant before she slumped against the wall. "I didn't think he'd do it again."

"You could have prevented what happened?" Rusty's voice rose to a shout.

"Maybe." She looked up at him with pain-filled eyes. "He told me he'd had counseling—I thought he was cured."

Rusty's coloring rose to a dangerous level. "Didn't you have any idea he was doing it again?"

"How would I know?" she cried.

Rusty flicked his hand at her in disgust.

"What should I have looked for? Garrett and I didn't even see each other very often. We weren't exactly close—you know that. Besides, you would have seen it before me. You're the one who was with him every day."

Her barb found its mark and Rusty took a step back.

"Did he ever do anything that made *you* wonder?"

"No. He seemed . . . normal." Rusty wiped his eyes with his fingertips. "But if anything happened to Kayla, I don't know what I'll do."

"You'll get her counseling and you'll see her through it," Fred cut in. He had no time to waste listening to accusations. And Rusty wouldn't accomplish anything by flinging them.

"With what? I can't even afford the damned baby doctor, Fred. You know that."

Olivia lifted her cigarette to her lips with trembling fingers. "I'm so sorry. If I'd had any idea he was still so sick, I would have said something."

"Would you?" Fred wanted the words to sting her, but she seemed to draw a challenge from them.

"Yes, I would have. But I can't expect you to believe that."

In spite of his desire not to, Fred did believe her. But the need to place the blame somewhere forced the next words from his mouth. "You haven't seen Alison lately, have you? You have no idea what Garrett's done to her."

"Don't I? Do you think this is the first time I've seen something like this?" She strode across the room and ground out her cigarette in an already full ashtray.

Fred drew in a deep breath and shook his head. "No, of course not. I know you were close to Jenny—"

Olivia barked a laugh. "Jenny. Yes, I had to watch her go through it, too. If I'd been a stronger woman then, I probably would have killed Garrett myself. I promised myself for years that I wouldn't watch it happen to someone I loved again. But when it came right down to it, I didn't have the guts."

Rusty shot Fred a look of confusion. But Fred had no idea what she meant, so he couldn't shed any light on the subject for the other man.

Olivia looked up at them. "You don't know, do you? Neither of you. You think Cutler's such a protected, safe little place. You don't think anything ugly ever happens here."

Fred didn't answer. She was leading somewhere with this, and he didn't want to derail her. But the hair on his scalp prickled with foreboding.

"When I was a little girl, I watched my best friend suffer after her father molested her. Over and over again, he came to her at night, and I was the only one she told." Tears filled her eyes and she wiped them away angrily with the back of her hand. "I made her tell her mother. I thought her mother would protect her. Instead, she denied it. She accused Rosie of lying. Said she made it up. So Rosie didn't tell her any more, and she stopped talking to me about it because she felt I betrayed her."

She fumbled with an open pack of cigarettes, managed to get one in her mouth, and struck the lighter half a dozen times before she got a flame. Inhaling greedily, she closed her eyes and held the smoke in her lungs. When she spoke again, the words and smoke came out together.

"She left town the day we graduated high school. I lost touch with her, but I heard later she never got over it. It ate away at her—made her crazy. And eventually she committed suicide."

Fred thought back thirty years, trying desperately to think of a girl named Rosie, but his memory failed him. Rosie. "Who was she?"

Olivia rubbed her forehead with the heel of her hand for a long, agonizing moment before she lifted her eyes to his again. "You really don't know?"

"Who was she?" he demanded.

"It's funny in a way, how lightning strikes the same place twice."

The hair on Fred's arms stood up and he battled the uncanny certainty that this would tie everything together.

Olivia looked from Fred to Rusty and then back again. "I'm talking about Rosie Devereaux."

twenty-five

Fred pounded on Margaret's door, waited half a beat, then pounded again. He heard footsteps moving inside, but he knocked a third time for good measure.

Rosie Devereaux. Suzanne's cousin. He couldn't remember her, but she would have been about Margaret's age. Margaret would remember.

His grandson Benjamin opened the door. "Grandpa?"

"Where's your mother?"

Staring openmouthed at Fred's unusual greeting, Benjamin gestured toward the center of the house. "In the kitchen." At fifteen, Benjamin already stood half a head taller than Fred, and it seemed like he grew another inch every week.

Fred started past him, but paused for a second to reach for the boy's shoulder and send up a reassuring smile. At least he hoped it was reassuring. It felt desperate.

Margaret sat at the table, a cookbook open before her, her usual glass of iced Diet Dr. Pepper at her right hand. She looked up and smiled when he entered. "Dad? Was that you making all that racket?"

"Tell me what you remember about Rosie Devereaux."

Margaret's eyes clouded. "Rosie Devereaux? What made you think of her after all these years?"

"What do you know about her?"

Margaret turned toward Benjamin, who must have followed him. "Fix your grandpa a glass of something, Ben. Dad, come and sit down for a minute. You look horrible."

"I feel worse." He gripped the table and met her eyes, hoping to convey his urgency. "What do you remember?"

Margaret's eyes flicked toward Benjamin again. "Not much. Why?"

"Do you remember ever hearing anything about her being abused?"

"Abused? You mean beaten?"

"Molested."

"Rosie?" Margaret's hand flew to her throat and her cheeks flushed. "No. Was she?"

"I think so."

"Not by Celeste?"

Fred shook his head. "By Arthur. Archie. Whatever the Sam hill his name was."

"Archie," she said automatically.

Out of the corner of his eyes, Fred saw Benjamin reach for an ice tray from the freezer and then sidle up to the counter to get a little closer.

"You don't remember anything?"

"I remember that she was always quiet. Not a lot of fun to be around. She never came to any slumber parties or anything like that. And when we got older, she didn't date much. She was too quiet for me. I sort of ran with a different crowd."

"She committed suicide. Later. After she left here. Do you remember hearing about that?"

Margaret nodded uncertainly. "I think so."

Benjamin dropped ice into a glass almost silently while he absorbed every word.

"What do you remember?"

She shook her head as if trying to loosen the memories. "I don't know. Just that she did it. And I remember that her father died not very long after that. That's what I remember most. There was a big story about him because it happened so soon after Rosie died."

"How did he die?"

"I don't remember. An accident of some sort. I remember seeing pictures of Celeste. You know—the tragic widow and that kind of thing."

Benjamin turned on the water tap—no more than a trickle—and stuck the glass under it.

"How long ago?"

Margaret tapped the fingers of both hands to her forehead in a gesture of exasperation and looked up at him. "I'd think you'd remember more than me. It couldn't have been very long ago. Ten years. No, it was before Douglas and Suzanne got married. Fifteen, maybe? Don't you remember?"

Fred shook his head. "No. I didn't pay much attention to local tidbits then. I was too busy. What else do you remember?"

Benjamin handed him the glass of ice water. "Grandpa?"

"What?" He tried not to sound annoyed.

"Wouldn't they have the old newspapers at the newspaper office? Maybe you could just go look it up."

"What?"

"I said, wouldn't they have the old newspapers—"

"Never mind, son. I heard you. Margaret, this boy's a genius." He took a healthy swig of the ice water and left the glass on the counter on his way out.

"Dad?" Margaret raced after him. "Dad? What's going on?"

"It's a long story, sweetheart, and I can't stop to explain it now. Douglas knows most of it. Call him." He stepped outside and started back down the sidewalk.

"Dad?"

He didn't turn around. He didn't have time. If he was right . . .

"Dad? You ought to call Enos."

He waved a hand over his head. Of course he'd call Enos. He'd promised to, hadn't he? But he'd already sent Enos off in the wrong direction once today. This time he'd wait until he had proof.

Fred pushed open the door to the office of the *Cutler Crier*, a weekly newspaper that had been put out by the Jeppson family since just after World War II. There had never been enough local news to justify more than weekly circulation. And even at that, the pickings were usually skimpy. But once in a while, almost by accident, they carried a newsworthy story.

Fred never read the *Crier*—he preferred the *Denver Post*—but Phoebe had read it regularly, and she had always kept him informed of the local news and the gossip. After her death, he'd let his subscription expire.

The wife of Jeppson's youngest boy—Fred thought her name might be Lisa or Lora—sat on a stool behind the counter. Her mother-in-law, Hettie, took up the position of honor at a desk in the back of the small room.

The younger Mrs. Jeppson beamed up at him from a cherub face framed by dark hair held back with a huge white bow. "Mr. Vickery. This is a surprise. What can I do for you?"

"Do you have any old issues of the *Crier* stored around here?"

"I think so." She looked at Hettie for confirmation. "Do we, Mama?"

Hettie scowled at him. "Of course we do, Fred. We do business like a real newspaper—no matter what some folks think."

He ignored her barb. "Can I look through them?"

"Look? No. We have back issues for sale, but you can't just come in here and catch up on the news by looking through them."

"Fine. I'll buy them. How much?"

"Which issues did you want?" She slid her glasses down on her nose and stared at him over them.

"I don't know. They'd have been out about fifteen years ago."

"Fifteen years? What do you want something that old for?"

"I'm trying to find out about something."

Hettie stood and crossed to the counter, leaning onto it with both arms. "We keep back issues for a year."

"You don't keep a . . . scrapbook or anything?"

"No, we don't keep a scrapbook."

"It's important, Hettie. Really important."

Hettie adjusted her glasses, but they immediately dropped again. "Just what is it you're trying to find?"

"I'd rather not say."

She harrumphed and sent a meaningful glance at her daughter-in-law. "Then how do you expect me to help you?"

"I didn't know you were going to."

"We try to be of service," she snapped. "To our subscribers."

"Do you have any papers that old?"

"We might."

"Hettie, please . . . What I'm looking for is really important."

She pushed up from the counter and walked to the end where she lifted a hinged piece to let herself pass onto Fred's side of the barrier. "Sterling might have some old issues in boxes in the basement. I suppose we could take a look."

"Thank you."

"Don't thank me yet. There's no guarantee we'll find what you want." She glanced at her daughter-in-law and nodded toward the front door. "You keep an eye on things while I'm helping Fred."

The young Mrs. Jeppson nodded and tried to look like she didn't mind being told the obvious. "I will, Mama."

Hettie led the way to a narrow stairway that cut through the center of the building and led toward a musty basement filled with boxes and off-kilter filing cabinets. "Don't know why I'm going to such a bother," she muttered. "But if we have 'em, they'll be somewhere down here."

At the bottom of the stairs she flicked on a single bulb hanging from a cord looped over a ceiling beam. The light bulb swayed and sent light skittering across the clutter.

"Point me in the right direction and I'll look through them. No sense your having to stay down here with me."

Hettie made a noise with her tongue and her teeth. "I can't leave you down here alone with the archives. It'd be as much as my hide is worth. I'll just have to help you, I guess." She propped her fists on her hips and looked around the room. "Besides, I don't have the foggiest notion where they'd be."

With a sigh designed to let him know just how much he

was putting her out, Hettie lifted the lid off the top box in a stack and dug through its contents.

"Should I start on these over here?" Fred needed her too much to annoy her, but he didn't want to stand idly by while she looked through every box herself.

She gave him a brisk nod.

An hour later, they'd checked nearly all the boxes without finding any archival records. They'd found trophies, old office supplies, files, receipts and bills, but no newspapers.

Hettie wiped her forehead with the back of an arm, leaving a dirt smudge in the place of perspiration. "Looks like I was wrong."

Fred tried not to let his disappointment show. "Thanks for your time anyway, Hettie."

She settled the lid on the box she'd been looking through and perched on the top of it. "Why don't you tell me exactly what you want to know."

But he shook his head. "I may be on the wrong track again."

"Listen, Fred, this is silly. You need information, and I've worked here every day for thirty-two years. Anything that's happened in Cutler during that time, I'll probably remember."

Fred weighed his options and decided that the odds of finding another source quickly came up short. He might as well give in. "Archie Devereaux. How did he die?"

Hettie pulled back in surprise, but answered briskly, "In a house fire."

"A house fire?" he repeated uselessly. He didn't know what he'd expected, but it hadn't been that.

"Oh, yes. It was a terrible tragedy. Poor Celeste had just gone through that awful business with her daughter—you remember that, don't you? Her suicide?"

He nodded, but didn't want to interrupt the flow.

"Those psychiatrists at that clinic made such a to-do about it, claiming she'd been suffering from depression or some-such all her life. You remember that part, don't you? She'd written all those poems and drawn pictures, and the doctors said they thought maybe she'd been molested as a little girl? Celeste really went through the wringer on that one, I'll tell you. It was ridiculous, of course. Archie and Celeste would never have done such a thing."

"A house fire," he repeated again. It wasn't enough. Coincidental, that's what Enos would say.

"Celeste barely made it out alive. Don't you remember?"

He shook his head. "What about Suzanne?"

"I don't remember if she was there at the time." She tilted her head and thought. "Her parents had that accident, you recall?"

He recalled.

"Suzanne might have been there . . . Yes, I think it might have happened when Suzanne was there. And after that, Celeste bought the house up here and they came back."

"What happened to Archie? If Suzanne and Celeste got out, why didn't he?"

"I believe he fell." She thought for a second or two, then nodded in a satisfied way. "Yes, I remember, he fell and hit his head . . . against the bathtub, I think."

"Hit his head?"

"It was so tragic."

"He hit his head?" Fred asked again. "Are you sure?"

"As sure as I can be. Mama Jeppson would remember. She can't remember what day it is today, but she remembers everything that happened in the past. Do you want me to call her?"

Fred's pulse thudded hard enough for him to feel it. "No, I think you've told me enough. I might ask Enos to come talk with you, though. Is that all right?"

Hettie nodded. "Sure. Whatever I can do."

Fred started up the stairway, clutching the handrail.

"Fred?"

He looked over his shoulder.

Hettie gestured toward the boxes. "I'm assuming you'll want me to start up your subscription to the *Crier* again."

Fred nodded. No sense fighting it. He knew when he was licked. "As a matter of fact, Hettie, I was going to ask you if you'd do that."

"You'll get this week's issue."

twenty-six

Fred emerged from the *Crier*'s offices to almost total darkness. Spring might be around the corner, but night still came early. He'd left home without a heavy coat, and now he wished he'd thought ahead. His thin jacket did little to keep the frigid night air at bay.

Two cars were parked across the street at Lacey's — Grandpa Jones's rattly old pickup and Suzanne's white Chevy. At least Enos had finished questioning her. The Copper Penny's parking lot was fuller. But most of the downtown area had emptied.

Fred walked quickly, hoping to catch Enos before he left the office. He had to deliver this news in person, and after the last wild goose chase Fred had led him on, getting Enos to listen might be tricky.

He had less than two blocks to walk, but when he reached the corner of Lake Front Drive and saw Enos's empty parking space, he knew he was too late. Just to be certain, Fred crossed the street and tried the door of the sheriff's office.

Locked.

He walked back to the corner and stared into the darkness that led home. Half a mile and he'd be there. Warm. Safe.

He looked the other direction. Less than half a mile past the church and the cemetery and he'd be at Enos's. Warm. Safe. All things considered, he'd be wisest to head for Enos's.

Stuffing his hands into his pockets, Fred bent his head into the breeze that cut through his jacket and stepped down onto the street. The sidewalk would make his walk easier for the first two blocks. After that, the forest scrambled down to the edges of the road and obliterated most signs of civilization.

Headlights from a car came up almost behind him and played over the street as the driver made a U-turn and headed back into town. He tried to look up, but the wind collected pieces of grit and sand and blew them into his eyes when he lifted his head.

Jessica would offer him cocoa—not his usual choice, but tonight maybe he'd accept. But she'd expect him to let her dog Magnum, a white piece of fluff with pretensions of grandeur, sit on his feet, and he hated that.

He practiced how he'd tell Enos what he knew. He tried a dozen different starts, pictured Enos's reaction to each, and thought again. Before long, he left the sidewalk and plunged into the darkness of the forest road.

Bits of moldy leaves and mud clung to his shoes and made his footing slippery. He scraped the bottoms of his shoes on a rock and trudged on, but within minutes he'd picked up enough new debris to make his feet slide when he hit a deep patch of winter leaves.

He caught his balance and looked around, trying to get his bearings. Less than half a city block ahead the church stood stark and white against the night sky. He calculated how far he'd come and figured he had two more curves in the road, with a long straight patch in between. Maybe a quarter of a mile, but uphill.

Giving himself a mental pat on the back, he lowered his head into the wind again. But by the time he reached the church, his breath was coming in gasps and his knees ached from his effort.

He paused, gulping air and letting his breathing slow. The road stretched out black before him, and he was still too far away from Enos's house to spot any lights through the trees.

After a moment he pushed on. One step after another. He cursed his age, his legs, his arthritis. He wished for the energy to bound up the hill the way he had as a young man. He pulled his hands out of his pockets and used his palms against his thighs to give his legs added strength.

At long last he rounded the first curve and started down the straightaway. In the distance he could see lights intermittently through the trees.

He thought about Jessica's cocoa. About how he'd spend half an hour watching a television comedy with her before he headed back. And about how he'd get Enos to offer him a ride home without admitting to his overwhelming fatigue.

He looked up again, trying to gauge his distance, but this time something else caught his attention. On the side of the road several feet ahead, a small white car sat in the shadows. It had been pulled far enough into the trees to escape his notice before.

He slowed his step. This road was too narrow to leave a car there. Even pulled that far off the road, other drivers would have to swerve to avoid it.

Squinting into the shadows, he tried to see it better. An elongated cross on the trunk glinted in the moonlight. A Chevy. Suzanne's car.

The taste of sick dread filled his mouth. It had been parked in Lacey's parking lot. It had probably been the car that came up behind him as he left town. She'd known exactly where he was going.

He didn't stop. That would only alert her. But he scanned the roadside carefully and made certain of his footing with each step. He was less than five hundred feet from Enos's house, but too far from any other civilization to be noticed. She'd chosen her spot well.

He passed the car, straining to pick up any foreign sound, any hint that she might be waiting nearby. But he heard only silence and the sounds of the forest.

Keeping his hands clenched tightly at his sides, he walked on. The cold bit at his fingers and numbed his skin, but he didn't allow himself even a moment's weakness.

The lights from Enos's house winked at him again, urging him to hurry. He walked a little faster. Maybe he could get close enough to raise their attention if he shouted.

Four hundred feet.

The trees backed away from the road, giving him a better

view of his surroundings, providing fewer places for her to hide. If he could just get past the next stand of trees—

He heard gravel crunch behind him. He ducked and turned, but something long and hard slammed into the small of his back.

He cried out as he fell. Landing on his side in the dirt, he slid a few inches. Rocks and twigs scratched his face and neck. He gasped for breath but could draw none.

He rolled again as the weapon crashed to the earth beside him, inches from his face this time. Clawing at the earth with frozen fingers, he pushed himself upright and listened for his attacker. He heard nothing but the night sounds and his own ragged breathing.

He turned, half crouched, hands out, ready for the next attack. Nothing.

Then he heard a sound, soft, almost indiscernible, but there. He tried not to turn in its direction, to act like he was searching for her somewhere else. He took a step away but kept his senses alert.

It came again.

He tensed, turned, and launched himself toward her, hands out and grasping for something to pull her down with. But he stumbled to the ground and the world fell silent again.

By breathing in shallow gasps, he kept the pain in his back under control as he struggled to his feet again. Darkness and shadows surrounded him.

He tried to shout for Enos, but his burning throat refused to make a sound. He started forward, limping this time. He had to get closer to Enos's house.

Every sense screamed to the alert as he walked. Leaves skittered across the road, wind whispered through the trees, a dog whined in the distance. He saw the lights on Enos's front porch, could make out a silhouette in the kitchen window, could see a glint of moonlight reflecting off their mailbox at the side of the road.

The scent of fresh, new soil floated on the air. The musty smell of leaves and old pine needles filled his nostrils. And then, suddenly, a new scent reached him. He ducked and twisted away, trying not to cry out as his knees strained with the effort. He eluded her and slipped into the cover of the trees.

He kept his eyes focused on Enos's kitchen light and struck out toward it. He tried and discarded a number of dead branches as he pushed through the forest. He thought about using a rock, but in the trees he'd never hit his mark.

He could hear her now, coming after him, crashing through the underbrush, frantic to stop him. She was younger and more agile, and she could keep him in sight. He could only hear her. And he had only a few seconds to locate a weapon.

In a narrow clearing he found a heavy branch nearly broken from a tall spruce. He snatched at it, but it hung fast. He needed something—anything—with which to defend himself.

He struggled to rip the branch from the tree's trunk as she burst through the trees. Besides age and agility she had another advantage over him: She wore a warm leather jacket and gloves to protect herself from the cold. Her fingerprints wouldn't show up on this weapon, either. At the sight of her face, his efforts became more frantic. But when she saw him standing there, she stopped. Her chest heaved from exertion and her hair hung limp into her face.

She took a step toward him. "I *liked* you, Fred."

He redoubled his efforts with the tree limb.

"Why didn't you leave it alone? I didn't hurt anyone who didn't *deserve* to be hurt. I didn't hurt anyone who hadn't *already* hurt someone else." She moved closer still.

The scent of her perfume reached him and he pulled on the tree limb again.

"They were *bad* men, Fred. Archie. Garrett. They *hurt* my girls." She pleaded with him to understand.

And part of him did.

"Don't tell. *Please*."

He thought of Alison and hesitated. She'd done this for Alison. Garrett had hurt the child in ways no woman should ever be hurt. He'd stolen part of her. "Why did you let Douglas take the blame?"

"It's not what I *wanted*. But I couldn't come *forward*, could I? They wouldn't understand. And *then* who would look after my girls?" She lowered the club slightly. "I didn't *mean* to kill him. I wanted him to admit how sick he was, but he *laughed*. About Alison. He laughed." Her voice dropped. "I couldn't stand the thought of what he did, but I asked him and he laughed."

Fred loosened the grip on the tree limb.

"He admitted it." Her voice rose again and her eyes glittered with hatred. "So I hurt him. I found that table leg on the floor and I hit him with it until he didn't laugh anymore."

Fred tightened his grip. "Enos would have made sure—"

"Enos? What could he do? Men like Garrett get slapped on the wrist and sent back out into society to hurt other children. They don't stop. Only one thing will ever stop them."

"No, Celeste."

"He hurt *Alison*."

"I know, and for that—"

"What? What would you have done? Tell him he's a *bad boy*?"

"No, but—"

She looked away, breathing heavily. "He *killed* my Rosie. As surely as if he'd held the gun to her chin *himself*. He was evil. *Sick*. He only cared about one thing. He *destroyed* her. And I promised myself I'd never let it happen again. *Ever.* But then Garrett came. He twisted Suzanne the way Archie twisted me. He made her doubt me. She denied what I told her. She refused to listen. He destroyed her marriage—"

"Suzanne and Douglas are divorced. Garrett didn't do that."

"But they would have gotten back together. I *know* they would have. That's why I told him to come."

"You told Douglas to come?"

"You didn't help me," she said softly, and the spirit seemed to drain out of her. Her shoulders slumped and she dropped the hand holding the club the rest of the way.

Fred took one cautious step toward her, but she didn't

react. He took another. He wouldn't feel entirely safe until he'd taken away her weapon.

"We could have made *everything* all right for Alison if you'd helped me."

Three steps away from her, he held out his hand for the club.

"*Why* didn't you want to help Alison?"

He took another step. "I did."

"No, you didn't." She shook her head in confusion.

"I was working to clear Douglas."

"*That* wasn't for Alison."

He touched the club, but didn't try to grab it yet. "Yes, Celeste. Having her dad go to prison for a murder he didn't commit would have hurt her."

"No!" She whipped the club up and brought it down on him.

He threw up his arms and blocked the blow, but pain exploded in his hands. He curled his fingers around the club and tried to pull it from her.

She ripped it away and raised it over her head again.

She'd kill him. This time she wouldn't stop. He jumped backward and nearly lost his footing on the slippery ground covering.

Celeste lunged at him. Fred dropped in front of her just before she reached him. She stumbled against him and tried to right herself. But Fred threw himself after her and used his weight and her momentum against her.

She hit the ground on her knees. Fred flew at her and used every ounce of strength he had left to wrench the weapon from her.

She used her hands then, clawing at his face and neck. But this time the gloves she wore protected him.

He threw the club aside. It did no good in such close quarters. She scrambled after it on all fours.

Fred staggered after her. Her fingertips brushed the club. He grabbed her by the waist and dragged her several inches back. She kicked out at him, landing blows on one thigh, striking him on the opposite knee. His grip loosened and she pulled away again. She stretched her hand toward the club.

Gripping her ankles, Fred tugged her away from it again. He threw himself at her, landing squarely on her back and pinning her arms to the ground with his hands. She twisted and tried to throw him from her, but he settled himself more firmly on top of her and kept her pinned to the ground.

He gasped for air, then immediately wished he hadn't. It burned all the way into his lungs.

Now what? He couldn't keep her like this indefinitely. She bucked beneath him, lifting her head and trying to bite his hands. He tried to shout for Enos, but nothing came out. Holding fast, he struggled to breathe, afraid he wouldn't be able to keep her down long.

Could he use his belt to tie her hands? Would that hold her long enough for him to get her to Enos? He heard a high-pitched whine and for a moment he thought Celeste had made the sound. The second time, he thought he recognized it. And the third, frantic barking confirmed his suspicions.

A moment later, Enos crashed through the trees and a blur of white fur scampered across Fred's boots and set up a ruckus in his ear.

Enos stopped in his tracks, pushed his hat back on his head, and looked down at them. Fred's relief at seeing him there weakened his grip. He sagged against Celeste for a moment until Enos started to laugh. "Good billy hell, Fred. Not again."

Fred knew what a sight they made, Celeste flat on her back, swollen and bleeding, and himself sprawled across her, but he could see nothing humorous about it. With unsteady arms, he pushed himself back up and glared. "If you're going to stand there and laugh, go back home. Otherwise, get out your handcuffs."

Enos sobered instantly and crossed to them. "What am I going to do with you, Fred?"

"Help me up."

But Fred managed to get himself upright again with little more help from Enos than a steadying hand on his back and a tug on one arm. Fred brushed mud and twigs from his pant legs. "How'd you know we were out here?"

"Hettie Jeppson called and asked me to pass on something her mother-in-law remembered about Archie Devereaux. She seemed to think you were on your way to see me. It was pretty obvious what you were up to, so I called your place. But when Douglas said he hadn't seen you, and that Maggie'd been asking all sorts of questions about Rosie, I decided I'd better come looking. I found Suzanne's car on the highway, but it was Magnum here who heard something and tracked you down."

Enos pulled Celeste to her feet and worked handcuffs over her wrists. She put up a token resistance, but nothing Enos couldn't subdue in an instant.

Dragging her a few steps away, Enos looked back over his shoulder. "Are you all right?"

Magnum danced across Fred's boots, darted to Enos and back again, and looked up at Fred with eager, expectant eyes. Fred reached down and thumped him on the side. "I'm fine."

"Maggie's going to come unglued."

"I know."

"What are you going to tell her?"

Fred dragged in a deep, steadying breath and put his hand on Enos's shoulder. "Me? I'm not going to tell her a blasted thing."

twenty-seven

Fred lifted his arm while Doc Huggins adjusted the blood-pressure band around it. "Well?"

Doc pumped air into the cuff, counted, and released the pressure. "Seems okay."

Fred glowered at Enos and Douglas who stood side by side in the open doorway of his bedroom. "I told you this was ridiculous."

"And I told you that I wouldn't say a word to Maggie about what happened up at my place last night as long as Doc gives you a clean bill of health," Enos said. "That was our deal, remember?"

"I remember." Fred fixed his gaze on Douglas. "What are you laughing at?"

"The two of you."

Enos's brows knit and he looked offended. "What about us?"

"I can't believe you're both afraid of Maggie. You're terrified she'll find out what you've been up to."

Fred breathed in and out while Doc nodded at intervals and listened to his chest. "I'm not afraid of my own daughter."

"Then why did you ask Enos to drag Doc over here to give you a checkup at eight o'clock at night instead of during office hours?"

"I don't mind," Doc said with a laugh. "I've been playing games with the grandkids all week long. I needed a night out."

Douglas made a noise of disbelief.

"There's a difference between fear and wisdom," Fred

said. "We're just smart enough to know when not to deal with an issue."

"Is that what you call it?"

"I think you're being too tough on your dad," Enos said. "You weren't here the last time he got himself roughed up and you didn't see what happened afterward. Maggie did real fine for the first few days, but after that she started watching him like a hawk. If she finds out he did it again, there's no telling what she might do."

"Well, I don't know how you think you're going to keep it a secret. Just look at him."

"I already told Margaret how I fell while I was taking a walk," Fred said.

"He just didn't mention that he had help." Doc motioned for Fred to sit up. Laying one hand on Fred's back, he thumped with the fingers of the other. "You're lucky Enos found you when he did."

"You're lucky Hettie Jeppson talked to her mother-in-law and called up to my place to tell you what she said," Enos insisted. "I'd never have known you were out there otherwise."

"I don't think you're going to get past Maggie looking like that." Douglas sounded skeptical. "Maybe we ought to tell her the truth."

Fred pulled himself up straight and put on his most intimidating expression. "You're in on it now, son. Clean up to your eyebrows."

Enos nodded solemnly. "No going back. We made our deal."

"Okay," Douglas conceded with some hesitation, "so Dad gets a checkup and we make sure he's okay. If he is, nobody tells Maggie what happened between him and Celeste. What do you guys get out of it?"

Doc stuck a tongue depressor into Fred's mouth. "He adds more vegetables to his diet and he only has breakfast at Lizzie's once a week."

"For six months," Fred added.

Doc nodded and tossed the tongue depressor into the garbage can. "For six months."

"And Maggie doesn't find out what happened, so she can't figure out a way to hold me responsible," Enos said. "Believe me, that's a hell of a good deal."

Douglas grinned. "What do I get?"

Fred slipped his arms into his shirt. "You get to stay here rent-free for a month while you look for a job."

Douglas's grin slipped. "Oh."

Doc looked up. "Is that what you're doing, Doug? Staying on, I mean."

Douglas nodded. "Suzanne's agreed to keep Alison here where she's already pretty settled, and Alison needs me. I've got to stay."

"I think that's a real smart decision. Are you getting her some professional help?" Doc asked.

"Suzanne's already made an appointment with a counselor in Denver. She's going to take her to a few appointments, but I've offered to take her whenever Alison's ready to be alone with a man again."

Doc smiled. "You'll work it out, and Alison's going to be all right. I have no doubt." He turned to Fred. "Well, you're okay—other than the scrapes and bruises. Looking at those knees, I can't figure out how you're still walking." He shoved a handful of equipment into his bag. "But this had better be the last time I have to do this."

Fred looked down at his buttons, matching them to the right buttonholes all the way up. "I don't plan on getting into any more fights for a while."

"Better make it for longer than that," Doc warned.

"I'll be dipped if I'm going to turn into an old man just because I'm a few years beyond my prime."

Doc opened his mouth to protest, but the sound of a car approaching stopped him. The car slowed.

Fred tensed and held his breath until he heard it turn into the driveway. "It's Margaret!"

Without a word, Enos turned and ran heavy-footed down the hallway. Douglas followed, his footsteps light, urgent. Fred shoved his shirttail into his pants while Doc threw the rest of his medical equipment into his bag and snapped it shut.

"Where—"

"Under the bed." Fred lifted the bedspread for Doc to slide the bag into place. "Get into the kitchen."

Doc trotted down the hallway and Fred spent a second smoothing his hair in front of the mirror before he followed. Halfway there he heard Margaret's footsteps on the drive and he quickened his pace.

He pushed open the kitchen door and slipped onto the empty chair, pulling a stack of cards toward him as he settled into place. Douglas had some money in front of him. Three sticks of gum, some loose change, and several bills marked Enos's spot. Enos shoved a small wad of bills toward Fred and Doc snatched up his own cards just as Margaret opened the back door.

She halted, surveying the room. "What's this?"

"Just playing cards," Douglas said.

She stepped inside and pushed the door closed behind her. "Cards? Since when do the four of you play cards?"

"We thought we might give it a try," Enos said. "You know, a night out with the boys."

"Really." She looked deep at him, but he wouldn't lift his head to meet her gaze.

She paced around the table, stopping behind Fred and looking at his cards. "How long has this been going on?"

Douglas looked up, remarkably innocent. He shrugged, sought confirmation from Enos, and looked back at her. "A couple of hours, maybe."

"Really." She took a couple of steps away.

Fred's heart sank. She didn't believe them. He studied his cards like he meant business. He held a Jack, a ten, two sevens, and a four. Nothing to speak of except the pair of sevens. If he held this hand in a real poker game, he'd get rid of everything but the pair and pray for better luck on the draw.

Margaret took up a place behind Enos. "What did the county attorney say about Celeste?"

Enos put his cards on his lap. "We've got a confession, but she made it before I read her the Miranda Act. If they can get her to confess again, we'll have the case sewn up."

"And if not?"

"Then we'll have to prove the case in court, without being able to use a blasted thing she said to us."

And Fred would have to testify and Margaret would know everything.

She gave Enos an admiring look. "I still can't figure out how you knew she did it."

Enos puffed up a little and glanced at Fred with a grin. "Just good old-fashioned police work."

Fred smiled back. "Oh, don't be so modest, Enos. There wasn't much to go on. It'd take someone pretty sharp to figure it out with so few clues."

Douglas started to laugh, but when Margaret eyed him suspiciously he ended with a cough.

Margaret looked at each of them in turn, wary, distrusting. Douglas and Enos both looked down and fiddled with their cards. Doc studied his hand and looked confused. Fred smiled at her in his most innocent manner.

She considered him for a moment. "Who's winning?"

Fred looked at each of their piles of money. "I am."

"So you're having a good night? That's nice. Especially after the fall you took earlier."

Fred mumbled his agreement at the same time Doc, Enos, and Douglas all put in their two cents' worth.

"Did you ask Doc if he'd look at those scrapes?"

"No. I didn't want to bother him—"

"I'll bet he wouldn't mind, would you, Doc?" She took a couple of quick steps toward the door. "Do you want me to get your bag out of your car for you?"

Doc shook his head vigorously. "No. He . . . I . . . ." He stopped, flushed, and glanced at Fred's face. "He looks fine."

"You think so?"

He nodded. "Yes. Fine."

"Oh." She stepped away from the door and came closer to the table again. "None of you are drinking anything? That's funny."

Douglas scanned the table, then beamed at her. "I just cleaned everything away a few minutes ago."

"Did you?" She locked her hands behind her back. "Well, good for you." She stepped slowly around the table and came to a stop behind Doc. "Who dealt?"

"Douglas," Doc said.

"Yep, Douglas did it," Enos agreed.

"I see." She dragged a kitchen stool into place and perched on top of it. "Mind if I watch for a while?"

Every one of them murmured their assent at the same time.

"Well, then I—" Douglas began, but the ringing of the telephone interrupted.

Margaret was closest, so she snapped the receiver off the wall phone. "Hello?" Her face lit and her eyes danced. "I'm great, how are you? . . . You're kidding? . . ."

It was Joseph. It had to be. Fred's heart sank. He didn't want to deal with Joseph right now.

"Yes . . . yes . . ." Margaret tilted back her head and laughed like Fred hadn't heard her do in months.

Maybe it wasn't Joseph. Joseph was a fine boy, but he didn't make anyone—not even Margaret—laugh like that. But the only person who did was sitting at the table holding a phony poker hand and watching her with a soft look on his face.

"You're kidding?" she demanded again. "Yes. Of course. Yes." She nodded eagerly, as if the caller could see her. But it didn't matter. Her delight was evident in the sound of her voice. "That would be wonderful. I'll talk to you Sunday, then. Here he is."

Without warning, she thrust the receiver at Fred and, almost reflexively, he took it. "Hello?"

"Hello?" the voice on the other end repeated.

"Jeffrey?"

"Dad?"

"It's Jeffrey," he announced to everyone who might not have heard him. "How are you, son? How are Corinne and the kids?"

"We're all fine, Dad. Corinne sends her love. I know you're busy, but I need to talk to you about something."

"Really? What?"

"I heard a vicious rumor earlier today. Thought I'd better all to confirm it."

Fred's delight faded a little. "What kind?"

"Well, it's ridiculous, really. Hardly believable. I heard ou were rolling around in the woods with some lady."

"Now, just a minute. I—" He broke off when he saw 1argaret staring at him with narrowed eyes. He cleared his hroat and lowered his voice. "Where on earth did you—"

"Doug called me earlier. He thought I ought to know what ind of behavior you were indulging in."

"That's not exactly right," Fred said, trying to sound asual.

Jeffrey laughed. "He said you'd chased this woman all ver town just so you could jump her when you got her lone."

Fred felt himself flush. "Jeffrey—"

"He said she'd had the hots for you ever since she came ack to town. And that you played hard to get until right at he end."

"That's absolutely not true."

But Jeffrey didn't seem to hear him. "He said . . ." His oice dropped. "He said you saved his life."

Fred smiled. "I don't know about that."

"No, he seemed pretty positive on that point. Are you all ght, Dad?"

"I'm fine, son."

"I take it Maggie doesn't know yet?"

"That's right."

"And you really think you can keep it from her?"

"Absolutely."

"Well, you're a braver man than I am." Jeffrey laughed gain. "You're sure you're all right?"

"Positive."

"This isn't the kind of thing men your age usually do. ou're aware of that, I suppose."

"I am."

"Good. I worry about you, you know. I don't want nything to happen to you."

"I know."

"Maggie's worried about you. She thinks you're going to hurt yourself."

"I know that, too."

"And when Joe heard you were trying to help Doug out he called us both. Did Maggie tell you?"

"She did."

"She thinks you've slipped off the deep end."

"Well, I never did like swimming in the kiddie pool."

Jeffrey chuckled. "He wants me to talk some sense into you."

"I see."

"I said I'd talk to you."

Fred didn't say anything to that, he just waited for his son to go on.

"So, tell me, Dad. Are you going to ever do anything like this again?"

Fred hesitated. He didn't plan on it, but he couldn't promise not to. And he didn't want to actually lie . . . "Not unless it's absolutely necessary."

Silence burned up the airwaves while Jeffrey digested his answer. "I see."

He shouldn't have said that. When it came right down to it, maybe Jeffrey wasn't any different from Joseph at all.

"Well, in that case, I just have one thing to say . . ."

Fred prepared himself for the lecture he felt coming.

". . . be careful."

"What?"

"I said, if you insist on acting like a man half your age, just be careful. Okay?"

Fred grinned. "Okay."

"And if you ever want a sidekick, call me."

"I just might take you up on that."

Jeffrey laughed. "I love you, Dad."

"I love you too, son."

Fred stretched to hang up the phone and every muscle in his back ached. Struggling to keep his face impassive, he settled back into his chair. Across the table, Enos studied his cards intently. Doc's confusion seemed to have grown, but

Douglas grinned and tapped his cards on the table. "Everybody ready now?"

Fred fanned out his cards. "Jeffrey said to tell you hello, Douglas. He said he hoped you were doing as well as the last time you called."

Douglas's smile slipped a little.

"He said you were telling him how you wanted to start getting up earlier in the mornings."

The smile faded altogether. "I . . . uh . . . Yes, I guess I did say that."

Fred pulled out all the cards except the sevens and dropped them on the table. "Maybe you'd like to go out with me tomorrow for my morning constitutional. It'll get you up early, get your blood pumping, start the day out right—"

Douglas shrugged. "Sure. If you want."

Enos pulled two cards from his hand and added them to the pile. "How about we get this show on the road?"

Douglas perked up. "Good idea. I mean, are we going to talk all night, or are we here to play cards?" He discarded one card and smiled up at Fred.

Margaret leaned forward and studied his cards for a couple of seconds. But when she couldn't find anything wrong, she leaned back again. "Who did you say dealt?" she asked.

"Douglas," Fred said confidently. "So you're first, Doc."

Doc smoothed the wrinkles of confusion from his brow when he looked up, but they fell into place again immediately. He looked back down at his cards. "Okay," he said.

They'd done it! They were going to pull it off. She'd never know . . .

Doc closed his hand, fanned it out again, and studied it for a moment longer. "Okay, Fred," he said at last. "Give me all your threes."